THE
BIG BOYS

THE BIG BOYS

A NOVEL BY

MAX EHRLICH

1981

HOUGHTON MIFFLIN COMPANY BOSTON

*Library of Congress Cataloging
in Publication Data*
Ehrlich, Max Simon (date)
The big boys.   I. Title.
PS3509.H663B5   813′.54   80-27399
ISBN 0-395-30525-X

Printed in the United States of America

D 10 9 8 7 6 5 4 3 2 1

FOR MARGARET

The characters, places, and
events in this novel are fictitious,
although the book is, in part,
based on a true incident.
Any resemblance to actual persons
or events is coincidental
and unintentional.

Statesmen forgot their Politics, Lawyers the Bar, Merchants their Traffic, Physicians their Patients, Tradesmen their Shops, Debtors their Creditors, Divines the Pulpit, and even the Women themselves their Pride and Vanity!

Viscount Erleigh—*The South Sea Bubble*

PREFACE

ACH YEAR makes its own history. But only a few achieve great drama and therefore stick tenaciously in memory. Because of some unique or cataclysmic event, each inherits a distinct personality of its own. Nineteen twenty-nine was such a year, and, like 1776, 1888, 1914, and 1941, it is clearly one to remember.

Most of those special years have been laid to rest forever. Some are briefly remembered on patriotic holidays. But the year 1929 has never really been interred. Now and then it stirs fitfully. It is a restless corpse indeed, always a ghoul threatening to rise from the grave. In periods when the market is shaky, when the economy seems overheated, when speculation runs high and inflation never seems to end, its ghost walks again. Sepulchral voices rise from every quarter: "Could 1929 happen all over again?"

In their history or economics classes, the young may have heard vaguely of what happened, or perhaps through the reminiscent gabblings of their elders. They may listen politely, but they are not really interested. They are participating in, or witnessing, other dramas. But to those who are old enough to have lived through 1929, memory has a loud voice. The trauma is still there, and always will be.

THE
BIG BOYS

PROLOGUE

IN ORDER to comprehend fully the incredible series of
events that took place at the Puritan Bank and Trust during
the year 1929, it is important to understand how the smaller
banks of the nation operated in those days.

The Puritan itself was then located on Main Street, just
opposite Court Square, in the city of Riverside, Massachusetts. Most of its business was done in cash. Checking accounts, as we know them now, were rather uncommon
among ordinary people of modest means. Deposits and withdrawals were made in cash, and bills paid in cash. The postal
money order was in popular usage. Business accounts and
large depositors, of course, used checks.

During this decade, the smaller banks, and even those of
medium size, were run in a rather relaxed way. It was a time
before elaborate computing and office machines had come
into being. The bookkeeping was done by people using ledgers. In the Puritan, for example, the only mechanical aids
were typewriters and adding machines.

Moreover, in the banks of the time, there was no thorough investigation of all employees in positions of trust.
Neither was there any bonding of people holding these

positions. The banks had not as yet installed careful internal audits of all financial transactions. They were occasionally checked by bank examiners from the state, but they did not have periodic audits made by certified public accountants.

The people involved in the bizarre affair at the Puritan Bank and Trust were not strictly innocents. Embezzlement is a harsh word, but let it be applied here. Yet, in retrospect, it can be seen that they were all tragically naive. They were all decent citizens. All of them, at one time or another, had gone to Sunday School. All of them, if not regular churchgoers, held membership in some house of worship. They regarded themselves as one big family. Loyal to each other, despite some human differences. And loyal to the bank itself. They, as well as their old New England city, were steeped in the Protestant ethic. And like their Puritan forefathers, they believed in the ancient virtues. Hard work. Self-reliance. A Man's Word is his Bond. And Honesty is the best Policy.

The truth is that all the participants involved were the victims of a mass insanity. They were infected by a nationwide virus against which immunity was almost impossible. Collectively, they were themselves a kind of American Tragedy—victims of their own innocent trust in one of our most sacrosanct institutions. If they were guilty of anything, it was their faith in American business and the future of their country.

In the winter of 1929, the Puritan Bank and Trust resembled a massive sandstone fortress. The good citizens of Riverside, on passing that institution, set their watches by the gold-embossed Puritan Clock located at the entrance. They must have taken real comfort in those solid walls. From the outside, an army division would have had a difficult time storming this bastion.

But any fortress, however impregnable, is vulnerable from within.

They did not know, and never dreamed, of the strange machinations already in progress behind those walls.

WINTER
1929

1

THE TIME WAS six o'clock in the morning. The date was the seventh of January, 1929. The place was the White House.

On this morning, punctual as always, the thirtieth President of the United States walked across the upstairs hallway to the Lincoln Room, wearing his long nightgown and slippers. There, he peeked through the window. It was still dark, but he could see his Secret Service escort and bodyguard, Colonel Edmund W. Starling, waiting on the lawn. Starling was on duty, as usual. And, as usual, he was going through his setting-up exercises while waiting for the President.

The President smiled bleakly. Starling was a great one for keeping in trim. He could outtalk that physical culture fellow, Bernarr McFadden, on the subject. The Secret Service man kept telling him, in his deferential way, not to slouch while he walked, to keep his head up and his shoulders back. The President paid no attention to Starling. A man walked the way he was born to walk. That is to say, naturally. He didn't hold with any exercise except walking. He did not play golf, ride horseback, fish, hunt, bowl, or even play billiards.

In the bathroom, he pulled the nightgown over his head

and studied his reflection for a moment. He had a fair complexion, abundantly freckled; blue-gray eyes; thin, straight, sandy hair; prominent nose; and somewhat rounded shoulders. His critics wrote that he had the kind of face you could lose in a crowd—nobody would turn and look twice—that, physically, he was anonymous and nondescript. One critic had even said that it was extraordinary how ordinary he looked. That was all right with the President. It was part of the reason he had been elected, back in 1924. He was the spitting image of the common man, and proud of it.

Now, studying his reflection in the mirror, he looked tired. Getting old, he thought. Be glad to be out of it soon, to go back home to Northampton, Massachusetts, again. Old Herbert can take over, come next March 4th, and good luck to him.

He lit a long black cigar, a particular brand of Perfecto he stocked, and began to dress. He had noted that the sky was heavy with lowering black clouds and there was the smell of rain in the air. The sidewalks were still slushy from a recent snowfall, and he put on galoshes over the high shoes he always wore. He put on his overcoat, and then his hat, a high-crowned brown bowler he favored. He adjusted it carefully, so that it lay perfectly level on his head. He did not like it to tilt to one side, even a little. He considered it frivolous.

Finally, he clumped downstairs and through the corridors, and out to meet Starling for his morning walk.

"Good morning, Mr. Coolidge."

"Morning, Starling."

After that, they walked in silence. Later, he might talk, if he felt like it. They had dubbed him "Silent Cal," and that was all right with him. A man talked only when he felt like talking, when he felt he had something to say. As they approached the gate, the President took the cigar from his mouth and flipped it onto the lawn. He loved the big black cigars; he smoked several a day. But he never smoked while walking outside the White House grounds. And he was never photographed with one, if he could help it. A President, after all, had to set an example. The public saw him as a thrifty, cautious New England Yankee, born a simple farm boy out of Plymouth, Vermont. A cigar was a symbol of affluence, of luxury, and it clashed with his image.

They walked up Sixteenth Street to Scott Circle. Traffic had started to become heavy, and Starling piloted the President carefully across the street. The drivers in the Model T Fords and the Marmons and the Packards waved at him, and he waved back. He smiled rarely, and now he did not even nod, showing only his famous deadpan. They were continuing west on Rhode Island Avenue when he saw a big chauffeured limousine roll past.

A lady wearing a cloche hat of red velvet was sitting in the back seat. Both men caught a glimpse of her. The President turned to Starling:

"That was ol' Frank Kellogg's wife, wasn't it?"

"No, sir. That was Mrs. Alice Roosevelt Longworth."

"You've got better eyes than I have, Starling. That was a mighty good-looking hat. You think Mrs. Coolidge might like it?"

"She might, sir."

"Tell you what I want you to do. You get in touch with old Mrs. Longworth. Ask her where she bought that hat. Then I can tell Mrs. Coolidge to go down and buy one for herself. That clear?"

"Yes, Mr. President."

Starling smiled. The President called everybody old something-or-other. Herbert Hoover was old Herbert, Andrew Mellon, his secretary of the treasury, was old Andy, and even the chief justice of the Supreme Court, Charles Evans Hughes, was old Charlie. None of this was by way of any disrespect. It was, Starling thought, just Mr. Coolidge's way. Probably a hangover from the President's early days in Vermont.

They stopped at a peanut stand. The President, who rarely carried any money, borrowed a dime from Starling, and they each bought a bag of peanuts. Later, the Secret Service man knew, he would receive a shiny new dime in one of the President's personal White House envelopes. Coolidge loved peanuts. He kept a supply in his room, along with crackers and preserves. And more than once, late at night, when he could not sleep, the President had invited Starling up for a talk and a repast. It was at times like this that the President liked to reminisce about the old days in Vermont and later at Amherst College and then in Northampton, where he had practiced law.

The President felt good on this particular morning.

Two years ago, in August, in Rapid City, South Dakota, he had issued his historic statement: "I do not choose to run." The Republican Party, his party, and his secretary of commerce, Herbert Hoover, had won a big victory in November. Al Smith—"Alcohol Smith," as they called him— had never had a chance. The Kellogg-Briand Peace Pact, renouncing war forever, had already been signed by fourteen nations in Paris and was due to be ratified in the Senate at any moment. His State of the Union message had been favorably received. The stock market was up again, the nation was in great shape, business was booming, prosperity was busting out all over. Everybody spoke of Coolidge Prosperity. It was now a household word. Many people actually believed that he, and he alone, had created the good times in which they now lived. He spent very little time denying it. Coolidge Prosperity. It, and it alone, would leave his imprint on history.

As he walked briskly along with Starling, the President

smiled at some of the things he had been called, by both
friends and critics. He had been called a Puritan in Babylon;
Mr. Average Man; a cautious, thrifty, reserved Yankee who
presided over a blatant and reckless age; a Rock of Morality
in a Sea of Sin. He had been called National Pinchpenny
because he had tried to save money in government and thus
cut taxes. Because the average man identified so much with
him, he was called Mr. John Q. Coolidge. He mystified his
critics, who complained that he seemed to accomplish everything by doing nothing. They called him Public Puzzle Number One, the inscrutable Yankee, unfathomable, unflappable,
the enigma in the derby hat.

Yessir, thought the President, it was a good time to be
alive. Aimlessly, he whistled one of his favorite tunes, "Blue
Skies," written by—what was the name of that fella—Irving
Berlin. Blue skies smiling at him, nothing but blue skies did
he see. In a little over two months, he would shed the cares
of his office, and old Herbert would take over. Then he and
Grace could go back home, back to Northampton. There he
could take his shoes off, walk around in his shirtsleeves, write
his autobiography, and not have to answer a lot of fool
questions. All through these years at the White House, he
had maintained the old duplex house at number 21 Massasoit
Street in Northampton. He had continued to pay rent on the
house, forty dollars a month, just to hold it. This had bothered him at times. It had seemed a waste of good money. But
now he was glad he had done it.

He liked to walk to F Street and window-shop with Starling. In order to get there, they had to pass the Treasury
Building. The sidewalk in front of it was in very bad condition. The flagstones were crooked and awry and formed
pockets that held puddles of rain from the night before. Both
of them saw a young woman get her stockings wet, the water
in the puddles splashing her legs halfway up to her knees.

Starling commented to the President that the sidewalk was an inconvenience and ought to be fixed.

"Yes," said the President. "I agree with you, Colonel. But more important, it is dangerous to the conduct of my government."

"Dangerous, sir?" Starling was puzzled. "To the conduct of the government?"

"Why, yes," said the President. He smiled one of his rare, northerly smiles. "By all means, the Treasury Department should level off those flagstones. If they don't, one of these days my secretary of the treasury, Old Man Mellon, is going to come by here and stub his toe. Maybe break a leg. You know old Andy. Never looks down to see where he's going because he's always counting his coupons."

*

Just after breakfast, the President quickly glanced through the newspapers.

An article in the *New York World* infuriated him. It was written by his mortal enemy, the author, critic, and iconoclast, H. L. Mencken. Mencken had a pen dipped in venom, and he used it like a dagger. This column was about the President. Mencken was reflecting on the end of Coolidge's term. He wrote that Coolidge had always played it safe by doing nothing and saying nothing, that no President had ever slipped into the White House so easily, nor had a softer time of it. That he was the luckiest nonentity in the world, a darling of the gods. That he had been on the public payroll for thirty years, and in the process had accumulated a fortune in his tight jeans. That he slept more than any other President, whether by day or night. There were a few idiots in the country who said he was such a typical American that he resembled Lincoln. But no matter how hard they tried, there was no way they could make old Abe out of old Cal. For openers, Lincoln was a lot taller.

The President threw down the paper, angrily.

The son of a bitch, he thought. That was stretching freedom of the press. Maybe he ought to call in his attorney general and see whether something could be done to shut up this loud mouth. As a public official for most of his career, he was used to attack, and even vituperation, but this was a little too much. He consoled himself with one thought. After the fourth of March, he would no longer be President of the United States, and Old Man Mencken wouldn't have him to kick around anymore.

From nine to ten, the President dictated memoranda to various departments of government and answered official mail. Then he met for a half-hour with the director of the budget. After that, a meeting with Senator Borah on the debate in the Senate over the Peace Pact. Then in quick succession, and at precisely timed intervals, the President received Chairman Adams of the Republican National Committee, fifteen minutes; Cody Allen, a granddaughter of Buffalo Bill, who presented with him yet another cowboy outfit—chaps, a red shirt, blue bandanna, a ten-gallon Stetson, spurs, and boots. Photos were taken, time ten minutes; a delegation of Boy Scouts, who presented him with an Eagle badge and a scroll to "our pal Cal," this also with photos, five minutes; the secretary of agriculture, pleading in behalf of the distressed farmer that a Federal Farm Board be created to drain off crop surpluses, one half-hour. And after that, a half-hour with Secretary of the Treasury Mellon and the President-elect, Herbert Hoover.

This was by far the most important meeting on his agenda.

The President was uneasy. Everybody was in the market, from tycoon to elevator boy. There was something close to a speculative orgy beginning to build throughout the country. The market had broken sharply on one fearful day in December. December 7th, to be exact. On that day, the ticker fell far behind the trading on the floor. Those who watched the tape in brokers' offices stood horrified, unbelieving, as Radio opened at 361 and then dropped 72 points; Montgomery Ward lost 29 points, International Harvester 60. But the disaster quickly turned into another thrust up. The story was that the Big Boys had sold, shaken the suckers out, and then bought in again when the prices were low.

Still, there were other opinions. Max Winkler, a financial pundit, made the comment that the market was discounting not only the future, but the hereafter. The President tended to agree with Winkler. And he expressed his concern to Hoover and Mellon. He opened the meeting on a sober note:

"Gentlemen, I am not an expert on the affairs of money, but you two are. It seems to me that speculation is getting out of hand. It's sopping up more and more of the surplus money in the country—in other words, inflating credit."

"I don't agree with you, Mr. President," said Mellon. Andrew W. Mellon was an imposing figure, tall, silver-haired, and aristocratic-looking. He was enormously rich. He had been head of the Aluminum Corporation of America and had served as secretary of the treasury under Warren G. Harding. He was a man of positive opinions and never hesitated to express them. "I think what you're seeing is not really speculation, but an enormous confidence in the vitality and future of American business. I should call it investment, not speculation."

"I agree with Andrew, sir," said Hoover. "Business was never better. I'll admit that the market is going up and that call-money rates are a little high, but I see no harm if people want to pay them. They simply want a higher stake in American business. And I cannot say that I blame them."

The President was silent for a long time. Every once in a while, he played the role of Silent Cal at these meetings, just for the sheer hell of it. Also, you learned when you listened. He was irritated at his two subordinates telling *him* about the strength and virtues of American business. That was *his* province. In a sense he owned it. He had always preached faith in American business. Let it alone, and it'll come home, dragging its profits with it. It was he who had uttered the classic statement, *"The business of America is business."* He thought it up one evening in bed, while paring an apple, and the press had caught it up, and then it had swept the country.

Finally Hoover, squirming a little uneasily in the heavy silence, said:

"Assuming you're right, Mr. President, what do you suggest?"

"Maybe, Herbert, we ought to ask the Federal Reserve people to raise the rediscount rate. Force the price of money up, discourage speculation, and reduce the volume of credit outstanding."

Now Mellon spoke up. "But sir, I must remind you that in July the Reserve banks had already raised the rate to five percent. Didn't discourage investors—or what you feel are speculators—one bit. Seems that people are willing to pay any sum for money if prices keep going up."

"Maybe we ought to try it anyway, Andrew."

The secretary of the treasury shook his head. "With all due respect, Mr. President, I think that would be a serious mistake. If we raise the rate still more, we run the risk of a serious drop in the market. We would be accused of deliberately bringing it on. I assume when you leave office in March you would want to see Coolidge Prosperity still intact."

"Yes, sir. I certainly would."

"Then my advice is let things alone. We'd be hurting business badly by forcing it to pay a higher rate for money. Further than this, if we accumulate more gold here in the United States, it'll have a negative effect on world trade. And there's still one more thing. As secretary of the treasury, I have a special concern about interest rates."

"Yes?"

"After all, Mr. President, we have our own financing to do. The government has to borrow money for its own day-by-day use. We'd have to pay higher rates just like anyone else. And you've always preached economy in government, and rightly so."

The President thought this over for a moment. Then he turned to Hoover.

"What do you think, Herbert?"

"I concur," said Hoover.

*

Just before lunch, Ira R. T. Smith, who had been chief of mails at the White House ever since the administration of William McKinley, brought the President two stacks of mail. One was personal, the other official.

The President thrust the stack of official mail aside. Here, in the final months of his administration, he was less interested in what was official than he was in what was personal. He rifled through the personal mail and then picked out one letter and opened it, chuckling as he did.

At lunch, he said to his wife:

"Grace, got a letter today from Old Man Hopkins."

"Henry Hopkins?"

"Yes, ma'am. Old Henry. Welcomes us back home, in March. Hopes to see us then."

"Oh. That's nice. It's always nice to hear from old friends. Did he say how Helen was?"

"Just fine, he says. But of course, she's put on a little weight. You know, Grace, I like old Henry. Haven't seen him or old Helen in a dog's age. Why don't we have them down for dinner one night, before we leave Washington for good? I think Old Man Hopkins would like that. Give him something to tell his friends about back home."

Grace Coolidge thought a moment. "I don't see why not, Calvin. I think that would be very nice."

Immediately after lunch, the President called his appointments secretary. Coolidge was not a man who made friends easily. Those he felt close to, those he trusted, were old friends, many from his college days. One of these was Henry Hopkins, who had been a classmate of his at Amherst. They had both been in the class of '95 and both brothers in the same fraternity, Phi Gamma Delta.

After that they had gone their separate ways, he into law and Hopkins into banking. But it was nice to know that after it was over, after he and Grace went back to Northampton, the Hopkinses would still be practically neighbors.

Henry Hopkins was now president of a bank called the Puritan Bank and Trust. And the Puritan was located in Riverside, a mere twenty miles from Northampton.

2

ON THIS SAME EVENING, the seventh of January, a man sat at a front table in the grand ballroom of the Hotel Astor. Along with some five hundred others, he listened to an after-dinner speech being delivered by James Walker, mayor of the city of New York.

The man's name was actually Charles Farnsworth Bennett, but Wall Street, and the country itself, knew him as C. F. Bennett, and in the newspapers, the simple initials C. F. were enough to identify him. He was, in fact, a legend, and even his superrich peers regarded him with awe. Some said his personal fortune rivaled that of Samuel Insull, the public-utilities magnate. But this was probably a gross exaggeration, since Insull was quoted at being worth $150 million.

He had a wife, and a huge mansion on upper Fifth Avenue. He had a villa on the French Riviera, a house in Palm Beach, and elaborate residences in London, Paris, and Rome. He had a shining yellow Rolls-Royce, and a huge yacht, only slightly smaller than that owned by J. P. Morgan. He was a rotund man, partly bald, in his middle fifties, and not particularly attractive. But his charisma was in his wallet. And women were drawn to him.

C. F. Bennett had made a fortune in the Chicago grain pits in the early twenties. He had pyramided this many times in the Florida Land Bubble. He had accomplished this by a massive selloff of thousands of underwater acres of real estate. He had managed this coup in 1926, just before the Bubble burst in a spectacular collapse.

After that he had gone into the stock market and multiplied his millions a number of times. And now he was titular head of the Sunrise Investment Trust, known as SIT.

C. F. Bennett smoked a huge Havana and sat patiently listening to Walker. The mayor, as was his custom, had arrived almost an hour late. He was dapper as always, wearing a sleek, pinstripe sack suit, white-on-white shirt, polka dot tie, and a carnation in his buttonhole. He started with a few witticisms, as usual, on the recent election, on Prohibition, and on the man in the White House. Then he got down to the nub of the meeting. The recently defeated candidate for President, Al Smith, and a syndicate of financiers were planning the world's highest skyscraper. It would be called the Empire State Building, some 102 stories high with it's shining tower, and would cement New York City's reputation as the greatest metropolis in the world. The building would need further financing. And thus this dinner.

His audience was composed of what the country called the Big Boys.

The investors in the bull market of 1929 spoke in hushed and reverent tones about the Big Boys.

These were the men who manipulated the market and ruled Wall Street—or so the public thought. They knew when to buy and when to sell. They always bought at the bottom and sold at the top. In fact, they arranged the market to suit themselves. As an investor, you tried to find out what they were doing and do likewise. Tipsters sold inside information on what the Big Boys were doing. Brokers claimed their suggestions came straight from the mouth of one of the Big Boys and thus fattened their commissions. Wall Street was flooded with rumors daily. The Big Boys were selling Fisk Rubber. They were buying Radio. They were buying Diamond Match and selling Atlas Tack at its high. And so on. Follow suit and ride the gravy train.

Some of the biggest of the Big Boys were present at the dinner on this particular night.

Actually, these multimillionaires were a mixed group. On the one hand, there were solid, conservative citizens, many of them representing old money and old family. This select group included people like Charles E. Mitchell, president of National City Bank; Thomas Lamont, of the firm of J. P. Morgan; Richard Whitney, vice president of the New York Stock Exchange; George F. Baker of the First National Bank and Albert H. Wiggin, head of Chase National; John J. Raskob of General Motors; and others. These were the men with a thorough financial or banking background.

But there were some celebrated names of quite another kind among the Big Boys. Names like William Crapo Durant; Arthur W. Cutten; Jesse L. Livermore, the former boy wonder and nicknamed King of the Bears; Michael J. (Mike) Meehan, who, among his other feats, opened a highly successful brokerage service aboard ocean liners; and of course, C. F. Bennett, who outdid them all. These were the plungers, the get-rich-tomorrow wheelers and dealers. They, more than the others, fascinated the investors. They made millions overnight and achieved a certain charisma. They seemed to be the darlings of Lady Luck. Everything they touched turned to huge profits. Many of them knew little about price-earnings ratios, cash flow, capital assets, or any of the other jargon of the market. What they *did* understand, and exploit, was human greed.

They were, in fact, the manipulators. They forced up the

prices of stocks in quick and dramatic runs, sucking in the general public. They squeezed out the short-sellers. Then, when they thought the time was ripe, they sold, leaving the investors holding the phone while the brokers screamed for more margin and sold them out. C. F. Bennett manipulated a number of these joyrides, in such stocks as American Smelters, Auburn Auto, and General Cable. Sometimes these pirates pushed the price of a thinly held stock by buying and selling to each other. They formed a pool, cornering the available supply of the stock, riding up the price, and later forcing the shorts to pay dearly or get out.

The Big Boys played the bull market like a church organ, pulling out a stop here, plugging one in there, sometimes playing a soft legato, sometimes a resounding crescendo. They held thousands of investors enthralled with their music, and in effect, a whole nation listened to their litanies.

Of them, more later.

*

After the speechmaking was over, C. F. Bennett chatted briefly with John J. Raskob, William Potter, head of the Guarantee Trust, and Seward Prosser, head of the Bankers' Trust Company. Raskob was a Democrat and had supported Al Smith in the recent election, and he was proof positive that you did not have to be a Republican to be one of the Big Boys. Raskob had recently written an article for the *Ladies' Home Journal* called "Everybody Ought to Be Rich." It had been reprinted widely throughout the country and had become somewhat of a sensation. It maintained that everybody could be rich by simply investing in the market.

C. F. Bennett made a special point of congratulating Raskob. After all, it was to his, Bennett's, advantage. The country had many people who still kept whatever savings they had in banks. This article would bring in thousands of new investors. And thousands of new investors meant millions in new and naive money.

Finally, with a great feeling of well-being, Bennett lit a fresh Havana and walked onto Broadway and into the night.

He had dismissed his chauffeur for the evening, and now he stood irresolutely on the sidewalk. He did not feel like going home yet, and especially to his wife. It was a cold night, but the air was sharp and clean. He found it refreshing after the stale, smoke-filled air of the ballroom. Around him, the Great White Way was living up to its name. Broadway was ablaze with light. Despite the cold, the sidewalks were crowded. The flashing electric theater marquees beckoned with such stage attractions as *Coquette,* with Helen Hayes; *The Front Page,* with Osgood Perkins and Lee Tracy; *The Royal Family,* with the Barrymores; and *Funny Face,* with Fred and Adele Astaire. In the movie houses, Gloria Swanson was starring in *Rain,* and Eisenstein's *Ten Days That Shook the World* was drawing in crowds of the curious. There was a new film starring the "It" girl, Clara Bow, and another with Gary Cooper, the sensational young actor who had risen to stardom in *Wings.*

C. F. Bennett glanced up at the illuminated moving newsbelt as it rolled and snapped around the upper part of the New York Times Building. On this day, the Dow Jones had risen two points. Tex Rickard, the boxing promoter who had made millions by putting on the Dempsey-Carpenter and Dempsey-Firpo fights, was near death after surgery. The Committee of Seventeen, an organization formed to enforce the Volstead Act, had cracked down on twenty-seven speakeasies and cabarets in night raids. Franklin D. Roosevelt, the newly elected governor of New York State, was planning a second message to the legislature. And King Alexander of Yugoslavia had suspended the Yugoslav Constitution and dissolved the chamber of deputies.

Bennett was feeling restless. He decided he needed a drink. For a moment he contemplated going to Jack Kriendler's Grotto on West 49th, which catered to people like Peter Arno, Jock Whitney, and Lucius Beebe, or to Tony's, a smart speakeasy frequented by Dorothy Parker, Bob Benchley, Monty Woolley, and Tallulah Bankhead. C. F. Bennett had cordial entry to both of these places. He was a bigger celebrity than any of their clients. He had had a hard day wheeling and dealing. And he decided that, rather than patronizing some quiet and discreet place, he needed a little action.

He decided on Texas Guinan's. Guinan's was just that kind of place. Besides, there was a girl in the small chorus, the second from the right, he had seen and admired. He wanted a second look at her before he made a decision.

He hailed a taxi and gave the driver the name of the club. The man was uncertain of the location. Texas Guinan's was periodically raided when someone failed to pay off the proper parties. The raiders would come in with axes, smash up the furniture, and padlock the cabaret. Then Texas would move the club to some new location and start business over again. She had done this several times, and sometimes it was hard to keep track of her. But C. F. Bennett knew the address of her latest location and gave it to the taxi driver.

When he walked into the club, Texas Guinan, big, buxom, and bejeweled, gave him the customary greeting: "Hello, sucker," and escorted him to a front table, as befitted his station. When it came to big spenders, no butter-and-egg man in all of New York could outdo Bennett. He was a fabulous tipper as well. Once, so the story went, he had signed a check at the Grotto, forerunner of today's justly famous "21." Its standards and prices were just as high as they are today. Bennett had never been there before, and the policy of the Grotto was strictly cash. When the waiter politely informed Bennett of this policy, Bennett nonchalantly took out his wallet and handed the waiter a $10,000 bill. The management, just as nonchalantly, had the change wheeled up on a silver trolley.

C. F. Bennett liked Texas Guinan's and patronized it often. And he liked its owner. Born Mary Louise Cecilia Guinan, she had a quick Irish wit, and her club was celebrated for indoor fun after midnight. Her battle cry was "curfew shall not ring tonight." And she liked to say her club was open every night from eleven to seven.

Bennett ordered a glass of iced tea. He was presented with a glass full of ice and a silver teapot full of "tea," which was actually Johnny Walker scotch whiskey, the real stuff and off the boat. For a while he watched the lady from Texas sit atop the piano and joke with her loud and happy patrons. She called attention to their bald heads, their fat stomachs and wallets, and issued dire warnings about their bills to come.

Finally the show came on. It opened with a singer named June Glory. Her gown was sleek and low-cut, her hips wiggled provocatively, and her already drunken audience, many of whom had heard her before, yelled and whistled and applauded. She was the kind of singer called a "belter," and now she shouted:

"Are you sober?"

And they all roared:

"No!"

Then, à la Ted Lewis: "Is everybody happy?"

They all roared yes. Then June Glory smiled provocatively. She wiggled her hips again and shook her breasts. The audience howled. Then:

"All right, you big butter-and-egg men, you baby dolls, what'll it be?"

With that, calls came from all over the club for the song "Prosperity." It was an old favorite at Guinan's, and it had been inspired by Raskob's now famous magazine article. She held up her hands to quiet the audience, smiled, and told them if "Prosperity" was what they wanted, "Prosperity" was what they would have. They all roared their approval and sat down, and then she started to belt out the song. The lyrics were highly contemporary and reflected the mood of the times:

> There's pie in the sky, baby,
> And I don't mean maybe
> A chicken in every pot
> A palace on every lot
> The Dow Jones is oh, so hot!

Here she motioned to her audience to join her in the chorus, and they did so willingly, yelling out the three lines with her:

> Prosperity! Pros-perity!
> Everybody's got that Wall Street itch
> Everybody ought to be rich!

> What did Cal Coolidge say?
> USA, we're on our way.
> You want a Stutz Bearcat,
> A hundred-dollar silk hat?
> A dreamy design by Chanel?
> Then what the hell,
> Buy American Tel and Tel!

> Prosperity! Pros-perity!
> Everybody's got that Wall Street itch!
> Everybody ought to be rich!

> General Electric and Atlas Tack
> Radio and Dupont, back to back,
> Buy General Cable, if you're able,
> And it's champagne and caviar on your table!

Again she sang the chorus, and her audience joined in. Then she turned with rump toward the audience and wiggled it. They roared in appreciation. Then she turned back for the finish of the song:

> American Can. I love you,
> Anaconda and Kodak, too!
> Trust the Lord and Montgomery Ward.
> Does Steel and Oil make you nervous?
> Relax with Cities Service!
>
> Prosperity! Pros-perity!
> Everybody's got that Wall Street itch!
> Everybody ought to be rich!

There was deafening applause. C. F. Bennett joined in himself. But actually, he was more interested in seeing the girls come on. Sometimes Texas Guinan, among her other attractions, used a small chorus to entertain her customers. In a few minutes, the chorus came on to a rousing reception, and began a cancan.

C. F. Bennett, as he had before, studied the second girl from the left. She was a brunette, young and lissome, with shaded, sleepy bedroom eyes. Her name was Dixie Day. She had been aware that C. F. Bennett had been watching her, and she pretended indifference, but her heart beat faster. She knew that the financier was fickle; he had a succession of girls. He loved them and left them, but he was also generous. It was said that, in order to sweeten the parting, he gave each girl either a large diamond ring or an apartment building.

After a while, apparently satisfied with what he saw, Bennett called a waiter and scribbled a short note. He gave the note to the waiter, along with a ten-dollar bill. Then he settled back to wait.

*

On a morning two weeks later, C. F. Bennett was having breakfast with his wife, Edna.

He was scheduled to leave that day for Florida and would be gone ten days on "business." He tingled at the thought; he could not wait to get aboard the train. He had reserved two compartments, one for himself, the other for Dixie Day.

His wife had wanted to come with him, but he had firmly vetoed this. This trip was going to be all business, and she would only be in the way.

At the moment, his wife was nagging him on a matter that annoyed him considerably. She wanted him to give her a tip on the market before he left. "You tell everyone else what to buy, dear," she said. "Why not me?"

C. F. Bennett was the kind of man who never talked business with his wife. He considered her too stupid to understand. And he was sure she couldn't keep a secret. Still, she persisted. She had some money of her own in the market, but she had invested it alone, on the advice of her broker and no one else. To her, this was ridiculous. She was, after all, Edna Bennett, the wife of C. F. Bennett.

He took off his dressing gown and put on his jacket. Then he went to a drawer and took out the railroad tickets for Florida. He glanced at the title on the envelope: *Seaboard Air Line.* His wife continued to nag him, and finally, on an impulse, he said:

"All right, Edna. All right. If you want something good, buy Seaboard Air Line."

Actually, this particular railroad was going nowhere on the market. It was relatively static. But, thought C. F. Bennett, anything to get her off my back. Then, just before he left:

"Edna, will you be here when I get back?"

"No, dear. You know I hate to be all alone in this big house."

"Then where will you go?"

"I'm going to visit my sister Mary while you're away."

"You know, dear," said C. F. Bennett, "I think that's a good idea. A very good idea."

Edna Bennett's sister lived in Riverside, Massachusetts. C. F. Bennett had never been there, but he pictured it as a nice, quiet place. In fact, from now on he would suggest that she make the visit more often. He couldn't be running to Florida all the time.

He kissed his wife gently on the cheek and then left. He hailed a taxi, and as he rode downtown, he aimlessly began to whistle "Dixie."

Already he could feel his groin harden.

3

HIS NAME WAS Freddie Mayhew, and he was twenty-four years old. He was the receiving teller at the Puritan Bank and Trust in Riverside, Massachusetts. He had held this position for three years. His salary was twenty dollars a week.

On this, the morning of February 6th, he awoke to the insistent and obscene buzzing of his alarm clock. It was seven-thirty. He rolled out of bed, padded to the window, and looked out at West Alvord Street. It was a gray morning, cold and overcast. Dirty snow still lay on the ground from the last storm. And this morning there was the threat of more to come.

If Freddie Mayhew had an inclination to be depressed, this would be a perfect day for it. But actually, he felt exhilarated.

All night long he had tossed and turned, thinking of Ellie Hopkins. She had driven him crazy the evening before, and was still doing so.

He went into the bathroom, took off his pajamas, and looked at his naked reflection in the full-length door mirror. He thought of Ellie, and his penis moved immediately to a horizontal position and stayed there. It was hard as a rock.

He studied it with pride. Ellie Hopkins had congratulated him on both its hardness and its size. She had gasped when she felt it, and curled her hand around it. "Oh, Freddie," she had said. "You're so big. You're *really* big."

They hadn't gone all the way. Not yet. But he felt that this would happen, any time now. He must remember to buy some condoms at Hellman's Drugstore, just to be ready. Just in case.

Ellie Hopkins was the daughter of his boss, Henry Hopkins, president of the Puritan Bank and Trust. Freddie had always admired her from afar, thinking how beautiful she was, how smooth and sophisticated. She was a graduate of Vassar, and he had never gone to college. His father was a postal clerk, and there never was enough money, and he had had to go to work right out of Central High School. He watched her driving around town in a Stutz Bearcat or a Premier Roadster with Yale men like Bud Studley or Albie Buckley, rich bastards who wore raccoon coats and lived in big houses on Maple or Longhill Street and belonged to the Longmeadow Country Club.

Funny what had happened to Ellie and himself.

He had seen her come into the bank now and then to see her father. She had been a vision of loveliness, black hair and black eyes, slender figure with full bust, and a soft, sensuous mouth. He had worshipped her from afar and, of course, had never spoken to her.

Then one night he had been in the Barrel, a speak over on Union Street. She had been there with a crowd of her friends, and they were drinking the homemade rotgut Tony was serving there out of tin cups. The boy she was with got drunk, and then quarrelsome and then sick, and somehow he and Ellie had begun to talk, and finally, seeing that her escort was in no condition to go anywhere, he had asked if he might take her home. He had had a few himself, and he was feeling full of courage. To his surprise, she accepted his invitation. He had no car, and he had asked Tony to call a taxi, but she had interrupted to say she had her own car outside and they could use that.

Although he had no car, he did have a driving license, and he drove her to her house on the Hill. He was a little drunk as it was. But he became even more so when he smelled her nearness, her flesh and perfume. She seemed immediately taken by him. She asked him about his work at the bank. She bluntly stated that her father was an old crank and a Babbitt. And after that she started to caress him and called him sexy. They parked in front of her house for a while, and they petted, and he was in seventh heaven. She made the point that she didn't give a damn who he was. She was sick of the social life; it was filled with bushwah and bores. What she liked about him was that he acted and sounded like a man. He was not only sexy, but sensitive and intelligent as well.

Then she drove him home, and they sat in her car and petted some more. That was the beginning.

Two days later, he called her for a date. He had some trepidation about this. She had been somewhat drunk on that first night, and perhaps in the cold light of morning, she had had second thoughts. But to his delight, she was glad to hear from him.

They met frequently after that, although surreptitiously, in out-of-the-way places, mostly speakeasies. He spent money on her, more than he could afford, and he was at least a month behind in his board money to his mother. They knew Henry Hopkins would violently disapprove if he saw them together or became aware of their relationship. Freddie Mayhew was sure that her father would fire him from the bank the moment after this happened. But now they were in love, and they agreed that in time they would face the old man with this fact. The thing was, he did not simply want to marry the boss's daughter and force Hopkins to subsidize him. He had too much pride for that. He intended to make it on his own.

And he had plans for that. Big plans . . .

In fact, he was already on his way . . .

He stared at his reflection a moment more. He flicked his penis with his hand, slapping it back and forth gently. It remained stiff. It thrilled him to think that Ellie's hand had been on it the other night, had touched it, held it, caressed it, stroked it, crooned to it, talked to it as though it were separate from him, as though it had a personality of its own. She had taken personal possession of it. She began to call it "my big thing." And while she had done this, he had one hand under her coat and her blouse, caressing her soft, smooth breasts. And he had run his other hand along her naked thigh. She had let him go no further, but it had been enough. Just in time, he had gotten out his handkerchief before he came.

She had let him know, obliquely, that next time they might go all the way. Not because he couldn't stop, but because *she* couldn't. Women were becoming freer now; it was a time of sex liberation. And she really wanted to "do it." Do it, with him.

He thought of Ellie's father and frowned.

One of these days, he thought grimly, I'll be out of that goddamn teller's cage in your bank, Mr. Hopkins. Just let the market keep right on going up, just let those shares I own of good old Radio Corporation of America grow and grow, and thank you very much, Mr. Hopkins. You can take your bank and your twenty dollars a week and shove it. You are now talking to Mister Frederick W. Mayhew, one of Riverside's dynamic new go-getters and businessmen, executive and man of vision, a potential tycoon of the future. Moreover, I'm thinking of marrying your only daughter and supporting her in the manner in which she is accustomed, and maybe even better. How do you like *those* apples, Mr. Hopkins?

He turned away from the mirror and shaved. He washed his face, patted on a liberal portion of bay rum, and studied his reflection in the mirror. He liked what he saw. Black hair, brown eyes, just a few freckles. Good nose, firm mouth, strong chin. But Freddie Mayhew wasn't interested in his masculine charms now, at least not from that point of view. He was interested in how he would look as a young executive, sitting at his big desk in his office-to-be, dictating to his pretty young secretary, or perhaps going over budget or sales figures with his first assistant. Maybe a mustache would help, he thought. Make me look older, a little more dignified.

He saw himself having lunch in the Highland Hotel or at the Kimball, with the other businessmen of Riverside, or sitting at a meeting of the Main Street Merchant's Association in the Chamber of Commerce Annex. Or even walking into the Puritan Bank and Trust now and then, to go into the vault and clip a few coupons. He'd be wearing a good three-button sack suit, Hart Schaffner and Marx, and smoking a full-bodied Perfecto. Henry Hopkins would leave his desk and come out to greet him, because big depositors like Frederick W. Mayhew were the lifeblood of the banking business. They would sit around and joke about old times, when Freddie had been a mere teller in cage number 3.

Then Henry Hopkins would again come to a point that had bothered him. "Freddie, as you know, this bank has always been family-run. I'm not getting any younger. In fact I'm thinking of retiring. I don't have a son to take over, but I *do* have a son-in-law, and that's you. How about selling your assets in that business of yours and taking over the presidency of the Puritan? I'm sure Ellie would like the idea. I've already talked to the board and they're for it a hundred percent. This desk is yours, son, any time you want it. How

about it?" And he would answer: "Sorry, Henry." He knew
that after he married Ellie, he could never bring himself to
call her father "Dad." "Sorry, but I'm doing pretty well
where I am. You know the kind of business I'm in—it's
growing so fast we can hardly handle it. The way our profit
statement is going to look this year, you couldn't pay me
enough. Besides, my partners simply wouldn't let me go. If
you insist, I *might* take an advisory position on the board,
just to keep my hand in . . ."

Of course, all this might never happen. It was entirely
possible that he would decide to have nothing to do with the
Puritan, but instead take all his business to the Union Trust
or the Third National Bank.

When the time came, he would see.

*

As he dressed, he thought again of how lucky he had been
to get in on the ground floor.

It had been a stroke of luck, pure accident, nothing more
nor less.

A few months ago, he and a friend, Johnny Nash, a cub
reporter on the *Riverside Union,* had taken the Sunday excursion train to New York for the day. They had gone in
order to see Babe Ruth and the Yankees play. It had been
a great day for the Babe. The Mighty Man had poled two
homers over the fence, and the crowd at Yankee Stadium
had gone wild. But it had been a greater day for Freddie
Mayhew.

Coming back on the New Haven, Johnny Nash had casually mentioned the fact that a couple of well-known businessmen in Riverside had decided to start a radio station. One
was an electrical engineer and contractor named Sam Ellinson, and the other was Carl Maynard, the owner of the
Worthy Hotel on Worthington Street.

"They've already got a license," Nash had said. "They're ready to start construction as soon as they can find a third partner."

Freddie had sat up at this. "They want another partner?"

"That's right. Kind of a junior partner. The idea is that Maynard will handle the business and administrative end, Ellison the technical and engineering part of it. But they need a third man, preferably a young guy with a lot of get up and go, to handle sales—you know, someone who can read a rate card and then go out and get the local merchants to put some of their money into radio advertising, instead of sinking it all into newspapers."

Freddie Mayhew had been fascinated. He had been a radio buff ever since it had started, from crystal set to super-heterodyne, and he had watched the progress of the industry ever since the first network had started. As everybody with any sense knew, radio was not only here, but it was growing fast as an entertainment medium. People were skipping the movies, staying home nights now to listen to Graham McNamee, or to Jessica Dragonette, or Roxy and his gang. Guy Lombardo and his Royal Canadians were getting mash notes all over the country for the Sweetest Music This Side of Heaven. And when the Happiness Boys, Billy Jones and Ernie Hare, came on, you could hear a pin drop in every living room in the land as the catchy jingle began: "We two boys without a care—entertain you folks out there—that's our hap-hap-happiness." People listened to KDKA in Pittsburgh or WJZ in Newark, or even WLW in Cincinnati, but the idea of Riverside having its *own* radio station—well, it was staggering just to think about it.

The next day he had gone up to see Maynard at the Worthy Hotel. At first the hotel owner had been skeptical about a bank clerk asking to be made a partner in a first-class business. He had been impressed by Freddie's enthusiasm but had expected the matter to end when he quoted the price. The investment on the part of a third and junior partner would be $20,000. The new partner would have to put up $2000 in cash within the month and the remaining $18,000 by the first of December.

Freddie Mayhew had been staggered by these astronomical figures. But he knew where he could get it if he had to. And much to Maynard's surprise, he agreed to meet these terms.

After all, he worked in a bank, and the one commodity in which the bank specialized was money.

Inside of a month, he had delivered $2000 in cash to the unbelieving Maynard. But he still had to come up with $18,000 more out of nowhere. And in these days, there was only one way to make that kind of money.

Freddie Mayhew had $7500 in Radio Corporation of America. His shares were held in his account by Charles Lothrop and Company, stockbrokers, over on State Street. Technically, of course, he held a lot more in actual shares, but he was on fifty percent margin. So that, in real money, he held seventy-five shares of Radio, which was now selling at about $100. Nobody knew about this little nest egg, not even his mother. She would faint dead away if she knew where he had found the money to invest. So would Henry Hopkins and that sharp-eyed bastard, the bank treasurer, Jonathan Keep. Freddie had been very careful in the way he had gone about it, and he had not overstepped himself by being greedy. A little here, a little there, so that no one would stumble onto anything. He had picked his spots carefully, studied each depositor who came up to his window, made his move when he was *sure*. He had sweated in the beginning. He imagined that the eyes of everyone in the bank were watching him, and he had had a few bad nights, haunted by the fear that somehow, somewhere, he had made a mistake.

But he had gotten over all that, and as he went on, his confidence increased. Pretty soon, if the market kept going, he'd be able to replace the money he had borrowed and buy his way into the radio station, too.

His mother called him to come down and have breakfast or he'd be late for the bank. He looked at the alarm clock and grinned. His mother always warned that he'd be late, but there was, as usual, plenty of time. He slipped into his BVDs, reached into the closet, and took out the blue double-breasted serge suit he always wore to the bank on week days. He noted again that the cuffs were becoming worn and that the wool was beginning to look shabby from too much dry cleaning. The elbows were shiny, and there was a big shine on the seat of the trousers. He thought of this as his "bank" suit, as opposed to his Sunday suit, a gray cheviot that now hung, alone and forlorn, in the closet. It looked less pristine than usual now. The jacket was wrinkled, and there was a smudge of face powder on the shoulder where Ellie Hopkins had leaned her face the night before.

One day he'd have five suits, and better than this one.

He went downstairs and had a breakfast of orange juice, cornflakes, and coffee. And once again, as he did every day, he thought of the secret hiding place he used at the bank, and what he was hiding there.

Once again, Freddie Mayhew reassured himself. Nobody, but nobody, would ever find that hiding place. Not in a hundred years.

He had no desire to go to jail for ten years. Not even five.

*

As receiving teller, Freddie Mayhew had to take in cash and register it for deposits. His basic equipment was a drawer that held a certain amount of paper money to be used in change and another with spare deposit cards. Added to this were a number of wooden racks filled with coins, a spindle on which deposit cards were impaled, and a number of rubber stamps.

Now Freddie watched Jonathan Keep out of the corner of his eye and waited nervously for the right kind of customer to come in. He had to be *sure,* it had to be just the right kind of depositor, and the situation had to be tailor-made. Otherwise, it wasn't worth the chance. The whole thing hinged on specific information, information that could only come from the depositor himself. And ever since he had gotten into this thing, it had been Freddie Mayhew's custom to offer a pleasant good-morning to every depositor who came to the window and engage him in conversation as he took the cash and made out the deposit slip. It was a fact that people who put money into the bank for deposit were a little more cheerful and garrulous than those who took it out. Those who withdrew funds were apt to be a little grim and surly, no doubt thinking of their depleted resources.

He struck pay dirt almost immediately.

A few minutes after the bank opened, a depositor walked up to his window. His name was Halsey, and he was in the trucking business.

"Good morning, Mr. Halsey."

"Morning, Freddie." The man took out five crisp new $100 bills from his wallet. "You can salt this away son, until I come back."

"Oh? You're going away?"

"Yessir. The wife and me are sailing for Europe. Going to be gone for three months. First vacation I've had in five years. Doctor said I'd better take it easy, for the sake of the old ticker. Can't drink any booze, can't smoke cigars, got to watch my diet from here in. Hell, I might as well stop living. But there you are."

"Then you won't be back till the end of April?"

"First of May, to be exact."

"Well, you have a good time, Mister Halsey. And take it easy."

"Thank you, Freddie. If I get a chance, I'll send you one of those French postcards. You're young enough to still appreciate it."

Freddie made out the deposit slip and handed it to Halsey. His heart was thumping. This was perfect, perfect. This meant that the account would be inactive for three months. It meant Halsey wouldn't be walking into the bank, say the day after tomorrow, to make a withdrawal.

When Halsey left, Freddie, his eye still on the lookout for Jonathan Keep, slipped the money into his pocket. Then he made out a deposit card for $500, credited to the account of Walter Halsey. Only this time he did not put the deposit slip through or enter it in the ledger. Instead he put the slip in his pocket, along with the money.

Now the sweat began to pour from his face. He felt himself trembling. Both the money and the deposit slip seemed to be burning a hole in his pocket. He imagined the mass of paper almost alive, wriggling in a struggle to be free. The oil paintings of the Hopkins' ancestors, lining the walls of the bank, all seemed to be glaring down at him now, the lips tight, the eyes ominous, the beards and whiskers bristling. He expected them, at any moment, to cry "Thief, thief." He turned to see Jonathan Keep, who was just coming out of the vault. It seemed to him that Keep was standing there, staring at him curiously. Had Keep seen something? Could he, from inside the vault, have looked out to see him thrust the money and the deposit slip into his pocket. *Did he know?*

He held his breath for what seemed to be a minute. Then he exhaled slowly. Keep had moved over to the file and records section and was now talking to Sarah White, the bookkeeper. Freddie Mayhew could have wept in his relief.

He was convinced now that Keep had seen nothing. There were a couple of more depositors waiting at his window. He could hardly keep his hands from trembling violently as he handled their transactions. Then, for a moment, there was a break in the traffic.

Now he called to Howard Fry, the paying teller, in the next cage.

"Howard, will you watch my window for a moment?"

"Sure. Take your time."

Freddie Mayhew turned and walked quickly into the men's room. It was empty. But just to make sure, he looked for legs under the door of the toilet booth. Then, quickly, he moved to the sink and sank to his knees, praying that no one would walk in. Not now, not for the next few seconds. This was the critical moment, the most frightening of all.

There were a number of loose tiles in the linoleum flooring under the sink. Freddie Mayhew had loosened them himself some time ago. Nobody could tell the difference. They lay flat and looked glued to the floor, as did the others. Quickly Freddie took the deposit card from his pocket and lifted one of the square tiles. There was a pile of other deposit cards hidden beneath. He added the card to the others and replaced the tile, patting it down to make it look as flat and innocuous as possible.

Then he washed his hands and face slowly in cold water. Those deposit cards were his insurance, in case he was asked to produce them by Jonathan Keep or anyone else in the bank, or by the bank examiner himself. And since the depositors like Halsey and the others would be gone for some time, he could always change the time of deposit on the ledger to some later date. For example, he now had $500 that was his for two months or more. Of course, he would have to replace it before Halsey came back, and the same was true of all the others. But a lot could happen to Radio Corporation in a few months.

He went back to his cage feeling better, much better. It would be nice, very nice, if he could get a few more setups, a few more depositors like Walter Halsey.

On the first of December, with luck, that partnership at the radio station could be a reality.

4

ER NAME was Hannah Winthrop. She was the descendant of an old and impoverished Riverside family, and she was thirty-two years old. For the last five years, she had been savings teller at the Puritan Bank and Trust. She had been able to acquire the job through family connections, and it was the kind of work that was considered respectable for a woman of her class. No one ever called her Hannah. She was always "Miss Winthrop," to everyone from Henry Hopkins, the bank president, to Joe Dailey, the guard. As impoverished old-family aristocracy, she was, they felt, entitled to this respect. She was also in charge of the Christmas Club and Vacation Club, and her salary was eighteen dollars a week. She lived in a tiny apartment on Oak Street. Her only company consisted of four cats, all from the same litter, and named Jo, Meg, Beth, and Amy, after the sisters in *Little Women.*

Her alarm clock had gone off exactly at seven-thirty on this, the morning of February 6th. Her cats were meowing loudly, jumping on her bed and rubbing their furry bodies against her face. But for the moment, she ignored them. She was thinking dreamily of the letter she had received yesterday, the letter which now lay on her bureau and which she had read and reread, at least ten times. The letter which could be the answer to her prayers and change her whole life . . .

The cats became insistent now, and she rose and fed them. Then she went into the bathroom, took off her long, high-necked nightgown, and studied her reflection. Her figure was still good, her breasts full and round, her legs firm and shapely. She wore clothes well. The other girls at the bank commented on her body, and the way she could wear clothes, with envy.

It was her face that was her misfortune.

She had been born with a faint harelip, and her nose was a little long and slightly hooked. There was nothing wrong with her complexion. But her mouth spoiled everything. Because of the harelip and some hidden tight muscle, her mouth had a tendency to slant crookedly to the right and remain fixedly in that position. And it slanted even more weirdly when she smiled. She was not ugly in a revolting sense and in no way resembled some kind of gargoyle. She was just plain unattractive. Men looked at her and then turned away. Not with disgust, but merely with a lack of interest.

In the last few years, Hannah Winthrop had been obsessed with her fear that she was destined to be a spinster and end her life in loneliness. She saw herself, chained in her tiny teller's cage at the Puritan year after year, growing old in the service of the bank, eating the same lunch she brought from home each day, the same sardine and tuna and ham sand-wiches in the privacy of the Employees' Room, taking the same Dwight Street trolley home, walking into the same empty apartment, feeding new litters of cats with other names as the years passed, knitting and listening to the radio and going to an occasional movie with one of the few female friends she had, and once in a while visiting her mother, now senile and helpless, at the Home for the Aged.

She had almost accepted the fact that because of her face, she would be manless, and she had begun to dream of other worlds where the men were all handsome, the women all beautiful. She dreamed of being young and lovely, chic and rich. And always some handsome young man, virile and daring and, of course, a millionaire, would come along and ask her to marry him. She loved to go to the movies, sit at the Capitol or the Majestic, and watch Norma Shearer or Greta Garbo or even Janet Gaynor get their men. She read all the movie magazines, and on her bureau were photographs of John Barrymore, Rudolph Valentino, Ramon Novarro. She knew that in this she was acting like some silly schoolgirl. But she didn't care.

Then, suddenly, she had met Edgar.

His full name was Edgar Morton. He was the assistant sales manager at the Apex Hardware Store on Columbus Avenue, and he was a widower of fifty. He was a depositor at the Puritan, and he had been coming into the bank, on and off, for about a year. But it was only a couple of months ago that they had really begun to exchange pleasantries. He was not a handsome man, not even attractive. But what did they say? Beauty was in the eye of the beholder. He was short, rather rotund, wore steel-rimmed glasses, and was almost bald. He lived in a rooming house over on Bridge Street, as Hannah knew by the address on his deposit slips. And she could see that he was lonely. He was not the kind of man who would attract beautiful women, and perhaps he felt on safer and more comfortable ground with her. Anyway, he had asked her, a little timidly, whether she would have dinner with him, and she had accepted. She considered him perhaps a little too old for her, but she was not prepared to be choosy at this point. He was, after all, a man.

After that they had gone out a few times. Sometimes to dinner, sometimes to a movie. And now and then, just for a ride in the country in his secondhand Graham-Paige. She had grown fond of him, and he of her. But what disturbed her was that he never attempted to make love to her, and, particularly, he did not try to kiss her. Then, about two months ago, it had happened.

She remembered that night bitterly, every minute of it. They had gone to the Strand to see Norma Shearer in *The Last of Mrs. Cheyney*. Then they had come back to her apartment, and she had allowed him in for the first time. She had served tea and cookies, and they sat on the couch, close together, and listened to Lanny Ross on the radio. She had waited for him to kiss her, and he did lean his face toward her. But then he turned away, and she knew he could not bring himself to do it. And, of course, she knew why. Actually, she could not blame him.

Anyway, that was the last she heard from him. He no longer came into the bank, and he withdrew his savings by mail. She assumed he did this so that he would not have to endure any embarrassing encounter. She hated him for it, of course, but she also understood him. And she hated herself more. Shortly after that, she had taken a week's vacation, just to get away from it all. She had gone to Boston, and there she had found new hope. More than that. A possible miracle.

She doused herself liberally with toilet water, and put on a heavy wool. Then she prepared her usual breakfast—orange juice, oatmeal, and tea without sugar. She picked up the letter from her bureau and read it once more:

Dear Miss Winthrop:
    As you know, Dr. Ricardi has a very busy schedule, and at present he is booked completely for almost a year. He can now

arrange to perform your plastic surgery on the tenth of December.

He has made a careful study of your facial contours, photographs, and models, and in his opinion, there is every reason to be optimistic.

The fee is $5000 for the actual surgery and postoperative treatment. Half of this is payable by October 10th and the rest upon completion of surgery. And, of course, you will be assessed for the short recuperative period in Dr. Ricardi's private hospital.

Will you notify us immediately, of your availability, since there are many patients seeking appointments?

Very truly yours,
Elizabeth Chandler
(Sec'y to Dr. James Ricardi)

It had been her sister who had suggested to Hannah that she consult Dr. Ricardi while she was in Boston. They were doing marvelous things with plastic surgery these days, changing faces as though they were made of soft plaster, lifting faces so that women looked ten years younger. Dr. Ricardi had a fine reputation in this field. His prices were steep. Only the very rich could afford him. There were very few men in this kind of practice, and he was one of the best. Hannah Winthrop was willing to wait a long time for a wizard like Dr. Ricardi to perform the surgery. Look at the society women he had taken care of, and the film stars. You'd never know them now. He had just peeled years off their faces, and off their lives.

She had gone to see Dr. Ricardi, and he had examined her. He seemed interested in her case, because of the harelip and that taut muscle that kept pulling her mouth to one side. He felt her face with his sensitive hands, measured its curves and contours with calipers and all kinds of strange instruments, and finally told her that she could, indeed, have a new face,

without twist and blemish. Not only new, but while he was
about it, a younger face.

She had almost wept with joy when he had given his
verdict. And she had asked, what would it be like, Doctor,
what would it really be like. He had drawn her a pencil
sketch of her new face, as he saw it, and when she looked at
it, she almost fainted away. It was beautiful—young and
beautiful—not Hannah Winthrop at all, but somebody else
entirely. The face of a stranger. And yet, yet it was *she*.

She had written her eager answer to the letter last night.
And now, all she needed was $5000.

Of course, on a salary of $18 a week, it was impossible to
save $5000 by the tenth of December. She had just *had* to
look for another way. Nobody, absolutely nobody, was going
to keep her from that appointment in Boston.

Finally, she had found another way. It was the way everybody was making money these days.

She stepped over her cats, who were waiting in the vesti-
bule, and went to the door. She opened it and picked up her
morning copy of the *Riverside Union.*

She turned immediately to the financial page, put on her
reading glasses, and ran her finger down the long lines of
agate type. She came to Fisk Rubber, which was quoted at
4. Then she called her broker at Charles Lothrop and Company.

"I want to buy some more Fisk Rubber."

"Yes, Miss Winthrop? How much?"

"Fifty shares."

"On the usual margin?"

"Please."

"Thank you very much. By the way, we're pretty high on
Fisk down here. We think it's going places. If you can see
your way to picking up some more . . ."

"You really think it's going up?"

"Well, we think the whole market's going up. The way business is booming, we don't see how the market can help but follow. Now, a security like Fisk is going begging at four. The high-priced stocks are pretty saturated. People are looking for bargains around this price. That means a buying trend. And so, if you can see your way clear . . ."

"All right," said Hannah faintly. "Make it a hundred shares."

"Yes, ma'am!" The broker sounded cheerful, as though this was a nice way to open his morning. "We'll put the order through right away, Miss Winthrop."

She made her bed, quickly, and picked up the cats' dishes and washed them in the zinc sink. Then she fitted a moulded turban on her head. Again, she wondered what Edgar Morton's reaction would be when he first set eyes on the *new* Hannah Winthrop. She was willing to wager he would come running then. And then, she thought cruelly, when I get my new face, why Edgar Morton? Why would I have to settle for him? Why, indeed? I could have my pick. Better men, richer men, younger men, more handsome men. She smiled at the thought. She couldn't wait until that first moment when he saw her, after the change had been complete.

She went downstairs and walked to the Dwight Street trolley stop. She would need money, of course, to cover that purchase of Fisk Rubber. She already had 2000 dollars' worth of Fisk, and she had gotten the money to buy all those shares in the same way.

Of course, she would have to be careful, as usual. The man to watch was Jonathan Keep, the bank treasurer. Thank heaven, she had those withdrawal slips hidden in a safe place, in a place where he could never find them. There was absolutely no way he could find them; she was totally secure in that. When you came down to it, she was only really borrowing the money. She intended to pay the bank back just as soon as possible. And when you came down to it, was it really wrong? She was doing the same thing everybody else in the country was doing. Investing in American business. Including the bank itself.

She had read Mr. Raskob's article in the *Ladies Home Journal*. And he was right. Absolutely right. Everyone should make as much money as he or she needed in these times of prosperity.

Again, she thought of her secret hiding place, right there in the bank, and she smiled to herself. Really, when you thought of it, it was very funny.

Still, she couldn't help feeling just a little uneasy. And when she finally got the $5000 she needed, she would repay every cent she had taken from the bank. There was no point in being greedy.

*

When Hannah Winthrop arrived at the bank, she wasted no time.

She liked to get to the business at hand early. Get it over and done with and face the rest of the day with a serene mind.

For a moment, she pondered the options open to her. As savings teller, she had access, of course, to the dormant accounts. But as Christmas Club and Vacation Club teller, there was a simple way to get the cash she needed. She could pocket the money given to her by some of the members of the Christmas Club and then simply fail to put the coupons through. After all, Christmas was many months away and she could replace the missing money by then. If necessary, she could rob Peter to pay Paul. That is, take money from the Vacation Club to make up the deficit in the Christmas Club.

She had used this technique before. But she decided now

to forego it, on the theory that one never overdid anything. She had drained the Christmas Club of at least a thousand dollars as it was, and there was always the chance that someone might come in and ask for their club money before the holiday came. That was all right. She had the coupons safely hidden away. If need be, she could always replace the cash from her own resources for the one or two club members who wanted their money before Christmas. The totals here would be no more than one hundred dollars, two hundred dollars at the most. The average Christmas Club member collected a hundred dollars at the end of the year.

This time, she decided to draw from the dormant accounts.

She took out the file, and started to go through the cards marked "dormant." She kept a weather eye cocked for Jonathan Keep, but she was not particularly worried. It was her job, as savings teller, to bring this file up to date. The file consisted of all depositors who had not made a transaction in five years or more. Nobody knew why. Some of them were dead, and the bank had not been notified. Some had moved to another part of the country and forgotten that they still had an account and money deposited at the Puritan. Once a year, the Puritan advertised these accounts, asking the holders to come into the bank and liquidate them. But despite the advertisements, a number of these depositors had never appeared. Nobody knew of their whereabouts, and in most cases, they were presumed dead.

On this morning, she found two cards with dormant depositors who had made no deposits or withdrawals in the past ten years. One was credited with $1000, the other with $600. She then made out two withdrawal slips, one for $200 and the other for $100. She made duplicates of the same slips, then took $300 from the cash drawer, and with a quick glance at Keep, stuffed the money in her purse. As far as the bank was now concerned, and if anybody asked, the long-dormant depositors had now shown up and withdrawn cash from their accounts. And Hannah Winthrop had the withdrawal slips to prove it. There was always a certain amount of danger to this, of course. And Hannah was haunted by it. One of these ghosts *could* walk in some day soon and ask for a statement of his or her account—walk in out of nowhere, so to speak. As long as she was present, she knew she could handle it somehow. But what bothered her, and kept jangling that tiny nerve, was the fact that the ghost might walk in, big as life, while she was absent one day—out sick, perhaps. Then, of course, there was a chance that the whole thing could blow up in her face. This was the perennial fear of the bank embezzler—to miss a day. You never knew what might happen in your absence. It was imperative to be at the bank *every* day. Even a vacation was out of the question as long as there were telltale records hidden around.

Now Hannah Winthrop went into the ladies' room. At the moment, Mary Burt, the proof operator, was in there. They chatted for a moment, and then the other woman left. And now, Hannah went immediately to *her* hiding place.

There was a cabinet on the wall, stocked with several dozen rolls of toilet paper in double rows on the shelves. She took a chair, stepped on it, and reached high up on the top shelf for the second roll of toilet paper in the back row, on the left. The tissue paper which covered this roll had already been broken.

She then put the chair back in the usual place in front of the mirror, retired into one of the toilet booths, and locked the door. She unrolled the toilet paper, about two yards of it, until she came to a pad of withdrawal slips she had put there at various times. She added the two withdrawal slips she had just made out and rerolled the toilet paper. Then she came out and peeked through a crack in the door to see if anyone was coming. When she was satisfied that it was safe, she replaced the roll of toilet paper in its original position. She knew that no one would be using that particular shelf for a long time, since the lower shelves were amply supplied with enough rolls to last for many weeks.

After that she stared at her face in the mirror, trying to imagine how it would look ten months from now.

5

AT EIGHT O'CLOCK on this same morning, Jonathan Keep, treasurer of the Puritan Bank and Trust, sat in a tattered bathrobe in his meager room and pored over his charts.

Now and then he would refer to the most recent copy of the *Wall Street Journal,* or *Barron's,* or one of the lesser financial journals piled high on his table. He peered at the print through his rimless glasses and then made rapid notations on a scratch pad which came from the bank and bore the figure of a Puritan on the top of each page. This was a likeness of Increase Hopkins, founder and symbol of the bank. Jonathan Keep hated to spend the money for these financial periodicals. But he had found them very worthwhile, and they had already paid for themselves many times over.

He was a careful and precise man, with an index mind when it came to figures and statistics. He believed in facts, not fantasies. Let the other fools run to their brokers on some offhand tip. Let them be gulled by every rumor that came along. He, Jonathan Keep, made his judgment and selection by other standards. How sound was the stock? What was its price-earnings ratio? Sales last year, sales this year, capital investment, debt outstanding, percentage of growth, product desirability, executive management, shares outstanding, performance of preferred?

He plotted his charts a few minutes more. Then he came to a decision. It was the same choice he had made many times before. He decided to buy fifty shares of Baldwin Locomotive, on margin. This morning it was quoted at 42, and in his opinion it was undervalued. In his opinion nothing adverse could really happen to it. The railroads in America were expanding, even though Henry Ford was turning out thousands of new cars in Detroit. Even in bad times, they would still be running, come hell and high water. There was a lot of talk that Lindbergh and Admiral Byrd had opened up a new air age, and that these airplanes would cut into the railroads one day. Jonathan Keep considered these people wild-eyed visionaries. How much freight could these airplanes carry? And who in his right mind would really fly in them as passengers? He liked to repeat the old joke: If you're in an airplane and you have an accident—where are you? But if you're in a *train* and have an accident—there you are.

This morning he would telephone his order in to Lothrop and Company, stockbrokers, from the pay phone at Wilson's Cigar Store, on his way to the bank. He didn't want Henry Hopkins to know his business. Besides, the employees of the bank had strict orders. They were forbidden to invest in the market, and that went for everyone from Henry Hopkins right down to the lowest employee.

Jonathan Keep was fifty-seven years old, and he had been with the Puritan Bank and Trust for over thirty years. He knew everything that was going on in the bank. He knew every nook and cranny, and he had a fiendish memory for exactly what was stored in every envelope, in every drawer and compartment in the vault.

He was a tall, emaciated man. He had a thin face and chilly blue eyes, over which thick bushy eyebrows beetled like the rims of two saucers. He was almost bald except for the tufts of gray hair leaping from his temples, and his speech was clipped and just a little nasal. Both his name and his appearance created a kind of odd caricature, rather Dickensian. And some people remarked that Keep reminded them of a twentieth-century Ebenezer Scrooge. He was conscious that people did not especially like him and that his personality grated upon them at times. But he was not looking for anybody's approval. He felt that he would rather live without it. If he was a lonely man, he liked it that way. He had his eye on the target; he knew what he wanted. And he intended to get it. This was all that interested him.

Each day he did his work at the bank and came home. He was a bachelor, and his rent for the single room at Mrs. Allen's was only three dollars a week. The rooming house was within walking distance of the bank, so he did not have to pay any carfare. He did his own mending and cooking, ironed his own shirts, packed his own lunch, which he ate by himself in the Board Room at the rear of the bank. He did not drink or smoke. Once a week he went to the movies, and this was practically his sole recreation. Once or twice during the summer, he would splurge by taking the Sunday excursion train to New York in order to see Babe Ruth and the Yankees play, and sometimes he would go to a Minsky's burlesque show. He had never considered marriage seriously, at any time. Women had passed him by—or rather, as he liked to think, he had passed them by. Occasionally he would feel the sex urge, and he would go to a whorehouse in Holyoke, in the paper mill district, where he knew a prostitute who was reasonable.

Although Jonathan Keep's official title at the bank was treasurer, it meant nothing. The title was high-sounding, but empty. He was actually the note teller. This meant that he was not even an executive of the Puritan, but simply another employee, even if he was second in command to Henry Hopkins. Banks were no different from other business institutions when it came to bestowing impressive titles upon employees in lieu of higher salaries. Keep's salary at the bank was forty dollars a week, and in the last five years, Henry Hopkins had never given him a raise.

For years, he had hated his job at the Puritan, and especially Henry Hopkins.

He hated his superior because by virtue of birth, just by being the descendant of Increase Hopkins, Henry Hopkins had been given the Puritan. It was a tight family bank, and a Hopkins had always been president, no matter how stupid. He, Jonathan Keep, had forgotten more about banking than Hopkins ever knew. He resented the fact that, after all these years, he had never been raised to the status of an officer nor been invited to sit in at the monthly board meetings. Here he was now, a man in his late fifties, still earning a pittance after all these years of hard work. He felt abused, set-upon, and humiliated, not only by Henry Hopkins, but by his cronies, the directors of the Puritan, the wealthy, poker-playing, whiskey-drinking descendants of Riverside's First Families. Jonathan Keep felt like a trapped animal in that first cage on teller's row, from which he could see the president sitting at his massive desk on the thick carpeted area behind the rail. The least Hopkins could have done, he thought angrily, was to give him a desk on the carpet, even a small one, so that he could *feel* like somebody.

Nobody in the bank knew it, but Jonathan Keep was a man with one great passion, one burning ambition, and that was to run his own bank.

For a long time it had been only a dream. But then he had begun to accumulate a nest egg by denying himself everything but the barest essentials and had started to buy Baldwin Locomotive. The market had gone up and up. And Jonathan Keep, torn between his conscience and the smell of opportunity, had decided to tap a new and much bigger source of cash, the bank itself. Of course, he would replace the money at the proper time, every dime of it. He did not look upon this as gambling with funds that were not his. He was merely investing in one of the giants of American business, and in this sense, in the country itself. If a company like Baldwin went, then the whole nation would go as well. And that, of course, was ridiculous.

To be president of a bank some day, he knew he would have to fill one requirement. He would have to "buy" the position, and he knew it would be expensive. Experience alone would not be enough. He would have to make a solid investment in money, a large deposit in his own name.

Now his dream had a chance of fruition. By fall he should have all the money he needed.

Keep was not worried about the state bank examiner, a man named Alfred Benziger. Benziger visited the Puritan once a year. He always stayed at the Worthy Hotel. He always came into town a day before his examination, and all personnel at the Puritan knew exactly when he got off the train and checked in. It was one of the duties of the desk clerk at the Worthy, for a slight fee, to phone the Puritan immediately when Benziger arrived. Thus alerted, everyone could "smarten up" the cash count and ledgers and get all accounts in order.

No, thought Keep, he could write off the bank examiner as a threat. Henry Hopkins was another matter, of course. But he, Keep, was prepared against any surprise. He not only had two sets of books, but if pressed, he could come up with a reasonable explanation for anything.

Anything. Except what he had hidden in a secret area of

the vault. But nobody would ever think of looking there. And only Henry Hopkins and he had the keys to the vault. He dressed, packed a brown-bag lunch, and went out. He stopped in at Wilson's Cigar Store and called Lothrop and Company. Charles Lothrop, head of the firm, answered. On an impulse, Keep ordered a hundred shares of Baldwin instead of fifty. Again, he asked whether his account would be held confidential, and once again, Lothrop assured him that the accounts of *all* clients were strictly confidential.

He walked out onto the street again and toward the Puritan. It was a square and massive building, made entirely of the sandstone indigenous to the region. Small windows were cut through the brown-colored stone, and the building bore two turreted towers, like some medieval fortress. It was entered by a short flight of wide granite steps, and these steps were bisected by a brass handrail that extended from the sidewalk level up the stairs to the doorway itself. Each day, this rail was polished till it shone to a dazzling brightness by Joe Dailey, a grizzled Irishman with a thick brogue who served both as bank guard and custodian.

On the sidewalk stood the bank's clock, a city landmark. The Puritan Clock was huge, perhaps five or six feet in diameter, and was set on a high sandstone pillar. The hands of this clock were in burnished gold leaf, and at night the clock was illuminated. It could be seen for several blocks up and down Main Street and kept what was known as Western Union Time. In the memory of old residents, it had stopped only twice. Once when the city had been hit by an earthquake tremor in 1906. And again, in 1915, when the clock had been struck by lightning. As the saying went in Riverside: "You can always set your watch by the Puritan."

Jonathan Keep was admitted to a side door by the custodian.

"Morning, Mr. Keep."

"Morning, Joe."

"Going to be a cold one."

"Looks that way."

Jonathan Keep went into the bank and headed for his cage. The bank had been built in 1881, and, actually, very little had changed since then. The main-floor area was stone, scuffed with the soles of heavy boots and shoes through many decades. Along the walls was a series of dull and sober oil paintings, all portraits of the members of the Hopkins clan, all of whom had headed the bank at one time or another since its inception. To a man, they were stern of visage, staring down with hard Yankee frowns, each bewhiskered or sporting a walrus mustache, each full-fleshed and portly, each wearing a heavy watch chain stretched across a vest covering an ample stomach.

But it was their eyes which bothered Jonathan Keep. They seemed almost alive, cold and suspicious. They seemed to follow him around the bank wherever he went. And they seemed focused on him, especially when he opened the vault, as though trying to catch him in the act.

Well, thought Jonathan Keep nervously, the hell with them. They're all dead. The only Hopkins he had to worry about was a live one.

Henry Hopkins.

*

As treasurer of the Puritan, Jonathan Keep had many duties. He was not only note teller and collection teller, but he was responsible for the books and customer ledgers, and he supervised the bookkeepers. When Henry Hopkins approved a loan, it was Keep who figured out the interest and collected payments on the loan. Now and then, if the president was not available, Keep had the authority to grant a small loan, as long as it was backed by proper collateral. The Puritan had recently put in a system of safe deposit boxes, and Keep was also in charge of this department.

Of all those who were "borrowing" money from the Puritan, Jonathan Keep's method was perhaps the simplest and most foolproof.

A half-hour after the bank had opened, a merchant named Chalmers came into the Puritan. He had borrowed $5000 from the bank, and now he wanted to reduce this loan by $1000. The treasurer was the man he had to see on this transaction. Keep took the $1000, which was in cash, and handed Chalmers a receipt. He did not enter the transaction into the books of the bank but simply pocketed the money instead. As far as the bank was concerned, Chalmers still owed the Puritan $5000 dollars instead of $4000. Since Keep calculated the interest—a routine job—Chalmers would receive a bill for interest on $4000 rather than $5000 and, as a result, would have no reason to suspect anything. And, Keep reasoned, there was plenty of time to replace the $1000, as well as the other sums he had taken. Clearly, Baldwin Locomotive was going no place but up.

In order to play it safe, Jonathan Keep kept two sets of books. In one, he manipulated the entries to suit himself and to present for Henry Hopkins' inspection, in case the president wanted to see any of the transactions. But he had another ledger hidden away, for the eyes of the bank examiner, just in case Alfred Benziger should happen to drop in out of schedule. This was highly unlikely, to be sure, but Jonathan Keep was not a man to overlook any hole in the dike, however small.

The hiding place in which he kept this doctored ledger was virtually foolproof. It was in the Safe Deposit Box Department, a caged area supervised only by himself. It was Keep who possessed the master key to the grilled door, and he was the only one empowered to admit clients to the area. He had issued strict orders to the custodian, Joe Dailey, never to clean the area unless he, Keep, was present.

The rows of safe deposit boxes rested on an iron base raised four inches from the floor itself. It was Keep's practice, whenever necessary, to linger in the bank a few minutes after closing time and after everyone had gone. Then he would enter the area. The ledger itself was taped to the underside of the iron base. By lying flat on his stomach and reaching into the air space between the base and the floor, Keep could draw out the ledger. Then he could make the necessary changes and retape the ledger in its hiding place. Sometimes, when he had to make extensive changes in the entries of this ledger—as well as the one he kept on his desk for Hopkins' inspection—he would come down to the bank on weekends, take out the hidden ledger, and do what he had to do. This was easy enough, since only two people in the bank had a key to the outside door of the bank—Henry Hopkins and himself.

Actually there was a third key, if you wanted to include Alfred Benziger, who had a duplicate key to every bank in his territory. But this was only a technicality. Hopkins was, under the circumstances, the only man he would really have to watch.

And so Jonathan Keep had good reason to feel totally secure. After all, no one was ever in here alone, without Keep's being present. And then, even if someone did get in here alone, he would never dream of looking under the safe deposit boxes.

Not in a thousand years.

6

WHEN HENRY HOPKINS awoke, he noted that the twin bed next to him was empty. He knew that his wife, Helen, had already dressed and gone downstairs. The sound of water running in the bathtub down the hallway told him that his nineteen-year-old daughter, Eleanor— or Ellie, as everyone called her—had also arisen.

He lay there quietly for a moment, feeling somewhat tired. He had not, in fact, slept very well, for a variety of reasons. He was just a little hung over from a dinner party held at the Longmeadow Country Club the night before. The bootleg scotch had not been of the first quality, and in the locker room a group of members had appointed Henry a committee of one to take care of it. He was also heavily invested in the market on full margin, his cash equity, at this time, amounting to some $50,000. This morning he was a little worried about the way things were going, not because the market was bad, but because it was a little too good. Despite one or two temporary setbacks, it continued to push upward. His New England sense of caution was deeply ingrained in him. He was, after all, a banker. And in his dealings with his own clients, he had always been highly conservative.

He rolled out of bed, heavily, and padded to the window

in his bare feet. The Hopkinses lived at 3 Overlook Lane in a large and graceful brick house of Georgian design, in the exclusive section known as "the Hill," along Maple Street. As always, and even on this gray day, he found what he saw greatly pleasing. On each side of his own house, he saw the Georgians or big white Colonials of his neighbors, and all of them had wide, sweeping, manicured lawns. Looking beyond and down the hill, he could see the city itself sprawling below, the roofs of its houses and factories clumped together in a warm huddle, and beyond them, the Connecticut River, now covered with ice. Across the river, he could see West Riverside, and beyond that, the broken line of the Berkshire hills themselves.

As a descendant of the original settler, Increase Hopkins, he could not help but feel a sense of pride, a proprietary interest in the city spread below. Increase, long ago, had shown an instinct for a fast dollar. He had bought what was now Riverside from the Nipmuck Indians. The price he had paid was eighteen fathoms of wampum, eighteen coats, eighteen hatchets, eighteen hoes, and eighteen knives. In return, he had given the Indians the right to take from the land fish, deer, walnuts, and acorns. The price was somewhat less than that paid for the island of Manhattan. All in all, it had not been a bad deal.

Finally Henry Hopkins turned away from the window and went into the bathroom. He was one of the few who had not yet succumbed to the advertising blandishments of Gillette, and he still used a straight razor. He liked to think of himself as an old-fashioned man, unswayed by all the new fads that seemed to be captivating everybody. And somehow the straight razor symbolized this. For the same reason, he wore a big Hamilton vest-pocket watch, one that had belonged to his grandfather, Ethan Hopkins. Let the others wear wrist-watches.

Henry Hopkins was fifty-five years old. He felt fit, and he

believed he looked it, for a man of his age. He was almost
six feet tall, gray at the temples, but otherwise totally bald.
His face had a hawklike cast, with a thin, sharp nose that was
perhaps a shade too prominent. But this was a Hopkins trait,
and all of his family had it, all the way back to Increase
himself. True, his body was a little on the fleshy side. He
could see the faint jowls under his chin, but he soothed
himself with the lie that they gave him dignity. What really
bothered him, however, was the look of his stomach. He had
somewhat of a paunch, which people at that time politely
called *avoirdupois,* or more rudely, a "bay window." But he
comforted himself with the thought that it was visible only
when he let his posture sag. And after all, he told himself,
he was no longer a boy. What could you expect of a man who
got very little exercise, who spent most of his day at a desk?
On this morning, he made his usual resolution, one that he
never kept. He swore to take an occasional weekday, get
away from the bank, and, in season, to play more golf—and
of course, to watch his diet.

He shaved and bathed and selected a gray three-button
sack suit, a conservative Kuppenheimer model he had
bought on one of his frequent trips to New York. Then he
went downstairs for breakfast. His wife was sitting at the
polished table in the big dining room when he entered. She
turned her cheek obediently to him. He kissed it lightly and
then sat down.

"Dear," she said, "I'll need some money."

"What for?"

"I'm going to the beauty salon this morning. Then I need
a new hat. *And* a dress. After all, we're having dinner at the
White House next week, and I don't want to look tacky. I'm
sure there'll be pictures taken, and I don't want my friends
to see me in something I've worn before."

"How much will you need?"

"Two hundred dollars."

"Helen, do you think I'm *made* of money?"

She looked at him coldly. Then, like a cutting knife: "If I still had my *own* money, we wouldn't have to go through all this, would we, Henry?"

He winced. "Must you always remind me of that?"

"I try not to. It's only when you get so stingy . . ."

"All right, all right," he said testily. Her barb had struck home. He felt guilty, humiliated, angry. "But I don't have that much cash on me. You'll have to stop by at the bank later." And he thought, I'll pay you back, madam, I'll pay you back every cent I took, if it kills me.

Helen Hopkins smiled sweetly and thanked him. She had a special use for that money, and it wasn't for a dress. Like many wives, she wheedled small sums of cash out of her husband for private reasons of her own, and thought, *what he doesn't know won't hurt him.* She was a matronly woman of fifty, and she, too, was descended from an old Valley family. She was a graduate of Smith and once had been a beautiful girl. But now she had ripened into a kind of over-maturity and ran somewhat to fat. Her plump neck was just a trifle baggy, and there were creases along the line of the jaw and around her eyes. Her husband no longer regarded her as a sexual creature. They were at that stage of marriage where they simply fitted each other, old shoes perfectly matched, taking each other for granted without too much irritation. Twice a week, she played mahjong with a group of other matrons whom she always called "the girls." And once a week, there was bridge at the club. Not auction, but the new game of contract that people now were so wild about. She belonged to the Maple Street Garden Club, the Tuesday Morning Literary Club, the Riverside Hospital Auxiliary, and all the other organizations thought worthy and proper for a banker's wife. Her hair was close-shaped and shingled, and on this morning she wore one of the new moulded silhouette dresses, in satin. It hugged her figure to the knees, so close that the stays of her corset could be seen underneath, and at the hem the dress flared pertly in circular flounces.

"Morning, Dad. Mother."

Ellie Hopkins came down the stairs and kissed each of them on the cheek. She looked tired, her face a little drawn. Her black hair was closely bobbed in the current mode. Her soft mouth was lightly touched with Chanel red, and she was dressed to go out, in a Godet knee-length skirt of dull satin, with Alençon lace yoke. It clung to her young curved body like a sheath. Satin was the thing this year. The hat she wore was a moulded-to-head creation of pointed-ear felt with glacé buttons, and she wore snake shoes, slave bracelets, and beads.

"Dear," said her mother, "you look peaked. You've got to get more rest."

"I'm all right, Mother."

"We've hardly seen you all weekend. You shouldn't be running around with all those boys and staying up so late."

"Mother, I *told* you I'm all right."

Mrs. Hopkins watched her daughter anxiously. She noted that all Ellie was having for breakfast was a cup of black coffee.

"Where are you going this morning, dear?"

"Out."

"I know. But where?"

"Just out. For heaven's sake, Mother, I'm not a child. I'm twenty-two. Do I have to tell you *everything?*"

"I'm sorry, dear," said Mrs. Hopkins, now contrite. "I didn't mean to nag."

Ellie Hopkins finished her coffee. Then she took a package of Sweet Caporals from her purse. She expertly flipped out a cigarette by jerking the package upward in her hand, tamped the cigarette once or twice on a painted fingernail, and lit it.

Her father watched all this with disapproval. He also noted that in the position Ellie was sitting, with her legs crossed and with her short skirt, she was revealing too much sheer silk and bare thigh. He adored his daughter. But now he felt that he had to straighten her out about a few things.

"Do you have to smoke, Ellie?"

"Daddy, we're not going into *that* again."

"I just don't think it's feminine for a young girl to smoke cigarettes."

"Oh, bushwah!"

"And that dress you're wearing—it's a disgrace. You women are all going crazy. The next thing you know, you'll be wearing them up to your navels."

"Henry," said his wife, "it's really a lovely frock. Very chic."

"By that," he said sourly, "I presume you mean stylish." Then he complained. "Chic. All these French words they're using these days. What's the matter with the good old American way of saying things?" Then he recalled something else. Early that morning, he had awakened to hear a car drive up. It had stayed parked in front of the house for over half an hour. It had been his daughter's car, and she had been in it with some boy. Henry Hopkins refused to admit it, even to himself. But a nagging nerve, somewhere deep below, told him that they had left the front seat and gone into the back seat of the car. Of late, he had been thinking the unthinkable. It was possible, just possible, that his daughter, his little girl, was no longer a virgin.

He tried to thrust the horrendous thought from his mind.

"You got in late last night. Two o'clock."

"All right, Daddy. What of it?"

"Who were you with?"

"Isn't that *my* business?"

Helen Hopkins quickly agreed with her daughter and told her husband so. Now he told Ellie that he was aware that she had lingered a half-hour with some boy in the car before she'd come in. And his daughter sighed in disgust.

"Daddy, you *are* such a stick-in-the-mud."

"Am I?"

"Terribly bourgois. A real Babbitt."

"Ellie!" warned her mother. "You know how your father hates that word."

"I'm as progressive as the next man," he said, irritated, "but you're just a kid."

"Oh, for God's sake," said his daughter. "When are you going to become part of it, Daddy? The world, I mean. This is nineteen twenty-nine, not the Dark Ages." She irritated him further with another French word. "You're passé, Daddy. Terribly passé. We're not Victorian lovers standing in the garden, dressed in long crinoline, swooning by the fountain, and waiting for our lovers to come. Haven't you heard of the emancipated woman? Why can't you be blasé about it, like everyone else, instead of playing the outraged father? There's no need to look so damned shocked."

"Will you at least try to talk like a lady?"

"Your father's right, Ellie," said Helen Hopkins. "It isn't really ladylike to swear."

"I'm leaving," said Ellie. "All I've been getting here is criticism."

He stared at her frock again. "That damned dress. It makes you look naked. Why don't you wear a corset or something?"

"Don't be silly, Daddy," she said, coolly. "Haven't you heard? The body is in. If I wear corsets, none of the boys will dance with me."

She glared at her father and walked out of the room. A

moment later, they heard the roar of her Marmon and the scrape of tires on the gravel driveway as Ellie drove away. Now Helen Hopkins looked at her husband reproachfully.

"Dear, you shouldn't have been so hard on her."

"Helen, I just don't understand young girls today. No manners, no respect, nothing. They're all going to hell on a raft, if you ask me."

This was the way Henry Hopkins, essentially a conservative and a fond parent, saw it. But he was not an anachronism; he had plenty of company. He and his fellow poker players at the club had often discussed the behavior of the young, and they viewed what was going on with alarm. Their daughters now rouged their faces, smoked, and drank gin. Sex had become the byword and the password. And they all agreed that the automobile had been responsible. The petting party in the back seat had become SOP—standard operating procedure.

The young people at the club, whenever it came to a dance, now insisted on jazz. The Hopkinses and the other elders stood around the dance floor and now listened, not to the romantic violin, but to the barbaric saxophone. The banjos twanged and the trombones blared and the clarinets piped their sensuous rhythms. Not just in respectable places like the Longmeadow Country Club, but in dance halls, speakeasies, and over the radios of the nation. And the lyrics! Hell, thought Henry Hopkins, they were all for the smoking car now. There was a new one out, for example:

Oooooooh, you bad bad boy, that was so nice,
Of course, I may scream—but please do it twice.

He had noted the way Ellie danced at the club, very close, cheek to cheek, in syncopated embrace. He had often wanted to grab the boy and throw him out one of the windows. And the trash they discussed. They were always talking this blah about the libido and the id, and companionate marriage, and this damned German (or was he Austrian) witch doctor, Sigmund Freud. And worse than that—they openly talked about homosexuality now.

"Helen," said Henry Hopkins. "I mean it. I just don't understand these kids today. They're absolutely without morals, don't even know right from wrong anymore. They've all gone hog wild."

*

After his wife had left, Henry Hopkins sat back and thought about the trip they would make to Washington the following Thursday.

The invitation from the President had been entirely unexpected, and both Hopkins and his wife had been surprised and flattered. The social and personal pages of both the *Riverside Republican* and the *Union* had carried stories of the invitation. Their friends were full of envy and could talk of nothing else. It would be nice to see old Calvin again, thought Hopkins, before he left office. And Grace, too. He and Helen expected to see a lot of the Coolidges after they moved back to Northampton. He knew the President cherished one thing above all—and that was his old friends. People like Henry W. Stearns; old classmates like Alfred Pierce Dennis, Dwight Morrow, Reuben F. Wells, and himself. And even simple people like James Lucey, the Northampton cobbler who had lined up votes for him in his early campaigns. He must remember not to call the President "Coolie," as he had in college days and for some years after that.

Now Henry Hopkins looked at his watch. He still had fifteen minutes before he would drive to the bank. He picked up the copy of the *New York Times,* to which he subscribed, and went to the red leather Morris chair in the living room. He adjusted it by means of a small lever at the side into a half-reclining position. Then he lit a cigar and settled back. This was a morning ritual, and he always looked forward to it.

He glanced quickly at the news items on the front page. But this was only a quick apéritif. Always, and deliberately, he delayed turning to the financial page immediately. It was a test of his own self-discipline, proof to himself that he, personally, was not infected by the market fever *that* much, to the exclusion of everything else. A man had to have a sense of perspective, he reasoned. After all, one should read the general news, if only to be informed as to the world around him, and *then* turn to the financial page. All this gave him the comfortable feeling that his head was still solidly on his shoulders, his feet firmly on the ground.

But the fact was that all of his assets were invested in the market. In the beginning, he had started to buy securities with his own money. Then, as time went on, he began to "borrow" other sums from the bank to buy more stock as new opportunities arose. In his mind, the money he took was for personal loans, although somewhat unorthodox. And, of course, he would pay them back in good time. The fact that there was no collateral to back up the money he "borrowed" did not particularly bother him. He himself made a few loans to borrowers without collateral. People he really trusted. He did this rarely, of course. But why not lend to himself? Why not indeed?

Now and then, he worried about the members of the board of directors. God help him, if *they* found out. But then, he was always able to reassure himself. He was covered, very well covered. He had always been very careful as to the way he handled these special transactions. Actually, the only man he had to worry about was Jonathan Keep. Keep was a snoop; he was always sniffing around. Henry Hopkins disliked him intensely. But he was a valuable employee, very valuable, and the Puritan could hardly get along without him.

At first Hopkins had made his investments with a brokerage firm in New York. This was to conceal the fact that he was in the market at all. People in Riverside, and notably the depositors at the Puritan, had certain strong opinions. And one of them was that a banker should stick to his own business and not play around in the stock market. The members of the board heartily concurred in this opinion.

The long-distance phone calls to the New York brokerage house had proved inconvenient. They were not only a nuisance, but expensive. He had therefore sought out Charles Lothrop of Lothrop and Company, the bigger of the two brokerage houses in Riverside, and taken Lothrop into his confidence. He had then opened a "dummy" account under the name of James Cooper. Actually it was the name of a distant uncle of whom the family had heard nothing for years.

There was nothing unusual in this. There were a number of other dummy, or confidential, accounts on Lothrop's list. The fact that Henry was occasionally seen with Charlie Lothrop, at lunch or elsewhere, meant nothing. They were both members of the club. They were both men concerned with matters of finance, and those who saw them together simply assumed they were merely matching notes on the state of the economy. Moreover, the Puritan had certain normal and routine dealings with Lothrop and Company on behalf of some of its depositors, who very often would instruct the bank to send assets to Lothrop by messenger so that stock purchases could be covered.

Even Henry's wife did not know he was in the market. He had his own private opinion about a woman's ability to keep a secret for long. Moreover, he had another, and much more personal, reason for not letting her know. Four years ago, he had sworn not only to himself, but to her, that he would never again be involved in anything that even smelled of risk or speculation.

In one sense, he had stuck to this promise. That is to say, he had bought only blue chips. There were no "cats and dogs" in his portfolio; each security was gilt-edged. He had learned *that* lesson the hard way. Some twenty months ago, he had bought securities like General Electric, American Telephone, Steel, and Westinghouse. He had smelled the boom early, and everything he owned had gone up. Now the value of his portfolio had doubled.

Four years ago, he had been caught investing in the disastrous Florida land boom and had lost some $200,000. Some of it had been his own money. But most of it had belonged to his wife, left to her in her father's will. Although she rarely mentioned it now, she had never forgiven him for it, and until he was able to recoup and pay her back, he could not rest. He was in the market, therefore, not just for profit, but for his pride as well. It was his intention to make up his Florida losses in the market, no more, no less. Then he would get out and stay out. The Florida speculation had taught him a bitter lesson. Buy only solid merchandise. The blue chips. Let the wild and woolly stuff alone. And after what he would always think of as "that damned Florida thing," he had sworn an oath.

Never again.

Now Henry Hopkins' eye quickly scanned the financial page. He looked over the quotations, but he was more interested, at the moment, in what the market analysts had to say. And on this morning, they were, almost to a man, highly optimistic. The bull market was strong, stronger than ever. It had not yet run out of steam, and probably it would not for a long, long time. After all, the economy was bursting at the seams, the gross national product soaring.

Yet he was disturbed to note that among the chorus of optimists there were one or two dissenters. He read what they had to say, and he felt slightly queasy. One of the dissenters was an economist named Roger Babson. An enterprising *Times* reporter had managed to get an advance copy of a speech Babson was to deliver before a business conference in early March. In it he stated that sooner or later a crash was coming and could well be catastrophic. He suggested that what had happened in Florida, back in '26, conceivably might soon happen on Wall Street. He predicted that the Dow Jones averages could drop anywhere from 60 to 80 points from the present level. And in a final burst of comforting cheer, he concluded that without doubt there would be a serious business depression.

He put down the paper and decided to call Charlie Lothrop.

As the connection was made, he could hear through the receiver the erratic sound of the ticker. It stopped and started, as though warming up for the opening of the market. He could hear also the buzz and hum of many voices, and already the place sounded crowded with people. Just listening to the hubbub sent a thrill of excitement through him, the same kind that possesses a bettor at a track just before the horses are about to burst from the barrier. Suddenly Henry Hopkins felt a hunger to be there, where the action was, so to speak. For a moment he toyed with the idea of stopping by for a few minutes on his way to the bank. But then, sternly, he suppressed it.

"Good morning, Henry. Good morning."

"Morning, Charlie. You seem to have a full house down there."

"Yes, *sir.*" Charlie Lothrop laughed. "The natives are restless."

"How does the market look?"

"Fine. Never better. Lots of big 'buy' transactions coming up. Big blocks of stock. Radio, General Cable, Gardner Motors. Looks as though the word for today is 'buy.' "

"Charlie, did you read that piece about Babson in this morning's *Times?*"

"I read it."

"Frankly, I didn't like it. I'm a little worried."

"Henry, look. There's no point in getting upset just because some wild man like this Babson makes an idiotic statement like that. He bills himself as an economist and statistician, but he's really an educator and philosopher—you know, one of those college professor types. He's made a lot of predictions before, and he's been wrong so many times that it isn't even funny. And at no time has he affected prices one damned bit."

"Then you think he's crazy?"

Lothrop laughed. "I sure do. Crazy as a fox."

"What does *that* mean?"

"There's a rumor around that my friend and yours, Roger W. Babson, the great prognosticator, is in the market himself to the tune of a few hundred thousand dollars. Only he's selling short, not long. Get it? Means that he's trying to depress the market so that he can come out with a big killing."

"You sure of that?"

"That's the story. And every broker in New York knows it. He's just trying to feather his own nest by scaring the devil out of everybody else."

"You think that's possible?"

"No doubt about it, Henry. No doubt whatsoever. You got any money?"

"Well, I suppose I could raise a little—yes."

"Then if I were you, I'd buy a few hundred shares of Graham-Paige Motors."

"Why Graham-Paige?"

"Because the inside word is that they're coming out with a sensational new model. Something like the Marmon, but a lot less money. Projection is it'll sell like hotcakes. If I were you, I'd get in on the ground floor, Henry."

"Graham-Paige, eh?"

"Tell you something else. I've just got a tip from a broker in New York. Old friend of mine. The Big Boys are starting to buy Graham-Paige. And C. F. Bennett has already taken a big 'buy' position in the stock."

"C. F. Bennett?"

"Straight from the horse's mouth. My friend, the broker, is close to one of the floor men on the exchange. Happens to know C. F. Bennett's coming in with a couple of more big 'buy' orders tomorrow. If you're smart, maybe you'll catch this swing going up."

"Maybe you've got something there, Charlie."

"Forget about Babson. He's an idiot." Then Lothrop crooned: "Haven't steered you wrong yet, have I?"

Henry Hopkins agreed to buy 100 shares. When he hung up, he felt better. What he needed now was something he did not have—a fistful of ready cash. Every spare dollar he had was already invested, but he knew where and how he could get it. He had always sweated a little in the process. But he had done it before, and he could do it again.

All he needed was the right situation, just the right depositor to come walking into the bank.

And to keep a weather eye peeled for Jonathan Keep.

7

IN THE PERFUMED feminine sanctuary of Mademoiselle Yvette's (Beauty Salon and Hair Coiffeurs), on the second floor of the Bright Building, just above Sanborn's Drugstore, Helen Hopkins was led to a curtained alcove by her hairdresser, an ample woman she knew only as Emily.

She always enjoyed coming to this cloister, with its contrasting color scheme of turquoise-blue and shocking pink, its buzzing gossip and its heady odor, an intriguing melange of cold cream, face powder, massage mud, seductive Chanel, and sensuous Patou. Now Helen Hopkins leaned back and sighed as the hairdresser made a quick survey.

"It looks very nice, Mrs. Hopkins. Very chic. We'll just give it a little more cutting."

"Isn't it pretty short now?" Helen Hopkins sounded dubious. "My daughter said that I was just being silly, trying to look too young."

"That's nonsense," said Emily, firmly. "These days, everybody can look young. I had a grandmother in here with a lovely shingle the other day. She looked exactly like her daughter. I mean, you simply couldn't tell them apart. She had her face lifted, you could see that, but still—well, why

not? What's wrong with living a little?" Then she came to a
professional conclusion. "Yes, Mrs. Hopkins. The thing to
do is cut it down and mould it even closer to the head." Then
Emily bustled away. "I'll be with you in a minute. Just have
to finish a combing in booth 3. My! You must be excited.
Imagine. Dinner at the White House!"

There was a pile of magazines on the table next to her.
First she picked up a copy of *Vanity Fair*. It featured two
lead articles, one of them "Joe College and Betty Coed—
Where Are They Headed?" and the other on the doings of
playboys Marquis Henri de la Falaise and Prince Serge
Mdivani, and how they had wooed and won Gloria Swanson
and Pola Negri. But the magazine under *Vanity Fair* was one
called *Personal Confessions*. It carried four lead articles:
"What I Told My Daughter the Night Before Her Marriage"
—"Indolent Kisses"—"Watch Your Stepins"—and "Mae
Busch's Secret."

Helen Hopkins decided on *Personal Confessions* and had
just settled back to read, when she heard the voice of a
woman in the next alcove. It was someone she could not see
and whose voice she could not identify. The woman was
talking idly to her hairdresser. She seemed to be rambling
along, almost in retrospection. But Helen Hopkins found the
subject of her conversation interesting.

"Now, I asked my husband: 'Darling, what do you think
I should buy now? I've got all those precious blue chips, you
know, General Motors and Pennsylvania Railroad, that kind
of thing. But darling,' I said, 'they're fine, but what I wanted
was a little more excitement. You know, a little *romance* in
my investments.' Well, my husband doesn't like to give me
advice, you know the way they are: He'll talk his head off to
his clients and tell them everything, but when it comes to his
own wife, butter wouldn't melt in his mouth, because he
couldn't keep the butter in, he keeps it closed so tight. I

mean, he knows all about these things, he's made a fortune buying and selling stocks, but I guess he just hates to see *me* successful. You know the way men are, always afraid that women will be competing with them. Well, I just wouldn't sit still. I just kept after him and after him, and finally he couldn't stand it anymore. I *knew* the market was going up, just like everyone else, and why shouldn't *I* get some of the velvet? After all, it was *my* money, not his. And so he finally yelled out the name to me. Just to get rid of me, I guess. 'Damn it, Edna,' he said, 'buy Seaboard Air Line. *Now* will you let me alone?' And that's just what I did. They say it's going way up, triple its price in six months. Charles thinks so, anyway, and if he doesn't know, who would?"

Helen Hopkins felt the gooseflesh prickle her skin. When her hairdresser came back to her, she whispered:

"Emily, do you know who that woman is in the next booth?"

The hairdresser knew that it was a Mrs. Bennett, a Mrs. C. F. Bennett, and that she was a sister of a rich widow named Mary Haggett who lived on Chestnut Street. It seemed that she was in Riverside for a few days to visit Mrs. Haggett, and apparently her husband was a very prominent stockbroker connected with Wall Street.

Helen Hopkins thought of the $200 she had wangled from her husband earlier that morning. She had never intended to buy a new dress at all. For a year, she had extracted bits and pieces of extra money by telling him little white lies—that she needed a new outfit for this or that—and then invested the money in the market. Henry Hopkins, like so many other husbands, really had no idea of the state of her wardrobe. She had often worn a frock many months old, only to hear him say that he liked her new dress. This, of course, had irritated her, but she had found his ignorance profitable. During the previous summer she had begun buying small quantities of a stock called Inspiration Copper, on margin. One of the girls at the bridge club had told her about it, and besides, she liked the sound of the name. Inspiration Copper was now selling at 47, and by buying it in dribs and drabs, two or three shares at a time, she had done very well. She had now accumulated just over 100 shares of it. And this morning, after her hair was done, she had intended to call her broker and invest her new bonanza of $200 in Inspiration Copper.

Now she could not wait. When her hairdresser returned, she asked: "Emily, do you have a phone in here?"

"Why, yes. Right over there on the counter."

"I mean a private phone."

"Well, there's one in the office." Emily nodded toward a door in the rear. "I guess it's all right if you use it. Nobody's in there now."

"Wait for me. I won't be long."

She untied the cotton sheet from her neck and went into the office, making sure to close the door behind her. Then she called the office of Lothrop and Company and asked for Mr. Curtis, one of Charles Lothrop's assistants. He had a pleasant voice and an ingratiating manner, and she always thought of him as "that nice young man." For reasons of her own, she would speak only to Mr. Curtis, and Mr. Curtis alone.

"Good morning, Mrs. Hopkins."

"Mr. Curtis, do you know a stock named Seaboard Air Line?"

"Of course."

"How much is it selling for?"

"Just a moment." There was a pause, and then he came back. "Seventeen and three-eighths."

"I want you to buy me two hundred dollars' worth. On the usual margin, of course. That would really be four hundred dollars' worth, wouldn't it?"

"Yes," he said. Then he sounded curious. "But why Seaboard? You've been buying Inspiration Copper."

"I've changed my mind," she said. "I like Seaboard now." Then she said, "In fact, I want you to sell all my Inspiration and put it all into Seaboard."

There was a surprised pause at the other end. Then: "Mrs. Hopkins, you realize you're making quite a switch here. You're sure you want me to convert it all into Seaboard?"

"Yes, I do, Mr. Curtis. The quicker the better. How long would it take?"

"Just a few minutes, actually." There was another pregnant pause at the other end. "Mrs. Hopkins, do you mind if I ask you a question? Where did you hear about Seaboard?"

"I'm afraid I can't tell you that."

Now he was insistent. "But *someone* must have tipped you off."

"Yes. Somebody very important. I think you call it—someone on the inside. But I can't tell you the name—it's confidential." She tried hard to keep the excited quiver out of her voice. "All I know is they expect it to triple in six months."

"*They* do?"

"Well, C. F. Bennett does."

Again, there was a long pause. Then slowly:

"Mrs. Hopkins, did you say C. F. Bennett?"

"Oh, dear," she said. "I'm afraid I've said too much already."

"Mrs. Hopkins," said Curtis. "You may have hit on something important. *Very* important. But of course, there are all kinds of rumors going on about the market, all kinds of people claiming they have information they really don't have."

"What I'm telling you, Mr. Curtis, comes—well, straight from the horse's mouth."

She told him of the conversation she had overheard. Once more, there was a long silence from the other end. Then she heard Curtis say, softly:

"Seaboard, eh? C. F. Bennett. Well, what do you know, what do you know."

"You'll take care of it, then?"

"Of course. Right away, Mrs. Hopkins."

"Oh," she said. "And don't forget. My account with you is secret. I don't want my husband to hear a word about this. I don't know *what* I'd do if he ever found out."

"Nothing to worry about, Mrs. Hopkins. As I've told you many times before, our personal accounts are confidential. Mr. Lothrop is the only other person who knows you have an account here, and he's told me to assure you that you need fear no disclosure from this office."

"Thank you, Mr. Curtis," she said, gratefully. "You're a very nice young man."

"Thank *you,* Mrs. Hopkins."

When Helen Hopkins put the receiver back on its cradle, she was unable, of course, to see what was happening at the other end. First, the nice young man, Mr. Curtis, scribbled down her transactions on two forms, one a buy order and one a sell order. Then he sat at his desk for a moment, staring out the window and thinking hard. After that he went to the files and took out a Moody's statistical report on Seaboard Air Line. He studied it for a moment, puzzled. A good, solid company, but he saw nothing to get excited about. Yet, he thought, he'd be a fool just to sit there and do nothing. These days, when you heard something good, it paid to act fast. As he had always told his clients: "Get in on the ground floor, or you'll miss the boat." Now he, as Mrs. Hopkins had done, looked for a private phone, and he found it in an empty office next to the Customers' Room. Naturally, he did not want his boss, Charles Lothrop, to know *his* private business. He put in a long-distance call collect to a brokerage firm in New York where he maintained a personal account. He then put in a buy order for 100 shares of Seaboard. *His* broker, a man named Fenwick, wanted to know why Curtis was buying Seaboard. Curtis told him where it had come from—straight from the horse's mouth—and swore his broker to secrecy. The minute Fenwick hung up, he called his floor man on the exchange. Then he put in a number of phone calls to each of his brokers, swearing *them* all to secrecy.

*

Back at Mademoiselle Yvette's, Mrs. Hopkins was now in her chair, relaxing under the soothing ministrations of her hairdresser. She reflected on what she had done. She was exhilarated. Of course, she thought, of course: It all made sense. Airlines were *the* things these days. Everybody said the future of America was up in the air. Aviators were very chic now. Look at what Charles Lindbergh had done. And the *Graf Zepplin*—look what *it* had done, flying across the oceans and all. The skies were simply full of all kinds of people now, flying to Alaska, across the country, in air derbies, and everywhere on the map. And that beautiful man, that terribly handsome and virile man, Commander Byrd, was even now getting ready to fly to the South Pole. One of the girls at the club this weekend had unequivocally stated, over the bridge table, that if it came to a choice as to whose shoes she would want under her bed, John Gilbert's or Commander Byrd's, she would take Byrd anytime. And look what the aircraft companies were doing in the market these days, stocks like Curtiss-Wright.

She leaned back in her chair, half-dozing, barely hearing the clip-clip of her hairdresser's scissors. She had no idea that

Seaboard Air Line had nothing to do with aviation, but was actually a Florida railroad.

And even if she had known, she wouldn't have cared less.

*

A few days later, C. F. Bennett was lying abed with Dixie Day in a small but posh hotel in Miami. As a matter of personal convenience, he had bought the Palm Surf Hotel so as to guarantee his own privacy. He registered Dixie Day and himself as a Mr. and Mrs. Ralph Wilson. C. F. Bennett rarely allowed himself to be photographed, and so he was not easily recognized. But if any employee of the Palm Surf knew his boss was lying in with his mistress, he also knew enough to keep his mouth tightly buttoned, or else he would lose his job, and more.

It was ten o'clock in the morning when C. F. Bennett awoke. He looked at the fresh young face of Dixie Day in repose, and studied her lithe, girlish body, half-exposed under the sheet. C. F. Bennett felt very tired this morning. Age was getting to him. He had had a great deal of difficulty getting it up for Dixie the night before. And, of course, she had noticed it. He tried to rationalize by telling himself that he was business-tired, that he had all these important and enormous deals swinging around in his head.

But he knew this was a lie. He cursed Mother Nature. She was ruthless and cruel when it came to men. A woman could screw at almost any age. All she had to do was spread her legs, he thought, and conjure up a little moisture, and she was in business. A man was out there, naked and exposed. He had to perform, get it up every time. But as time went on, Mother Nature began to lower the boom and cruelly humiliate the boys. It was embarrassing to stand there as Mr. Limp when your lady was waiting.

The phone rang and he answered it. Only one man knew

he was staying at the Palm Surf. And that was his executive assistant, Paul Morell. Morell was also his senior financial advisor at Sunrise Investment Trust. He could only suggest, but C. F. Bennett made the decisions. He knew Morell would never call him at the Palm Surf unless it was extremely important.

"Mr. Bennett, what do you know about a stock called Seaboard Air Line?"

"It's a Florida railroad. I came down on it. Why?"

"It's started to move up. Two points day before yesterday. Another two points today."

"But that stock's just been lying there . . ."

"That's my point, sir. Suddenly, there's interest. Suddenly, everybody's talking about it. Somebody must know something we don't know. There's a rumor on the Street that it's going to double. Nobody knows why, there aren't any statistics or events to support it. We've researched it from here to hell and back again. But somebody must know something we don't know. Anyway, they're talking Seaboard all over the place. There's even a rumor you've bought it."

"Well, I'll be damned," said C. F. Bennett. "Now that's really something. Some of these bastards on the Street will do anything to sell anything. Still—you've heard talk that Seaboard may double?"

"I've heard more than that, Mr. Bennett. I've heard that in three months it may even triple."

"From reliable sources?"

"From the best."

C. F. Bennett thought for a moment. Funny. He had recommended this stock to his wife as a kind of joke. It just went to prove that sometimes you never knew. What was that old cliché? Sometimes strange chickens came home to roost. He was the kind of man who made decisions on hunches rather than statistics. He had a smell for success, it had made him a millionaire many times over. And this Sea-board Air Line had just that kind of smell. The public was buying it on rumor alone. He liked to catch this kind of stock at the beginning of a rise. He liked to take a big position in it, let it float up, then suddenly sell and let the suckers catch it coming down.

He was a man who made decisions quickly. He told Morell to buy a million shares at the market. Later on, Sunrise would come in for more.

The conversation about Seaboard had stimulated him in a strange way. He always felt a certain excitement when he went in for a gamble of this sort, when he made a big buy like this. There was an inner thrill to it; it was like sex. In fact, it *was* sexual.

He looked down at his penis. It had been flaccid a few moments ago. Now it had hardened. He studied Dixie Day speculatively. Now she was stretching and yawning, blinking at the morning light. His erection continued to hold fast.

He jumped into bed with her. This time, he knew his performance would be adequate. If not superb.

8

HENRY HOPKINS leaned back in his chair and thought again about the money he owed his wife.

Once again he thought of how sweet it would be to pay her up in full—and that time was not too far away now. Then he could tell her, once and for all, to shut up. The Florida disaster would become a thing of the past.

A lot of people in town thought Henry Hopkins owned the bank. This was not true. If he did, he wouldn't have to scrounge for the money he needed to play the market. In a sense he was himself an employee, responsible to the board, although he was a partner as well. His duties were many. Outside of presiding over the board, he was the only loan officer. He opened the big accounts, sought new business, and okayed overdrafts. He was the investment officer who decided where the surplus funds should be invested—subject, of course, to the approval of the board. And he controlled the transfer of funds between the Puritan and other banks, although the technical details of this operation were actually handled by Keep. All mail was delivered to him, unopened. And he, and only he, opened it first.

An hour after the bank had opened, Henry Hopkins found the opportunity he had waited for.

It came through the door, as though delivered by some dazzling Providence, in the person of a man named Ralph Mackey. Mackey, who owned a hardware store on Fort Street, was well known to Henry Hopkins. They had done business before, and they were on a first-name basis. Mackey started to sit down on one of the stiff-backed leather chairs just outside the rail, but Henry waved at him.

"Come on in, Ralph."

"Thank you, Henry." Mackey took the seat across the desk and mopped his brow. "Going to be another cold one."

"Yep. Smells like another snow."

They chatted a few moments more in pleasant fashion, in the way of old friends. Then Henry Hopkins leaned back and came to the point.

"Well, Ralph? What can we do for you this morning?"

"Like to borrow some money."

"Well, sir, you've come to the right place. How much?"

"Five thousand."

Henry Hopkins did not change expression, but a nerve twitched. Five thousand dollars would make a nice little addition to his kitty. Now he bent forward, smiling expansively, trying to keep the eagerness out of his voice.

"For how long?"

"Six months."

"May I ask what this loan is for?"

"I need more room at the store, Henry. Figured I'd break through the back and build another section. I'm developing a line of machine tools and mill supplies—you know, drills and taps, that kind of stuff. The mills can't get enough these days, what with the production they're getting out, and I figure I can take a piece of the business away from Valley Mill Supplies. But I need all the room up front for my meat-and-potato merchandise. Mostly, for the new line, I'll need shelving and storage room. But I figure with the extra business, the investment might pay off with a fifteen or twenty percent increase in my annual gross."

"Nothing wrong with that kind of percentage on *any* investment," observed Henry Hopkins.

"Unless you're in the market. Then it might look a little slow."

"I know. But personally, Ralph, I like a little caution and prudence. You try to tackle the whole hog, and it might slip through your fingers altogether. For my part, I'm the kind who's glad to settle for a few choice cuts of the bacon."

"Then you'll grant the loan?"

"We'd be pleased. What do you propose for collateral?"

"I was afraid you'd ask me that."

"Were you?"

Mackey grinned. "I thought you'd give me an unsecured note. Just on my character."

Henry Hopkins smiled back. "I have a very high respect for your character, Ralph. But I'd much rather secure this note with a little collateral. You'd agree if I issued loans on the character of every man who walked in here—well, it'd be a hell of a way to run a bank."

Mackey laughed. "Henry, you're a real Scrooge. General Motors securities all right?"

"Good as gold."

Henry Hopkins continued to banter with the hardware merchant. But his brain was whirling, and he felt the tension building.

He took out a pad of loan forms, scribbled the amount of the loan, the date it was taken, and his signature. He gave it to Mackey and held his breath. As always at this particular and ticklish moment, he could feel the perspiration popping out of his skin. He was gambling on the fact that the hardware merchant would not bother to read the fine print at the bottom of the loan application. If Mackey had, he would have noted that the form was for an unsecured loan. It simply indicated that the Puritan Bank and Trust had lent Ralph Mackey $5000, on character alone, and had received no collateral whatever. It had been Henry Hopkins' experience that whenever he presented these applications to borrowers, they always accepted them without question and never read the fine print. They would sign any document thrust at them in the same way, when it came from a banker. It was natural for the borrower not only to trust a banker but also to assume he knew what he was doing.

Mackey signed the application and then opened a manila envelope he was carrying. He counted out ninety-three shares of General Motors, more than enough collateral to cover the loan. On this day, General Motors had a market value of seventy-five dollars a share. Henry Hopkins picked up the securities quickly, thrust them into a drawer of his desk, and locked the desk.

It was only then that he remembered to find out where Jonathan Keep was and what he was doing.

He looked quickly at the first cage. It seemed to him, in that split second, that Keep, who had been dealing with a customer, had been watching him. He couldn't be sure, but he thought he had seen Keep's head turn away quickly. Now Henry Hopkins began to sweat profusely. *Had* the treasurer seen him put those securities in his drawer? Or had it just been his imagination? Mentally, he cursed himself for his stupidity. He should have checked to see what Keep was doing *before* he put away those securities.

He stared hard at Keep. The treasurer was busy completing some transaction with his customer. He gave no sign that he had seen anything. His face was impassive. Hopkins gave Mackey another form to sign, this one converting the securities so that they would be negotiable to anyone who presented them. This was obviously routine, since the bank might find it necessary to cash in the securities in case Mackey defaulted on the loan. When this was over, Henry Hopkins leaned back and drew a long inner sigh of relief. He was home free.

"All right, Ralph," he said, "as of now, your account is credited with five thousand dollars."

After Mackey had gone, Henry Hopkins sat at his desk thinking through what he had done, as he had so many times before, when it came to this kind of thing. He would give the document Mackey had signed to Jonathan Keep, who would simply enter it as an unsecured loan. Now, he had almost 7000 dollars' worth of General Motors stock in his desk—and nobody else in the bank knew he had it. In effect, it was now his to do with as he wished.

In a day or two, he would deposit the stock into his account at Lothrop and Company. This would cover his purchase of Graham-Paige. Long before the due date of the loan, he would naturally replace the stock and deposit it in the bank vault, where all collateral was kept. But for six months, he would have the use of it to further build his profits in the market.

There was, of course, one remote possibility that could be unsettling. Suppose Ralph Mackey found some loose money somewhere or inherited some money from a rich uncle? Then he might walk into the bank and ask to redeem his loan before it matured. If he paid it off, he would ask for the General Motors securities he had given to Henry Hopkins as collateral. It was up to the bank to return these shares to Mackey on demand. But of course, Henry Hopkins would not have the shares to deliver. In that case, he would have to stall off Mackey. Give him some story. Tell him that the securities were in the vault of the Puritan's cooperating bank in Boston, the Atlantic Trust, and that it would take a day or two before it could be mailed to Riverside and delivered to Mackey. He had no doubt that the hardware merchant would accept the short delay and find it entirely reasonable. And this would provide enough time to phone Charlie Lothrop and have him send the securities over by messenger. Or if Lothrop had sold them, he could always buy new shares of General Motors out of the market profits he already had, to replace the old securities.

He had turned this trick a number of times now in order to build up his investment in the market. He reasoned that actually he was only borrowing the money from the bank, not stealing it. He did not see himself as an embezzler. If the thought intruded into his unconscious mind, he thrust it out, resolutely. What he was doing was slightly irregular, perhaps. But dishonest? No. He was simply using the stock certificates that Mackey owned, and those of others before him, instead of letting them gather dust in the vault. He was a banker, and this was sound banking procedure. What good was money or negotiable securities unless you put them to work? And after all, while the loans were outstanding, the collateral in the vault was actually the property of the Puritan Bank and Trust until the loans were repaid, and so, in that sense, he was using the bank's resources, not someone else's.

Another thing. He was in a position to replace that collateral, or its equivalent in money, any time he wished. All it took was a call to Charlie Lothrop to sell some of his securities. The bank, he told himself, could lose nothing by this, nothing whatever. Meanwhile, he was pyramiding his profits, and everybody was happy. It wasn't as though he were borrowing the money and spending it on booze or women. He was buying the prime blue chips of American business, backed by the Big Boys like J. P. Morgan, Bernard Baruch, Charles Mitchell, and Richard Whitney. If gilt-edged investment stocks like Graham-Paige or Radio or Baldwin went under, then the dollar itself would go under. So would the whole country, for that matter, and everything after that would be purely academic, anyway. He felt that he was investing in the nation's future, and how could you go wrong in that? What was it Calvin Coolidge had said? *The business of America is business.*

He continued to study Keep. The more he thought about it, the surer he was that Keep knew nothing about those securities he had just locked in his desk. He called to Keep to come over to his desk and handed the treasurer the copy of the application he had just made out for Mackey. His hand was steady, and he watched Keep's eyes.

"File this away. It's a loan for five thousand, six months, Ralph Mackey."

Keep glanced at the slip. "Unsecured."

"Yes. But Mackey's got a fine record. I think he's good for it."

"I agree, Mr. Hopkins. He's never had to default yet."

Jonathan Keep's face was impassive. Henry Hopkins saw nothing, not even a flicker of the eyes. As Keep turned to go, Hopkins was relieved.

Yet he was sweating at the neck; his collar was damp with it.

9

HIS NAME WAS Patrick Nolan. He was a big, barrel-chested man with a florid complexion and fiery red hair. He had been born shanty Irish, the son of a railroad worker who had emigrated from the Old Country. As a boy he had lived on Hungry Hill, an area in Riverside populated by those who had emigrated at the turn of the century to escape the potato famine in Erin. Since then, by using his combined assets of hard knuckles and muscle, plus a native shrewdness and a burning desire to improve himself, he had graduated to the lace curtain variety of Irish, as they were known throughout Massachusetts. Now, at the age of fifty, he spoke softly and courteously. His suits and ties were conservative and in the best of taste. He lived well, if not ostentatiously, in a big house in Forest Park, one of the better sections of the city.

He was Riverside's leading bootlegger and highly respected in the community.

Pat Nolan was well heeled, very well heeled. All his assets were in cash. Nobody knew how much he was worth, since he maintained no bank account anywhere. There were guesses of a million to three million. He had no intention of making it easy for the tax collectors to pry into his financial affairs. It was assumed that he kept his money in some mattress somewhere. He was one of the few people of means in Riverside who had not invested a cent in the market. He was not interested in anything that smacked of risk, or that was recorded on paper for others to see. In his business, Pat Nolan sold only for cash, and for a huge profit. All in all, a nice clean business, and no questions asked.

He was proud of the fact that he ran a "class" business, and he sold only to the carriage trade. His competitors sold whiskey cut many times, which they claimed was "just off the boat." They sold alcohol which had been cooked in hideaway stills located in barns, caves, corncribs, rendering works, and even old churches. It was stuff which delivered a kick, to be sure, but it could also possibly blind and paralyze. It was the kind of booze that was called such diverse names as White Mule and Jackass Brandy, Panther Whiskey, Goat Whiskey, White Lightning, Soda Pop Moon, Yack Yack Bourbon, Straitsville Stuff, and Jamaica Ginger.

But Pat Nolan sold only the legitimate and the best. He handled Canadian whiskey smuggled across the border, and gin and rum brought in from ships out of Bimini or St. Pierre and then transferred to fast motor boats which could land in any protected cove. He rarely sold to individuals. His customers were the best speakeasies, politicians who liked to throw big parties, and organizations such as the Elks, Kiwanis, and the Chamber of Commerce—not to mention hotels and so-called roadhouses, where the whiskey ultimately ended up in teacups and hip flasks.

On the morning of the twentieth of February, Pat Nolan startled his wife with an idea he had been nurturing for some time. He was making a large amount of money, and all in cash. What he proposed now was to approach Henry Hopkins at the bank. He would ask Hopkins to put up his name for membership on the Board of Directors of the Puritan

Bank and Trust. It would be a long chance, of course, but Patrick Nolan was a persistent and determined man, and his ambition was to have the name of Nolan on the bank stationery. His wife, Rose, was naturally skeptical.

"You haven't got a chance, Pat."

"No? And why not?"

"Well, first, you're a bootlegger."

"It's a respectable business. And you'd be surprised how many respectable businessmen in town are trying to get into it, Rose."

"Second, you're Irish. And those people at the Puritan are all Protestant, old family, and high society, up on the Hill."

"That's true. But there's one thing they love, more than anything else. And that's money. I'll be able to offer them a blank check, write in your own figure, for a seat on the board."

"They're all rich men in their own right. They don't need your money, Pat. All they'll see in you is a pushy Irishman."

"Let them. You never get anywhere in this world, Rose, unless you push."

"If you *must* be a bank director, why don't you try the people at the Third National, Pat? They're not so high and mighty . . ."

"No," he said. "It's the Puritan I want, or nothing. It's the best, and I won't settle for anything less."

Pat Nolan was an aggressive man, and a proud man. He had long suffered from a feeling of inferiority. The Irish who had imigrated to Riverside during his father's time, the Irish just off the boat, with their shirtsleeves and their brogue, had been held in contempt by the old Yankee citizens of the community. In those days an Irishman often was not even called by his proper name, but was summoned by the humiliating term of "Paddy." They had not, until recently, even been allowed to serve on juries. They had settled in the Flats or on Hungry Hill and had been employed only in the most menial labor, working on the railroad or digging ditches. The straight-laced descendants of Increase Hopkins and the others saw in them only Rome, Rum, and Rebellion. They regarded the Irish as ignorant, brawling, and drunken second-class citizens.

But things had changed since Pat Nolan's father's time. The Irish were coming into their own now, and one of them, Al Smith, had even been nominated for President. They had become policemen, firemen, strong in the civil service, and many had thrown away the shovels and become important men in the construction and heavy-industry business in Riverside. The prejudice against them had become less obvious, far more subtle. But it was still there.

It was Pat Nolan's intention to break that barrier, and he was determined to do it, no matter what it took. And he thought, Goddamn them all, the whole bunch of them, those snooty Episcopalian bastards up there on the Hill and at the club. They were sitting pretty now, on their fat asses. But you never knew, he reflected. Things could change, life was funny that way.

So far, he had had to come to them. Maybe some day, they might have to come to *him*.

10

AT SEVEN O'CLOCK on the evening of this same day Henry and Helen Hopkins entered the grounds of the White House through the main north entrance.

The porte-cochere and veranda were illuminated. A number of reporters chatted and smoked in the shadow of one of the tall Grecian columns that supported the portico. They were waiting to interview Senator Borah, who was in conference with the President. Two policemen stood guard.

The senator came out and the gentlemen of the press crowded around him. The Hopkinses approached the great glass door, and a white-gloved usher opened it. He asked for their name, although he obviously knew who they were. He took their hats and coats, and they were passed on to another usher. They were then led into the Red Room, where they sat and waited for the President to come down from the family quarters on the second floor.

Shortly thereafter, the President emerged from the elevator and entered the Red Room, followed by Mrs. Coolidge. They greeted their guests warmly and with obvious affection. The party moved immediately to the great paneled dining room. At the door, they were greeted by Rob Roy, a huge white collie, who bounded across the room to meet the President. He patted the dog and ordered him to sit on the hearth of the fireplace while dinner was in progress.

The President's taste in food was simple, and the meal reflected it. A consommé, a veal cutlet with string beans and potatoes, a lettuce-and-tomato salad, chocolate cake, vanilla ice cream, and coffee. For a time, Grace Coolidge took over the bulk of the conversation. She had an olive complexion, her eyes were large and brown, and her hair was full, wavy, and streaked with gray. In all respects, she was a gracious woman and a fine hostess. The national press was very fond of her. Those who met her were impressed by the great contrast between herself and her husband. She was social, she liked entertaining conversation, and she had great warmth of feeling. In contrast, the President was regarded, in a social sense, as a cold fish. Almost at once, Grace Coolidge made Henry and Helen Hopkins feel at home.

Finally the President himself began to talk, and now he belied his image of "Silent Cal." He began to reminisce about the old days when he and Hopkins had been classmates at Amherst. And later when they had begun their professional careers in Northampton, he as a young lawyer and Hopkins as a young banker. Both of them had lived near Round Hill, and they walked down Elm Street together each morning. On hot weekends, they took the open trolley up to Mountain Park. The President remembered how cool the ride was as they bowled up to the crest. He recalled the band playing while the peanut roasters hissed and young girls screamed on the roller coasters and giggled on the merry-go-round. In those days, Hopkins and he had dined together modestly in a little room in Rahar's Inn and went to community meetings in the Draper Hotel. Henry Hopkins had been at the President's wedding. And later, when Hopkins had the opportunity to head the Puritan Bank and Trust in Riverside, and the President was soon to leave for Boston to take up the governorship, they had said goodbye in front of Kingsley's Drugstore.

Henry Hopkins had an idea in the back of his mind. Something he felt would be a coup for the Puritan Bank and Trust. But first, he maneuvered the conversation around to the state of the economy. The market had broken twice, once on December 7th, and once on the second of February. Now, he asked the President whether he saw any storm clouds in this. Hopkins was still thinking of Babson's comment and of the securities he owned.

The President was optimistic. Business was the key, he said, and American business was strong and getting stronger. The future looked good, prosperity was here to stay. There was this new installment credit plan that had taken root in the country ("You furnish the Girl, we furnish the Home"). And that was all to the good, as far as business was concerned. It enabled people to buy more and thus boost the economy. As to the market, of course there were some excesses, but these would be corrected. You could not, said the President, cure some people, who lived in the fantasy they could become rich without work. There was no way you could prevent some Americans from being foolish, any more than you could stop them from drinking wood alcohol or killing themselves and each other with their cars on the highways. But the economy, and therefore the market, was fundamentally sound, because business was. Even now, the President was sure the Federal Reserve would move in and correct the recent excesses. Personally, he, Calvin Coolidge, didn't have a dime invested in the stock market. He was an old Vermonter. He liked his money either in his pocket or in the bank. And he naturally assumed that Henry Hopkins, being a hard-headed man and president of a bank, felt the same way.

Hopkins hastened to assure the President that, naturally,

as head of the Puritan, he had stayed away from the market. Then he asked the President a favor. In a few weeks, Coolidge would leave the White House and retire to Northampton. Would the President honor him, Hopkins, and his bank, by becoming a depositor? It would be great prestige for the bank if Coolidge would consent to do so. The name stood not only for prosperity, but solidity and stability. The word would get around, and the business of the bank would boom.

The President thought for a moment.

"So you want me to become a depositor, Henry?"

"Yes, sir. I would consider it a great personal favor."

A sly grin spread over the President's face.

"Tell you what, Henry. Suppose I keep my money in my pocket and just become an *honorary* depositor. Wouldn't that serve your purpose just as well?"

This was, of course, Coolidge's idea of a joke. He would be glad to oblige Henry. Why not? What were old friends for?

*

The last few days of his term in the White House, the President became withdrawn and irritable. On March 4th, 1929, he rasped out a goodbye to the White House servants, whom Mrs. Coolidge had gathered outside the room where he was dressing.

Afterward he descended to the Blue Room, where Herbert Hoover and Vice President-elect Charles Curtis were waiting, along with other officials and their wives. He shook hands with some of them, and then said brusquely:

"Time to go."

It was drizzling slightly when the President and President-elect rode to the inaugural ceremonies. They said little, if anything, to each other. Calvin Coolidge offered no advice, and Hoover asked for none.

After attending the ceremonies, the Coolidges went directly to Union Station, where they boarded a train for

Northampton. He spoke briefly, saying only, "Goodbye, I have had a very enjoyable time in Washington."

During the rest of his lifetime, Calvin Coolidge would see the city only once more.

*

So the Presidents parted, one to the abdication heartlessly prescribed by law, the other to what he hoped would be glory.

Yet, from what the journalists of the time wrote, Herbert Hoover seemed to feel nothing of his new and eminent station. There was no smile on his face. He was aware of the cheers but did not really listen to them. His head told him that he was now President of the United States, but he did not seem to sense the august meaning of these words.

Now the thousands of onlookers waited for the new President to arrive at the White House, no longer touching elbows with his predecessor. It began to rain, perhaps an augury of ill. The crowds filled the bleachers or jammed the sides of the avenue. They jostled each other and stared at the familiar sights: the streetcars passing, the rain-washed Ionic pillars and columns of the Treasury.

The rain became heavier. People in the left section of the bleachers, who occupied the best seats, began to raise their umbrellas against the rivulets of water seeping down the plane trees, now denuded of leaves. The slope became a pastel of colored umbrellas blurred red, green, and violet.

The avenue itself became sleek and shiny, reflecting in grotesque images the now pressing and impatient crowd. Peddlers passed through the mob vending tacky souvenirs, medals, dolls' heads on sticks, flags, and pennants. And almost everyone wore a button or a badge with Herbert Hoover's round, thick face inscribed on it. The rain continued to fall. Women folded caps out of their newspapers and fit them over their hats to save them from the rain. Everything smelled damp—paper, coats, fur, the flesh of the onlookers themselves.

Then finally the shout: "Here they come!"

A craning of necks, the clatter of horse's hooves, the new President is arriving. The old king is dead—Long live Mr. Hoover! Now the open car approaches in the rain. Mrs. Hoover sits beside her husband, radiant, clearly excited, charming, waving to friends. She is the queen of the festival, knows it, and appreciates it. Behind them, in the car following, is Vice President Curtis, openly delighted, ready to laugh in his exuberance, waving his tall hat at the crowd with exaggerated gestures.

But there is the great man himself. Mr. Hoover. Now President Herbert Hoover. He holds his hat in his hand and he is dripping and sodden in the rain. He seems still without enthusiasm, in a kind of rigid spasm, as though not comprehending who he actually is now and how he got there. He manages to bow and smiles mechanically, a jerky puppet responding to a hurricane of applause.

He might have at this moment envied his former employer, now on his way to peace and retirement. He might have been awed or frightened. He might have suspected that Calvin Coolidge had gotten out just in time, leaving him, Herbert Hoover, holding the bag.

He might have even had mystic foreboding of things to come. Instincts, visions, a troubling of the unconscious.

And could there be an omen in the fact that it rained on *his* Inauguration Day?

SUMMER
1929

11

IN THE SUMMER of 1929, the big bull market continued its dizzy climb.

The nation itself was in a state of euphoria. There were now 120 million Americans, and the word was buy, buy, *buy*. Even though Herbert Hoover was now President, they continued to call it Coolidge Prosperity. Business boomed everywhere. New industries grew, skyscrapers began to rise from the Main streets of one-time villages, shiny new cars choked the highways, great power lines spanned the hilltops to give life to thousands of new labor-saving machines. The installment plan had come of age, and the citizens of America cheerfully went into hock, on the theory that good times were forever.

It was estimated that there were some 23 million automobiles on the highways and dirt roads of the nation. There were Model A Fords, of course. Millions of them. But there were also Graham-Paiges, Cadillac V-16s, De Soto Sixes, Pierce Arrow Straight Eights, Gardners and air-cooled Franklins, Packards and Buick Marquettes. And of course, the legendary Stutzes, which claimed a total of forty-six body styles, including the famous Stutz Bearcat, the Stutz Blackhawk, the Stutz Custom, and the Stutz Salon. You could buy a De Soto Six for $845, or the Dictator Six, a Studebaker closed car, as it was then called, for $1200.

The summer of 1929 was the beginning of the air age as well.

The *Graf Zepplin* had begun a world tour. Charles Lindbergh had married Anne Morrow, and together they were flying off into the wild blue yonder. Admiral Byrd was waiting in the darkness of Antarctica for his chance to fly to the South Pole. Flying schools sprang up everywhere, and flying circuses toured the nation. Daredevils stood on their heads on the wings or swung into the air hanging from the struts. Myriad fliers prepared to fly the Atlantic once again, as well as the Pacific. Airmail was now routine, and only a short time after the Lindbergh flight, the market price per share of Wright Aeronautical Company soared from $25 to $245.

This was the last summer of what has since been called the Era of Wonderful Nonsense. Flagpole sitters like Shipwreck Kelly still were in the news. An inventor named Walter Critchlow claimed his new "moisture humidifier" and carbon eliminator would make any Ford go 42 miles on a single gallon of gas. The Duchess of Bedford, in a single week, flew 10,000 miles to India and back to England to keep a dinner engagement. In Rumania, Miss Universe burst into tears because the Rumanians thought she was too thin. On Pathé News, audiences in movie theaters saw a bizarre experiment conducted at the Westinghouse plant in Pittsburgh. There was a box, and in it was a picture screen about three inches wide. On the tiny screen appeared something that looked like an old-time picture on a kinescope, obscure and full of what appeared to be a snowy effect. They could barely make it out, but the picture was that of Krazy Kat doing a dance. They called it by a new name, television. And some crazy visionary predicted in a newspaper article that one day there would be

movies in every American home. The American public was
properly skeptical, and there was no rush whatever to buy
Westinghouse stock.

On the world scene, both Mussolini and Stalin were tight-
ening their holds on their respective countries. Fighting
broke out between Arabs and Jews in Palestine, in Jerusalem,
Hebron, Haifa, and elsewhere. It was reported that Arabs
attacked the city of Safed and killed twenty-two Jews. On the
national scene, the President had appointed the Wickersham
Commission to investigate law enforcement in general and
prohibition in particular. The Harding Oil Scandals had
come to a head, and Harry F. Sinclair was now languishing
in jail, although it was reported that he took daily trips in a
luxurious motor car. Governor Franklin D. Roosevelt can-
celed all appointments because of pains in his leg. In
Northampton, Calvin Coolidge had started to work on his
autobiography. He had signed a contract for its publication
while still in the White House, first as a serial in Hearst's
Cosmopolitan, and then in book form. He was to be paid five
dollars a word.

In sports, Gene Tunney was the heavyweight champion of
the world, having beaten Jack Dempsey two years before.
Bill Tilden was the king of tennis, and Helen Wills, she of
the deadpan face and green visor, was the queen. Bobby
Jones dominated the world of golf with his magic putter,
Calamity Jane, but Walter Hagen was not far behind. The
average man was now beginning to take up golf on the new
so-called public courses, and he could buy a complete golf
outfit, five clubs and a bag, for $6.95. Babe Ruth was still
hammering out home runs, but Graham McNamee, on his
radio broadcasts, glorified the exploits of Lou Gehrig. And
Gallant Fox was the Horse of the Year.

In fashion, when it came to hairstyles, the shingle was out,
the bob was in. In hats, the turban, moulded to cover the

entire head from the nape of the neck to the eyebrows, was all the rage. But some women preferred the pointed-ear felt. The new zipper suits for fall were a sensation. Velvet was the thing for the fall, as well as satin, and dresses and coats were both cut in the moulded silhouette look, knee-length and no longer.

Clothes for men underwent certain changes as well. Knickers were on their way out on the golf course or on the estates of country squires. Men wore two- or three-button tailored sack suits by Hart Schaffner and Marx, or Kuppenheimer, in heather-brown or Scottish gray. Men still wore separate collars on their shirts, but the attached variety was coming in fast. White pants with a thin stripe, and a blue blazer, was the standard costume for the young gentleman.

In the summer of 1929, much of the music was upbeat, reflecting the buoyant and optimistic mood of the time. Irving Berlin reflected the euphoric mood of the nation with his "Blue Skies," and indeed, they seemed to be smiling, not only at him, but everyone else. "Happy Days Are Here Again" was a hit, as well as "With a Song in My Heart." Libby Holman sang "Moanin' Low," and it was a sensation. So was "Singin' in the Rain," "Stardust," "There's Danger in Your Eyes, Cherie," and "Ramona." Rudy Vallee was a sensation, and a national hearthrob, when at the Heigh-Ho Club he sang "I'm Just a Vagabond Lover."

On the radio, people tuned in their Model 20 Compact Atwater Kents and found a wide diversity of programs. There was "Roxy and His Gang," "The Friendly Hour," "Tea Time Tunes" sung by Lanny Ross, the Edgewater Beach orchestra, and of course, "Amos 'n Andy." Paul Whiteman and his Rhythm Boys, among whom was a young man named Bing Crosby, commanded a huge audience. On Broadway, *Street Scene* and *Journey's End* were solid hits, and a young comedian named Eddie Cantor was big box office in a show called *Whoopee,* as was Helen Morgan in *Showboat.* In the ornate movie palaces, Janet Gaynor and Charles Farrell captivated audiences from coast to coast, and everybody was singing "If I Had a Talking Picture of You."

In the summer of '29, *All Quiet on the Western Front* was the big book of the season. The intellectuals talked of sex and more sex, and the new emancipation of women. They argued about Hemingway, Gide, Lytton Strachey, Virginia Woolf, Arnold Bennett, and Robinson Jeffers. They scorned the Philistines, who were motivated only by greed. They had only contempt for the current materialism and the effect of standardization and mass production upon American life. Yet they, too, participated in the bonanza. Most of them were secretly in the market themselves. The artist who was once enraptured with the work of van Gogh had a few shares of American Car and Foundry laid aside and would buy more if he could sell another painting. The editor of the small literary or poetry quarterly stopped by his friendly neighborhood broker often to find out how Fairbanks Morse or American Water Works was doing. They too, became involved in the national insanity.

Prohibition was a toothless law. People laughed at it and ignored it. Some died because of it, through drinking either wood alcohol or other poisonous concoctions. Or they dropped dead by gunfire, or were fragmented by a bomb thrown into some speakeasy that did not pay its dues to whatever mob was in power. In the city of New York, Police Commissioner Grover Whalen estimated that there were 32,000 speakeasies alone. One of them, on the East Side, was fronted by an exterior that looked like an orthodox synagogue, with an inscription in Hebrew over its entrance.

The Volstead Act continued to spawn and nourish crime in the summer of '29. In Chicago, the government was beginning to harass Al Capone, and he offered to settle all grievances for $4 million. The government refused. The Unione Siciliana still carried muscle in Chicago, the Purple Gang was the power in Detroit, and people like Bugs Moran, Machine Gun Jack McGurn, Hymie Weiss, and John Scalise became household names. The gangland feud in New York City hit its zenith in 1929. The big city spawned other household names, some of them up and coming—Frank Costello, Lucky Luciano, Waxey Gordon, Longy Zwillman, and Lepke Buchalter.

For the general public, it was a good summer. The nation enjoyed high employment. Henry Ford paid a flat five dollars a day to each worker on his assembly lines. A good clerk could make eighteen dollars a week, and a male bookkeeper twenty-five. And in the summer of 1929, the price was right. One could buy a good man's suit for forty dollars, certain brands of cigarettes for fifteen cents a pack, or two for a quarter. Arthur Murray advertised his famous course in dancing for five dollars, and the price of the *Saturday Evening Post* was five cents a copy.

And if this were not enough, your friendly neighbor and bootlegger would sell you a quart of genuine Johnny Walker or Usher's Green Stripe scotch whiskey for two dollars and twenty-five cents, or two quarts for four dollars.

*

But the big news of the season was far and away the great bull market.

It was the prime topic of discussion in every home and restaurant and on every street corner in the nation. A special survey by one magazine revealed that on the local commuter trains coming into Pennsylvania or Grand Central stations, two out of every three newspapers left on the seats were turned to the financial pages. The old measures of a common stock had long been outmoded. If a stock valued at 50 went to 100, what was to stop it from going to 200 or 300 or 500? Why not ride the gravy train with it, and retire rich?

In the summer of 1929, millions of Americans held stock on margin. The prices of issues soared into the stratosphere. There were a few economists and financial experts who cried "wolf, wolf," but nobody listened. The happy music of the stock ticker drowned them out. Time after time, the Federal Reserve Board tried to alert the public to the possibility of inflation. Nobody listened. The whole idea of inflation was ridiculous. Maybe some time far in the future. But not now. Not with American business and industry going full blast. The Federal Reserve Board raised the rate for call money to the highest it had been since 1921. After a shock and a set-back, the market rallied and went even higher.

The lesson was clear. The public refused to be shaken out of the market. Everyone ought to be, and expected to be, rich. Time and again, the investor was reminded of the golden harvest a man would have reaped if he had bought a hundred shares of General Motors when it was first listed on the market and simply held on. And everyone was re-minded, again, that one of the Big Boys, one of the really Big Boys, George F. Baker, had never sold *anything*. As for the danger of speculation, ex-Governor Stokes of New Jersey, in a well-publicized address, proclaimed to the nation that Co-lumbus, Washington, and Thomas Edison had all been speculators.

Meanwhile, the Big Boys rode high and wide on the boom.

They created the so-called investment trusts, much like the present-day mutual funds, and these multiplied. In the summer of 1929, there were nearly 500 of them, with a back-log capital paid in of some $3 billion and holdings of stock worth another $2 billion. The idea was simple enough. Why should the ordinary citizen try to pick out stocks when the experts, indeed one of the Big Boys, stood ready and able to do it for him, through an investment trust?

Some were honestly managed, like the Blue Ridge Corporation. This was an investment trust sponsored by the highly respectable banking firm of Goldman, Sachs and Company, who offered to exchange its stock for those of the leading blue chips even at the current high figures—324 for Allied Chemical, 293 for AT&T, 395 for General Electric, and so on. Other investment trusts were highly speculative concerns launched by ignorant or venal plungers and promoters. Still others existed for the sole purpose of absorbing securities which the men running the trust found hard to sell in the open market. The Sunrise Investment Trust, headed by C. F. Bennett, specialized in this.

Bennett was known as a plunger and seemed to buy on hunches. But his success was phenomenal. Seaboard Air Line, for example, in which he had invested heavily, had a spectacular rise. Sunrise, or SIT, pyramided to three times its value in nine months. Investors followed Bennett like lemmings. He may have picked his stocks out of dreams or from a crystal ball. No one seemed to care. In a year, Sunrise had pyramided to a paid-in capital sum of $200 million, and was still growing.

C. F. Bennett continued to maintain his air of mystery, and people found the legend awesome. He was known to make frequent business trips to Florida with an attractive secretary. His yacht was sometimes seen cruising the waters around the Bahamas or the islands of the Caribbean. Even the other Big Boys did not know too much about him. But if there was one thing known about C. F. Bennett, it was this: He had the Midas touch.

The people who bought shares of Sunrise and the other investment trusts were grocers, truck drivers, automobile mechanics, waitresses, and elevator operators, as well as those more richly endowed. All of them had the innocence of amateurs, but all of them had the Great American Dream. The man holding a hundred shares of Blue Ridge or Sunrise would someday be a C. F. Bennett, in his own small way. He would sell his SIT shares at a tremendous price, and buy a mansion in Palm Beach or perhaps on the Riviera, and purchase three or four big, shining cars, and hire the servants he needed, and lie on the beach and to hell with everything. Others, of a more serious bent, saw the future of America as a nation set free. Not from crime, or war, or from control from the bureaucrats, or from corruption, or from manipulation, or from propaganda and ballyhoo. What they saw in this dream was a new America—a model for the rest of the world—a nation all of whose people were actually free at last from poverty and back-breaking labor.

The summer of 1929 could be called the last of the best— the siesta season of great and golden expectations. It was a summer to remember for its innocence and its happy euphoria. It was the last summer in which Americans were at their buoyant peak, so uninhibited and confident, so sure of the future. Truly, the sun had never shone so bright.

And never would again.

*

During this summer, all of the four embezzlers prospered, and far beyond their wildest expectations. Their investments in the market never stopped going up—and at dizzying speed.

Freddie Mayhew had run his nest egg up to $15,000 by steadily buying Radio on margin. By Labor Day, Radio Corporation of America had soared to 101. The work on the broadcasting station atop the Hotel Worthy was well in progress. It was to open officially early in January, and Freddie had staked out an office with two windows, overlooking

Main Street and the Post Office. He wanted to buy a car now, a Marmon or a Stutz. But he did not dare. He knew it would look too conspicuous. People would ask how a bank clerk on a salary of $20 a week could afford a luxury car. It would be better to wait until he resigned and then became an executive.

By now he was deeply in love with Ellie Hopkins, and she with him.

The night had come when she had moaned in his arms and begged him to "do it." After that, they did it everywhere—in the back of her car, in a Lovers' Lane on Mount Tom, in a canoe on Watershops Pond. They did it in the sawdust under an icehouse on the same pond. They did it in the woods near Riverside Park after one of the big bands had come there to play. They did it in a roadhouse, and they did it on the floor of an empty office owned by a friend of Freddie's. Now, instead of buying Trojans in packages of three, he bought them by the dozen. Once or twice, when in his own excitement his fumbling fingers botched the job of rolling on the condom, she impatiently told him to forget the awful thing and hurry up, she just couldn't wait another second. Freddie Mayhew found that delicious, but a little scary too.

But they were in love. There was no doubt of it. She talked of getting married as soon as possible. They would elope and *then* tell her father. But Freddie Mayhew held back. Ellie did not know what he was doing at the bank. She had only a vague idea that he might become associated with a radio station. She had no idea that he would actually be a full-fledged partner, and he wanted to surprise her. He would wait until he resigned and took his new position, before he proposed to her. Then it did not matter whether her father approved or not. By then, he could take care of himself—and her. He planned to move out of his mother's house and buy a nice Colonial up in the Forest Park section, and he planned to take Ellie to Bermuda or Nassau for their honeymoon.

As for Jonathan Keep, he had pyramided *his* holdings in the market. By Labor Day, the stock he was buying, Baldwin Locomotive, had reached the dizzy height of 63-3/4, and Keep now had $100,000, on paper. He had learned that a new bank was to be opened in Westfield, some nine miles from Riverside. It was to be called the Citizens Bank of Westfield, and it expected to get its charter from the state banking commission about the middle of December. Keep had put in an application with the new board of directors. He wanted no less a job than president of the new bank.

At first, there was stern objection. The board felt it would like some local man, someone who knew everybody in town, belonged to the Westfield Country Club, and so forth. Much of the banking business, the members pointed out, depended on loans, and for that it was important for a bank president to know the local people, their assets and reputation.

But Keep pointed out that as far as he knew, there was no one in Westfield to match his forty years of banking experience on an executive level. It was all very well to install an inexperienced president, if they wished. That was their prerogative. But shrewdly, he pointed out that the Massachusetts State Banking Commission was very fussy about this kind of a thing. Banking was a responsible business. Bankers dealt in other people's money, and the members of the Massachusetts State Banking Commission were very rigid on this particular matter. They liked to see a highly experienced man at the helm, and it was possible that they might withhold a charter until this condition was met. The board was impressed. Then Keep struck home. He offered to put $100,000 of his own money in the capitalization fund. After that, the vote for Keep's installation was unanimous.

As for Hannah Winthrop, her investment in Fisk Rubber had paid off handsomely as well. By Labor Day weekend, the stock was selling at 8, and her nest egg was very close to the fee she would have to pay Dr. Ricardi to have her face done. The fee, of course, would come out of pure profit. She would have to replace the Christmas Club and Vacation Club money before the holiday season. But now that was no problem.

She could not wait until the Day. She kept the pencil sketch of her new face, the face Dr. Ricardi had drawn for her, in the drawer of the end table next to her bed. She looked at it every night before she retired and every morning when she arose. She had already told Henry Hopkins that she wanted a three-week vacation in December, although she did not tell him why. She had told no one of her coming trip to Boston. She was entitled to only one week with pay. But Hannah Winthrop said she would take the other two at her own expense. She told Hopkins she had an aged mother in Boston who was sick and needed her care for a while. Hopkins agreed to give it to her. It was a little white lie, of course, but understandable.

Henry Hopkins' profit position in the market was now almost $200,000. This was, of course, on margin. But he was confident that he was on course, that soon he would have enough to pay his debt to his wife. Meanwhile, the Puritan Bank and Trust was doing tremendous business. Hopkins had advertised that the Puritan was the bank in which Calvin Coolidge put his money. There was a large sign on the rear wall of the bank: CALVIN COOLIDGE BANKS HERE, and the same legend was put in all the advertisements and embossed on the bank stationery. The President himself had visited the bank on three separate occasions and had been duly photographed.

Labor Day weekend came, and the four embezzlers rested

from their labors, sure of the future of the country, and now secure in their own.

They did not know—they had no way of knowing—of the sinister black mote, yet unseen, approaching in the high, blue summer sky.

AUTUMN
1929

12

ON TUESDAY MORNING, the day after the Labor Day weekend, Freddie Mayhew was rudely awakened by a phone call.

It was from Ellie Hopkins. She sounded very upset.

"Freddie, I'm sorry I've called you this early. But I had to. I just *had* to. Can you talk?"

"Yes."

There was a strange sound in back of Ellie's voice. Freddie could not identify it. He was puzzled and asked her where she was calling from. She replied that there was a long extension on their upstairs phone and she was calling from the bathroom. She had the water running in the bathtub, just to make sure her folks couldn't hear. And then she said:

"Darling, I still haven't fallen off the roof."

"You're sure?"

"Yes. I've tried everything. Hot baths. Jumping up and down. Running up and down the stairs. Taking castor oil, everything. And nothing. Nothing's happened." Then a wail: "I think I'm pregnant, Freddie. What am I going to do?"

"How long has it been now?"

"I'm three weeks overdue."

"Look, Ellie," he said desperately. "Don't give up. Keep trying. Promise you will. I don't know much about these things. But I've heard women can get nervous and upset or something, and you know—not be on time. Maybe it's one of those . . ."

"False pregnancies?"

"Yes." He hesitated. "Maybe you ought to see a doctor and find out for sure. I don't mean one in Riverside. But maybe you could see someone in Holyoke, or Hartford, or somewhere. Someone who doesn't know you."

"You think I should?"

"Only way we can find out for sure, Ellie."

She thought it over for a moment and then remembered that she had a friend who had been caught in the same situation. She recalled that the friend had seen a doctor in Hartford, and she said she would try to make an appointment and drive down during the morning. She told Freddie Mayhew she loved him, and he told her he loved her, and they agreed to meet that night at the Blue Door, a speakeasy on the road between Feeding Hills and Southwick.

He had tried to stay calm on the telephone, to reassure Ellie that everything would be all right. But inside he was disturbed. If Ellie was really pregnant, it would present complications. He needed the job at the bank, at least until December, to buy his position at the radio station, and he was still some distance from that. He would marry Ellie, of course. And secretly. He was sure that the minute Henry Hopkins found out what had happened to his daughter (*if* he found out), he would fire Freddie on the spot. And sooner or later, Ellie would give herself away by the usual symptoms —morning sickness and things like that. And of course, later on she would show.

He could only hope that it was a false alarm.

When Freddie Mayhew left the house, he already felt

somewhat limp from the weather. It was hot and muggy, and he pictured what kind of a day this would be at the bank. It would be absolute murder. Unlike the Union Trust and the Third National Bank, the Puritan Bank and Trust had not yet put in one of those new air-cooling systems. Eventually it would be forced to, in order to meet the competition. People liked to step off the hot street into cool interiors— banks or stores, or whatever. But Henry Hopkins still did not want to put any money into an air-cooling system, at least not this year. Freddie Mayhew cursed him as a tight bastard.

Now the Walnut Street trolley came along, showers of sparks flashing from the contact of the trolley spindle with the electric wire above. It was an open-air car, and Freddie could see the motorman spin his brass brake handle around to bring it to a stop. It was crowded with passengers this morning, filling the long wooden seats lined at right angles along the car. Others stood on the front and rear platforms, and a few men hung on by means of brass rails along the sides, so that their bodies tilted crazily away from the car, hanging over the street at almost a forty-five-degree angle.

He was aware that the men on the trolley were staring at him curiously. And for a moment, he could not imagine why. Dimly he began to realize that the others looked different, somehow. Suddenly he understood. Not one of them was wearing the usual summer straw hat, and he was. He had forgotten that traditionally, in Riverside or elsewhere, you always put away your straw hat after Labor Day. Unofficially, although the calendar said otherwise, it was the end of summer. He felt a little embarrassed. He took his hat from his head and tucked it under one arm, holding onto the car bar for dear life with the other.

The trolley moved along Walnut, turned left on State, and headed down the long hill toward Main Street and the center of the city.

He got off the trolley just opposite the bank and bought a copy of the *Riverside Union*.

He turned to the financial page and smiled at what he saw. Everything was coming up roses. Radio was going through the roof. The financial columnist of the *Times* made the point that there had been no summer lull in the market this year. The direction had been up, up, up. The volume of trading had been 4 and 5 million shares daily. All this seemed to be a testimonial to the rising wealth and vitality of the American economic system. And men who seemed to know, men like Bernard Baruch, John J. Raskob, and Charles Mitchell, predicted that in September the market should be even stronger . . .

Everything was going so right, thought Freddie Mayhew. Except for Ellie Hopkins' condition. Again, he hoped fervently that it was a false pregnancy. He knew he was going to have a bad day until he heard for sure.

He walked into the bank. Even before he went to his cage, he headed for the men's room. He did that automatically now. Just to see that those tiles were intact.

Just to see that everything was all right.

*

Once again, later that morning, he found the right kind of customer. A woman he knew, a Mrs. Drummond, came in and deposited $400 in cash. She was going to Florida and would stay through the fall and winter with her daughter, who had a house in Sarasota. And she would not be back till April of the following year.

He took the deposit slip into the men's room, after making sure no one was around—or at least he *thought* no one was. He looked under the two toilet booths to make sure they were unoccupied. Then he took the deposit slip from his pocket, lifted the linoleum tiles, and started to put the slip with the others.

It was then that he heard heavy footsteps outside just approaching the door of the men's room. He went into panic. He just managed to replace the tiles and dash into the toilet booth, when the door opened. To his dismay, he noted that the lock on the toilet booth door was broken. In his panic, and without thinking, he tore up the deposit cards. They were made of very heavy paper, and this was not easy for him to do. He heard the man outside move to the sink and start to run the water. From the weight of the heavy steps and the sound of the ponderous shoes, he guessed it was Joe Dailey. It occurred to Freddie Mayhew that Dailey might, just might, enter the toilet booth. If so, he, Freddie Mayhew, would be caught red-handed with the goods. He flung the torn pieces of the deposit cards down the toilet and pulled the chain. The water spun and gurgled, but the pieces of heavy paper would not go down. He pulled the chain again. Still, they would not flush. On the third try, they were reluctantly sucked under.

Freddie Mayhew stood there, rigidly, until he heard Dailey—if it *was* Dailey—leave. His collar was wilted, his whole shirt was soaked through with sweat. And trembling, he went back to his cage.

At two o'clock, when he received the phone call from Ellie Hopkins, he was still in partial shock at his close call. What she had to tell him shook him up even more.

She had seen a Dr. Edgerly in Hartford, and there was no doubt about it. She was pregnant.

13

WHEN HENRY HOPKINS arrived at the bank on this same morning, Joe Dailey was watching for him through the window. The guard swung open the big door.

"Good morning, Mr. Hopkins."

"Good morning, Joseph."

"Going to be a real hot one today, sir."

"Yes, indeed. It certainly looks that way."

Hopkins went directly to his desk. The first thing he did was to take from his suit pocket the two freshly starched detachable collars he had brought from home and put them in the top drawer. It was already oppressively warm in the bank, and he knew that later he would have to change his collar. His desk had a glass top, and he liked it to be entirely clear when he started the day. He was by nature a neat man, almost prissy in this respect. Not even a paper clip marred the surface of his desk, and as he looked down, he could clearly see the full reflection of his face.

Now Jonathan Keep came over.

"Morning, Mr. Hopkins."

"Morning, Jonathan."

"Looks as though it's going to be a big day for withdrawals."

"It always is, the day after Labor Day."

"Yes, sir, no doubt about it. Our paying teller's going to have his hands full. Same as he did Friday, before the weekend." Keep smiled sourly. "People go crazy and spend every cent they've got at the beach, or at the mountains, or fixing up the flivver to go riding, and nothing on this earth is going to stop them."

"Better make sure we've got plenty of cash on hand, Jonathan."

"Just checked the vault, Mr. Hopkins. Got all we need." He grinned thinly. "Barring of course, any run on the bank. Never saw so much cash around, in my memory, and I've been around a long time. You'd think people were growing money in their backyards like tomatoes."

"Coolidge Prosperity," said Henry Hopkins. "Seems to be still with us. Of course, a lot of it is in the market—on paper."

"Don't believe in the market," said Keep. "Never cottoned to the idea you could make something for nothing. Sooner or later, it's got to come a cropper."

"I agree with you, Jonathan. Personally, I wouldn't touch it with a ten-foot pole."

They discussed some routine bank business and joked about an item both of them had read in the morning newspapers. A gang of bank robbers had successfully robbed a bank in Bellows Falls, Vermont; another in Laconia, New Hampshire; and still another in Lenox, Massachusetts. This kind of thing was rather unusual in New England. Somehow it belonged in places like Kansas and Oklahoma, or elsewhere in the West. The recent robberies had taken place in small towns where the banks had poor security facilities. The Puritan had just installed the latest security system only six months ago. But what amused Hopkins and Keep most was that the leader of the gang had a girlfriend who also participated in the robberies. Some headline writer on one of the

New England newspapers, in a wry moment, had facetiously called the bank robbers "Bunny and Clive," a takeoff on the notorious Bonnie and Clyde, who, more and more, were showing up in the headlines. The nickname stuck, and every newspaper now used it.

On the dot of ten, Joseph Dailey, who had been watching the hands of the big Puritan Clock on the sidewalk outside, swung open the doors to the public.

At the Puritan Bank and Trust, the business of the day had begun.

*

The last appointment of the long, hot day, as noted on Henry Hopkins' calendar, was with the city's leading bootlegger, Pat Nolan.

He watched Nolan wince a little as he told the Irishman that the board had decided not to take on another member at this time. Again, Nolan repeated that he was willing to buy in on the board, and he was ready to offer the bank a blank check, fill in your own figure, for the privilege. Again, Henry Hopkins gently made the point: It wasn't a question of money. There just wasn't room for another member of the board. Hopkins tried to soften the blow.

"Of course, if a vacancy comes up, if one of the directors leaves town or dies, then I'd be glad to go back and propose your name again."

"Sure, I understand." Nolan was tight-lipped. "And thanks for trying."

Hopkins wondered why Nolan had even made the attempt. He knew, and so did the Irishman, that there wasn't a chance, not the ghost of one. The mere fact that he was Irish was enough to insure a Yankee blackball, at least at the Puritan. And his being a bootlegger raised the barrier still higher, although this was not really an important factor. All over the country, there were bootleggers sitting on the boards of banks, men who wanted this kind of status and could buy their way in by the sheer power of money.

The board had held its meeting on Friday, and Henry Hopkins had told the four other members that Nolan was making application. They were all friends of Hopkins', neighbors who lived on the Hill, wealthy businessmen, cronies at the club. They had looked at each other incredulously and then started to chuckle. Sam Porter, who owned and published the *Riverside Republican,* had laughed outright, and said, "Well, I'll be goddamned. Now *that's* what I call brass!" Arthur Herrick, who owned the Mayflower Textile Mill, had agreed. "The shanty Irish are starting to take over Boston. But they'll never do it here—except over my dead body. I'll say this for Nolan. He's got one hell of a lot of gall. Next thing you know, he'll try running for mayor!"

They had, of course, voted it down unanimously. After that they had gone about their routine business, approving large loans, reviewing old ones, deciding matters of policy. Then, at the end of the meeting, Arthur Pynchon, the head teller, was ceremoniously ushered into the Board Room. He carried a small money tray, and on this tray rested five twenty-dollar gold pieces, one for each man. He passed the tray around, and each man, in complete silence, took one of the gold pieces and slipped it into his vest pocket. After that, they had all gone to lunch at the Mansion House, still amused by Pat Nolan's overweening ambition.

After Nolan left, Henry Hopkins had some paperwork to do, so he stayed an hour after closing time. The entire personnel of the bank had left, except for Hopkins and the bank guard. It was one of Joe Dailey's duties to remain on the premises and lock up after everyone had gone.

Now, as Hopkins rose and prepared to go, Dailey came over to his desk. The burly guard's face was apologetic.

"Sorry to bother you, sir. But we've got a couple of problems."

"Yes?"

"I've just come from the men's room. We're very low on toilet paper."

"All right. Then order some more."

"Sir, if I may make a suggestion. The ladies' room is oversupplied. There must be more than five dozen rolls in there. I thought that maybe I could switch some of those rolls into the men's room before I go home. Save us ordering a new batch before we need it."

"Fine, Joe," said Henry Hopkins. "You handle this any way you like."

"Now, sir, there's something else."

"Yes?"

"The toilet in the men's room. Something wrong with it. Somebody threw something in it they shouldn't. Anyway, it's overflowed. There's water all over the floor, and it's loosened some of the tiles on the floor."

"Damn it," said Hopkins, irritated. "We just had those tiles put in six months ago. Tell you what you do, Joe. Call the Riverside Flooring Company. Tell them to have some people over tomorrow to replace those tiles. Oh, and don't forget a plumber. First thing in the morning."

14

THAT NIGHT, Freddie Mayhew and Ellie Hopkins
drove to the Blue Door. Normally, they would have patronized the Barrel. But the Blue Door was not considered chic
and thus was a speakeasy not usually frequented by any of
their friends. On this occasion, they were in no mood for
frivolity or social chitchat. They wanted to be alone.

At the door, a slit opened to their knock, and a pair of eyes
studied them. Freddie said, "Eddie sent me" and presented
a card for the eyes to study. After that they were admitted.

Freddie ordered a gin rickey and Ellie a Cuba libre. Both
of them were still stunned by what had happened. They
stared at each other, trying to hold back what was very close
to panic. Finally, Freddie said, half to himself, still unbelieving:

"So you're going to have a baby."

"We." She corrected him.

"We."

"There's no doubt about it?" he said, desperately. "I mean,
this doctor in Hartford . . ."

"He was positive, Freddie. He was absolutely positive."

Then: "What'll we do?"

"I don't know."

"*Think* of something."

"I was thinking of what your father's going to say when he hears of this . . ."

"My God," she said. "He'll kill me. *And* you."

They both knew how and when it had happened. On a night over a month ago, they had parked at a secluded spot overlooking Watershops Pond. Freddie had spread a blanket on the ground, and in spite of the nippy autumn air, they had made love. At the crucial moment, Freddie had fumbled in his coat pocket for one of the thin rubber condoms he always carried. To his horror, he realized he had left the Trojans in another jacket. But there was Ellie on the ground, her skirt pulled high up, her legs spread, and moaning for him to hurry and put it in, put it in. As for Freddie, at that moment, his swollen penis was ready to explode. Somewhere, a small voice warned him not to thrust it home, to relieve himself in some other way. But he was wild with desire for her, and he could not help himself. He thrust his burning shaft deep into her, as far as it would go.

Freddie ordered another gin rickey. Then, almost apologetically, he made a suggestion. Maybe Ellie could get an abortion. Indignantly, she rejected this possibility. It was an ugly thing to even think about. It was illegal and dangerous. One of her girlfriends had paid $100 and had almost died in the hands of a sleazy butcher who called himself a doctor. Her girlfriend could never bear a child again. She, Ellie Hopkins, was going to have the baby, no matter what. And Freddie agreed to this, although his heart really wasn't in it.

She went on with a dismal scenario of the near future. Her father would be furious. He would fire Freddie and perhaps disown Ellie. He might insist on an abortion. At the very least, he would send her away to some distant rest home to have the baby and then give the child out for adoption. He would not have the Hopkins name sullied in Riverside, she told Freddie. In 1929, a daughter who had a child out of wedlock could disgrace the entire family. Her father would go to any lengths to prevent this. Certainly he would see Freddie as a fortune hunter, trying to worm his way into the Hopkins wealth and position. Certain magazine articles had appeared lately, advising young men how to climb the ladder and be a success. Basically, the idea was not to work hard. The easiest and surest way to get ahead was simply to marry the boss's daughter. Henry Hopkins was certain to see Freddie in precisely this light.

Freddie listened quietly to her wailing. But by the time he had finished his third gin rickey, he was no longer disturbed. He began to see clearly that their situation, his and Ellie's, wasn't so bad after all. In fact, he now wondered why he hadn't thought it through in the first place. If you looked at it a certain way, both Ellie and he had a glowing future. In a few minutes, and after the third drink, Freddie underwent a complete change in his attitude. Now he became cool, confident, even cocky.

He reached out and took her hand, trying to comfort her. "Ellie, there's no point in getting yourself all upset."

"Oh, that's all right for you," she said, her eyes blazing. "But I'm the one who's pregnant, and I'm the one who'll have to break the news to Daddy. And to my mother . . ."

"Look, in a few weeks our troubles will be over."

"What do you mean?"

"Simple. We'll get married."

"Oh, Freddie," she said.

They were sitting close together, and she embraced him and kissed him passionately. Then she drew back, jarred by a sudden brush with reality.

"But what'll we live on?"

He told her he had made some money in certain investments. In a month, perhaps two on the outside, he would have enough to support both of them. Then he could tell her father to take his job and shove it. He was also slated to take a certain executive position after he left the bank. Then he grinned at Ellie:

"How do you like those apples, *Mrs. Mayhew?*"

"But Freddie. Where did you get all that money?"

He shrugged, and then, in a modest way told her again that he had made certain investments. But for the moment, and for certain important reasons, he had to keep them secret, even from her.

Ellie, naturally, was not satisfied with this explanation. She wanted to know why they could not be married instantly. If her father would not consent, they could always elope. Freddie now opened the door a little. He told her he had made this money in the market. She did not press him any further, since this was entirely reasonable. Everybody was making money in the market. He told her again that he needed just another few weeks before he could be entirely sure of his investment. Then they could be married, without worry or uncertainty as to their future. Freddie Mayhew was not ready yet to tell anybody what he was doing, not even Ellie. And if things turned out the way he expected, he'd never have to tell her.

Finally, and reluctantly, she accepted the delay. But she warned Freddie not to wait too long. The time would come when she would start to show. He wanted to know when that would be, and she told him somewhere around three months. But they had better be married long before that. If they were, perhaps they could get away with some explanation that the baby was premature.

Still, she had seen the surge of confidence in Freddie, and, magically, it rubbed off on her. And just to celebrate, he had his fourth gin rickey, and she had her second Cuba libre.

On the way home, Freddie was roaring drunk and exhilarated. Ellie was driving. He became very amorous. He suggested that they stop and spread the blanket. He took one of her hands and put it on his swollen crotch. She slapped it away. She told him, first, that she wasn't in the mood. Second, that it was too cold outside and it was too cramped in the back seat of the car. And third, she became perverse and primly told him there would be no more "going all the way" until they were married. Perhaps she hoped in this way to bring about their legal union much earlier than Freddie had planned.

When she let Freddie off at his house, he barely made it up the stairs. He threw himself on his bed, fully clothed, and almost instantly he fell asleep.

*

The next day, Freddie Mayhew had a tremendous hangover.

His head ached, and his throat was thick with nausea. He had a tremendous desire to vomit. He put on an old bathrobe and filled a hot-water bottle with ice and put it to his aching head. He groaned aloud and wished he were dead. And he swore that he would never patronize the Blue Door again. He was convinced that their gin rickeys were spiked with fusel oil, or something else, God knew what.

He phoned the bank and left a message that he was ill and would not be in to work that day.

Here he violated the classic credo, the ironclad rule of the embezzler. Never miss a single day at the bank. Because that could be the day the roof falls in, unless you're there to protect yourself. The classic Murphy's law always haunted the embezzler when he was absent: *If anything can possibly go wrong, it will.*

Early in the afternoon, Freddie Mayhew received a phone call. Now, with a towel soaked in cold water and tied around his forehead, he answered. It was Henry Hopkins.

"Freddie, I want you to come down to the bank immediately."

"But sir, I've already phoned in. I'm sick."

"I don't care how sick you are, boy," said Hopkins. His voice sounded cold, ominous. "I would advise you, for your own good, to get down here at once!"

Hopkins hung up abruptly. Dread began to tickle Freddie Mayhew's body with creeping fingers. He felt a chill crawl up his spine, and his mouth went dry. Gooseflesh popped up all over him.

He wondered what had gone wrong. A depositor who hadn't been in the bank in five years might have picked this particular day to check his account and make a withdrawal. Or a depositor may have died suddenly, and the Internal Revenue people may have been in, quick as a flash, to impound the depositor's bank records and seal his safety deposit vault for further examination of assets. There could be any number of unpleasant, sweaty situations.

Slowly and painfully, Freddie Mayhew began to dress.

*

When he arrived at the bank, he was immediately led into the Board Room by Henry Hopkins and Jonathan Keep. Their faces were set and grim. Henry Hopkins locked the door behind them.

Then, wordlessly, Hopkins took from his pocket a handful of deposit cards. They were water-stained but still legible. Hopkins told Freddie that the toilet in the men's room had overflowed, loosening the tiles. The floor men, in repairing the tiles, had come across these deposit cards, hidden under one of the tiles. Freddie went pale. The deposit cards were easily identified as his.

Now Hopkins said, "I want the truth, boy. The whole truth, and nothing but the truth."

Freddie Mayhew looked at the impassive faces of the two men watching him. His head ached more than ever, and there was a knot in his stomach. He knew they knew what he had done, but apparently they wanted to hear it from him. Freddie realized that now he was finished. There was no use in putting up any kind of defense. They had him cold, and that was that. And so, in despair, he made a full confession.

They listened quietly and without interruption, and when he had finished, Hopkins said:

"Let's be plain about this, Freddie. You know what you are. You're an embezzler."

"Yes, sir."

"And we could send you to jail for this," added Keep.

"Yes, sir. I know that."

After a pause, Hopkins said:

"What do you expect us to do about this, boy?"

"I don't know, sir," said Freddie manfully. "I suppose I'll have to take my medicine."

For a moment, Freddie Mayhew thought of telling Hopkins that he intended to be Hopkins' son-in-law. That Ellie was pregnant. Throw himself on the mercy of Ellie's father and hope Hopkins might think twice about sending a future member of the family to jail. There was always the Hopkins name to consider. But at the last moment, he decided to keep silent. It would be a desperate gambit, and it could backfire. Hearing this news, Henry Hopkins, in his anger, might even be more eager to see that he went to jail.

For a while there was silence. Freddie Mayhew shrank in his chair and waited for the verdict. Finally Hopkins said:

"You realize we could file a complaint with the police, Freddie."

"Yes, Mr. Hopkins."

"And embezzlement is a serious crime."

"Yes, sir."

Hopkins looked at Keep. There seemed to be some kind of understanding between them. Then he said:

"I've talked this over with Mr. Keep here, Freddie. And we've come to an agreement. We've decided not to prosecute . . ."

Freddie stared at them incredulously.

"You mean, you're not going to . . ."

"No. For a number of reasons, boy. First, you're young. Something like this could ruin your whole future. You've shown yourself a thief, but it's the first time, and we understand that you didn't have the strength of will to resist the temptation. We felt there was little enough mercy in this hard world, and we thought this was the time to show some."

"I'm very grateful, Mr. Hopkins."

"Second," Hopkins said, "you told us you fully intended to replace the money you took from the bank. Speaking for myself, I believe you." He turned to Keep. "And you?"

Keep nodded. "I'm inclined to believe the boy, too."

"This determination to replace every cent," continued Hopkins, "we find commendable. And we're taking it into consideration. If we bring the police into this and prosecute, we shake the confidence of our depositors. We would create a scandal and excessive publicity. The state banking commission would immediately be on our backs. They would conduct an exhaustive investigation of the bank's books and perhaps create all kinds of difficulties. And again, the Puritan would make all the newspaper headlines. We're a quiet bank, Freddie; we serve our depositors quietly and with dignity, and Calvin Coolidge himself banks here. We like to keep our light shaded, and the last thing we would want is adverse publicity. You see, boy?"

"Yes, sir. I certainly do."

"Now, of course, you're through here, at the bank. Unfortunately, we can't give you a recommendation, so you'll have to look for some other kind of work. I'm going to ask you, Freddie, to stay on two more weeks until I get a replacement for you. It'll take at least that long."

"And naturally," added Keep. "We'll expect you, by that time, to cash in your securities and replace the money embezzled from the bank."

"Yes, sir. I'll certainly do that, Mr. Keep." Then he hesitated for a moment. "Only . . ."

"Only *what?*"

"What about the profit I made?"

Hopkins and Keep looked at each other. Freddie was quick to see they were both in agreement.

"You're to return that money to the bank, too."

"But it doesn't belong to the bank. It's money I made in Radio . . ."

"You made it with the bank's money," said Keep, "and in that sense, your profit is the bank's money. When you borrow money, boy, you have to pay interest. We'll just call this interest."

"*Some* interest," said Freddie, bitterly. "I'm talking about thousands . . ."

"We're letting you off easy, boy," said Hopkins. "You've got to understand that. That profit of yours was obtained illegally. Of course, if you want to oppose us on this point . . ."

"No, no," said Freddie quickly. "Take it all. I'm very grateful to you, Mr. Hopkins. And to you too, Mr. Keep."

Hopkins unlocked the door. It was toward the end of the banking day, and Freddie left. He had come out with his skin. But in spite of the reasons they gave, he wondered why they had been so lenient. Especially, Jonathan Keep. He was as tough and cold-blooded as they came.

It wasn't like Keep. It wasn't like Keep at all.

*

The employees of the Puritan bank normally stayed from a half-hour to an hour afterward, balancing their books, sifting out the deposit and withdrawal cards, and counting the money deposited for the day.

At four o'clock, Hannah Winthrop put on her hat, preparing to go. She had a date at the hairdresser's at four-fifteen, and she was the last employee left in the bank. Then she saw something that stunned her.

The door to the ladies' room was open, and Joe Dailey was coming out of it. He was wheeling an office cart piled high with toilet paper from the ladies' room into the men's room. He did not notice her presence in the bank. Apparently he thought everyone was gone.

His task finished, he shut the door to the ladies' room and wheeled the cart into a back room at the bank.

Hannah Winthrop froze in horror. Then she almost fainted, holding the edge of a desk for support. But even though she was dizzy with fear, she had all the instincts of a survivor. She was desperate, and she knew she had to act quickly to avert a disaster.

She ran into the ladies' room. With a quick glance, she saw that all the rolls of toilet tissue on the top shelves, including *her* roll, were gone.

She heard a door close. She knew that Joe Dailey had reentered the main area of the bank. She opened the door a crack and peeked out. Dailey seemed satisfied that everyone had gone. He never checked the employees as they left, since they left at various times. She watched the guard as he lit a cigarette. Then she saw him enter the men's room. A minute or two later, he emerged, buttoning his fly. He paused to take one long look around the bank. Then he went to the big main door, deactivated the alarm, unlocked the door, using three keys to do so, and set the alarm again. Then he locked the door from the outside and left.

Now Hannah was alone in the bank. She still felt dizzy. She washed her face in cold water and tried to think through what to do next—not that there was very much to think through.

She had to have that roll of toilet tissue. *Her* roll. And there was only one way to get it.

She left the ladies' room and went out into the main area of the bank. Now that it was empty, it seemed eerie, ghostly. She knew she was alone, but fear whispered loudly in her ear. The eyes in the oil paintings, generations of Hopkinses, were all watching, all staring at her accusingly. But then, she told herself that her fear was ridiculous. She had to keep her nerve. There was only one way to assure her safety and that was to find that key roll of toilet tissue, no matter how long it took.

She entered the men's room. The faint smell of urine assailed her nose, and she recoiled at the sight of the single urinal. She had never been in a men's room before. She looked at the cabinet that held the rolls of toilet tissue. It was exactly like the one in the ladies' room. And all four shelves were fully stocked. It was impossible to tell one roll from another—she had never written any distinguishing mark on her roll because she knew exactly where it was—and she did not know quite where to begin. And she knew, unless she was very lucky, that she could be here half the night before she found what she wanted.

She took a roll of toilet paper from the top shelf and bowled it across the floor of the men's room so that it unreeled by itself. No Christmas Club slips. She rerolled it and put it back on the top and did the same with the next one.

Each of the shelves had two rows of toilet paper. In an hour, Hannah had finished the top shelf.

And no luck.

Frustrated and close to tears, she started on the second shelf. A few minutes later, just as she was about to again bowl a roll of toilet paper along the floor, she heard a door close in the outer bank. Startled, paralyzed with fear, Hannah listened. She heard steps moving through the bank, fading as they moved toward the rear. Clutching the roll of toilet tissue close to her chest, she went to the door, opened it a crack, and peered out.

She saw a man at the steel gate of the vault. His back was turned toward her and he was taking out a bunch of keys.

It was Jonathan Keep.

She watched him as he opened the grilled gate, which admitted him to the inner door of the vault itself.

Once inside, he twirled the big dial on the vault door to the required numbers and swung open the door. He left the big steel door wide-open as he entered.

Now Hannah Winthrop watched, fascinated, as Keep unlocked the cash compartment. He used a tiny flashlight, and she saw him reach in and take out a packet of money wrapped with the official Puritan bank paper binders designed to hold together packages of bills in various denominations. He stuffed the packet into his pocket and started to close the cash compartment. He hesitated a moment and stood there deep in thought. Then Hannah Winthrop saw him shrug, as if to say "What the hell," open the compartment door again, take out a similar pack of currency, and stuff it in another pocket. Then he closed the door and locked it.

But there was still more to come.

Hannah stood riveted to the spot and watched Keep drop to his knees in front of the iron base supporting the rows of safe deposit boxes. Then he lay flat on his stomach, reached underneath the base, and extracted what Hannah could see was a ledger. He had to pull it out with some effort, since it had been held firmly to the bottom of the base with heavy tape. He stripped off the tape, took the ledger to the desk nearest the vault, and, still using his tiny flashlight, made a couple of entries. Then he went back into the vault and retaped the ledger into place.

At all this, Hannah Winthrop went into a kind of shock. It wasn't real, it couldn't be. This was a play of some sort. In a moment, the curtain would come down, the lights would go on, and the audience would file out onto the street and into reality.

But it *was* real. And that *was* Jonathan Keep, treasurer of the Puritan Bank and Trust, who appeared to be stealing the bank's money. She continued to watch, and she saw Keep pick up the phone, ask for a number. It was a number familiar to her.

"Hello," Keep was saying. "That you, Lothrop? Glad I caught you. Working late, I see." Then after a pause: "Reason I'm calling is this. I want you to buy me another fifty shares of Baldwin Locomotive, first thing tomorrow morning." Then, after another pause: "Right. On the usual margin, of course."

She watched Keep as he hung up. He stood by his desk for a moment, deep in thought. Then suddenly, to Hannah's horror, he began to walk straight toward the men's room.

It was too late for her to slip out. Wildly, she looked around for some place to hide. There was only one place she could find shelter. And that was in the single toilet booth. She rushed into the booth and saw, to her dismay, that the lock was broken. It was possible that Keep wanted to use the toilet instead of the urinal. In that case, she was trapped.

The toilet booth had a partial door, so that by looking underneath, you could see the legs and feet of anyone sitting on the toilet seat. Hannah Winthrop, now close to hysteria, realized this. She stood on the rim of the toilet itself, since the seat had been left standing in an upright position. Her footing on the slippery porcelain rim was precarious, and she teetered this way and that. But in her present position, Keep could not see her head or her legs.

She prayed that Keep would use the urinal instead of the toilet booth. Her prayer was answered. He went to the urinal, and presently she heard him urinating. The obscene sound of the liquid stream splashing against the hard surface of the urinal unnerved her. Suddenly she slipped and lost her balance. She uttered a small scream as she fell, and tried to regain her perch. Her foot missed the rim and plunged into the water of the toilet itself. The roll of toilet paper she held against her breast slipped from her grasp and started to unroll. A streamer of paper emerged from under the toilet booth and rolled out onto the floor of the men's room. Unfortunately for her, this was *the* roll, and it spewed out the Christmas Club deposit slips she had hidden.

Jonathan Keep, still at the urinal and not quite finished, stared in disbelief at this. He had heard Hannah's slight scream, and now this roll of toilet paper emerging from under the booth startled him still more. With an effort, he contracted his muscles and was able to stop urinating at midflow. He noted the Christmas Club slips on the floor and picked one up to look at it. Then he cautiously approached the toilet booth.

Now thoroughly alarmed, and realizing there was someone else in the bank, he pulled open the door to the toilet booth. Hannah Winthrop was sitting on the rim of the toilet, her legs spread grotesquely, her hat askew on her head. She glared up at him defiantly. Then her eyes moved downward, and she saw that Keep's fly was unbuttoned and his penis still partially hanging out. She screamed and turned her head away, and he quickly buttoned his fly.

He looked at Hannah accusingly and showed her the Christmas Club deposit slips. Then he said:

"I think you'd better explain this, Miss Winthrop."

But Hannah Winthrop was not cowed. Not in the least. Her manner, to his surprise, was defiant, even insolent.

"And maybe *you'd* better explain something, Mr. Keep."

He stared at her. "What are you talking about?"

"The money in your pockets. The money you took from the vault. I saw the whole thing," she said. "And if you report me, Mr. Keep, then I'll report you."

At this, Jonathan Keep recoiled as though hit by a hammer. To use the hoary phrase, he was the pot calling the kettle black, and now he was suddenly upended. He knew Hannah Winthrop meant exactly what she said. Clearly, they were in it together now, as each other's hostage. From now on, silence would bind them together. Finally Keep said:

"Maybe we ought to talk this over, Miss Winthrop."

"Yes, I think we should, Mr. Keep," she said firmly. "I most certainly think we should."

Suddenly her cheeks flamed as she realized how ridiculous she must look to Keep, sitting as she was, on the men's toilet, one leg soaked almost to the knee with water. She rose, set her hat straight, walked out of the toilet booth, and gathered together her Christmas Club deposit slips. Then she rerolled the roll of toilet paper, *her* roll, and without saying another word to Keep, walked out into the bank. Then she went into the ladies' room, where she replaced the roll temporarily until she could think of another hiding place.

Meanwhile, as Keep waited for her to emerge, he must have started to ponder on what seemed to be developing. At this point, he knew that both Freddie Mayhew and Hannah Winthrop were now "borrowing" funds, as well as himself. Hannah did not yet know that Freddie Mayhew was also involved, but she would soon find out. Thus, three of the

bank's employees were involved, and Jonathan Keep knew
—or rather suspected—a fourth.

The Puritan Bank and Trust had some fifteen employees
on its payroll. It was highly possible that others might be
involved, given the temptations of the market. But of course,
Keep could not be sure.

15

ON SUNDAY MORNING, September 29th, Henry Hopkins dutifully attended services at the First Episcopal Church with his wife, Helen. The pastor preached a rousing sermon on morality versus Mammon—the latter, in this case, representing materialism, and especially the market. The people of Riverside, as well as those in the rest of the country, were clearly far more interested in reading the financial pages than the Bible. They hung on the words of new disciples like John J. Raskob, Bernard Baruch, or C. F. Bennett, rather than Matthew, Luke, and Peter. Listen to the real prophets, and not these Philistines. So thundered the Reverend Charles Moorehead. And his congregation listened with bowed heads.

But it is questionable whether very many resolved to go out and sin no more. By this time, the Sunday edition of the *New York Times,* with its world-famed financial section, had reached town via the New Haven Railroad, and they were anxious to get home and read the latest prophecies of the financial gurus and analysts on which way the market would go—whether it was headed for heaven or hell.

Henry Hopkins drove his wife home. He had a hurried

lunch and told her he planned to drive to the club and play a little poker with some of his cronies. Instead he turned the car off Maple onto State Street and from there headed down-town toward the bank. The fact was, he needed a quiet hour or two alone at the bank to catch up on certain work locked in his desk.

Again, like all embezzlers, he needed to keep two sets of books. One for himself and a doctored version in case there was a sudden audit or if the bank examiner happened to show up unexpectedly. He could not work on these two sets of books during the business day for the obvious reason that he might get caught. And he could not take them home with him because that created certain risks. Not only must he physically be at the bank every day, but so must his books.

Driving down Main Street, Henry Hopkins was in both an angry and depressed mood. At the Cup Dance at the club the night before, his daughter Ellie had drunk herself into enough courage to tell both her father and mother that she was in love with Freddie Mayhew and intended to marry him shortly, if not sooner. That had been one hell of a shock to them both. That damned pipsqueak had taken advantage of his little girl and of himself, Hopkins told himself. If he thought he was going to get ahead by marrying the boss's daughter, Mayhew had another think coming. Hopkins had changed his mind. He intended to keep Freddie on at the bank. At least there he could keep his eye on him. He was as involved as Mayhew was—birds of a feather, so to speak —and if Freddie made some kind of foolish slip, he, Hopkins, might possibly be involved as well. But he would make the young whippersnapper sweat for his arrogance. Helen had become hysterical at Ellie's announcement and he had had to take her home early. His daughter had told them that if they did not give their consent, then Freddie Mayhew and she planned to elope and be married by a justice of the peace.

Henry was further upset by the fact that during the last week the market had taken a sharp turn downward. Downward, in fact, was a polite word. It had plummeted for four days, and only on Saturday, the day before, had it steadied. On Friday alone, Westinghouse had slipped eleven dollars a share; Allied Chemical had about the same loss; General Electric had dropped almost thirteen dollars a share; and Columbia Carbon closed at seventeen below its opening price. Everything had gone way down, including Henry's portfolio. In Saturday's *New York Times,* it was reported that thousands of calls had gone out from brokers for more margin for overextended buyers. Some speculators who had bought up to their necks on margin were wiped out and ruined. Others owned stocks which were hardly worth the money borrowed from the brokers to buy them in the first place. An analyst for the *Times* pointed out, as prices fell, that the loans from brokers should have dropped as well. But the contrary had happened. And this seemed to indicate that stock was passing from the knowing hands of the Big Boys into the inexperienced ones of small investors or speculators.

At any rate, thought Henry Hopkins, it was hell on wheels to stand by and watch your assets begin to melt away like a hanging icicle in the noonday sun.

But of course, the market would turn around. It always had, he reassured himself. And the thing to do was not to panic, not to sell, but to hold on.

There was only one bright note to temper Henry Hopkins' gloom.

On Tuesday, the Riverside Chamber of Commerce was holding its monthly luncheon meeting in a special dining room at the Highland Hotel. The chamber was in the habit of rotating its prominent members as chairman of the month, and it was Henry's turn. There was usually a speaker at the monthly meeting, and Henry had set about finding one. He had been struck by a sudden inspiration. It was a wild chance, but not impossible. He put in a telephone call to Calvin Coolidge. Would his old friend come down to Riverside and be a guest at the luncheon? To his delight, the President, or ex-President, out of his old friendship with Henry Hopkins, accepted. Coolidge hadn't even moved from his house on Massasoit Street lately. He was busy writing a syndicated column, 200 words of common sense each day, and was working on his autobiography. He was at the moment a little bored with what he was doing, and it would be refreshing to get away for a day. But as a stern condition, the President, or ex-President, exacted a promise from Henry—no speeches. Coolidge was finished with speeches; he had had too many of them in his years of office. Henry asked for only a few words, but Coolidge remained firm—no speeches.

All this was a lift for Henry's ego. There would be photographs of himself standing next to the President, smiling and shaking hands. It would not only enhance Henry's personal prestige, but all this would mean great publicity for the Puritan Bank and Trust. Coolidge already banked at the Puritan, having a modest amount on deposit, and all the depositors, old and new, could sleep soundly, knowing their money was secure.

*

There were very few people in downtown Riverside on Sunday, but Henry took the precaution of parking his Pierce Arrow two blocks away. There was no point in being too conspicuous.

He walked to the bank, unlocked the door, and entered. But to his surprise, he suddenly found that he was not alone, that someone else had come down to do a little extra work on a quiet Sunday.

Jonathan Keep was at his desk, working over two sets of books, and he was just as surprised as Henry. For a few moments, the men simply gawked at each other. Then the unexpected meeting became a confrontation. It was instantly apparent to Henry Hopkins that his treasurer had a doctored set of books before him, and he indignantly accused Keep of hanky-panky. He thought he knew what his treasurer was up to—it was quite obvious—but he demanded an explanation. Keep, however, was unruffled. He coolly accused Hopkins of coming down to the bank for the same reason—to doctor *his* double set of books. He told his superior he knew all about that General Motors collateral and the unsecured loan Henry had made to Mackey, as well as to others. In short, they were both involved, and who was calling whom an embezzler?

At this point, they decided to talk it over. Both Hopkins and Keep knew Freddie Mayhew was an embezzler, but Keep knew about Hannah and Henry did not. Hannah knew Keep was an embezzler, but did not know about Freddie or Henry. And Freddie did not know that anybody else was involved except himself.

After some discussion, the two men decided that a meeting of the four people involved was vitally necessary. And that it should be held in the Board Room after banking hours the next day so that the other employees of the bank would have no idea what was going on.

The point was that they were all in possible jeopardy; they were all hoeing the same garden. Everyone had to protect everyone else, and all cards should be laid on the table—and thereafter, some action taken.

*

The next day, Monday, September 30th, Henry Hopkins called a special meeting in the Board Room, just after the bank closed. The meeting was held behind locked doors. Present were Hopkins, Keep, Freddie Mayhew, and Hannah Winthrop.

The Board Room itself was paneled in oak and served as a conference room as well. On the wall were photographs of ex-President Coolidge and the present chief executive, Herbert Hoover. Once a week, usually on Friday mornings before the bank opened, Henry Hopkins ran a staff meeting of all personnel, so Freddie and Hannah were no strangers to the impressive room. The four sat in straight-backed chairs around a long polished table.

All of them had suffered horrific losses in the market of the previous week. Their mood was depressed and not a little fearful. They were suffering from a kind of aftershock. The bears had, at least for the moment, driven the bulls from the pasture.

Freddie Mayhew was quietly informed that he would keep his job at the bank, for the time being. Now he, as well as Hannah Winthrop, was mystified as to the purpose of the meeting. Occasionally, the president of the Puritan *did* call a special meeting, but again, it was usually when the entire staff was present. They were further intimidated by the grave and tight-lipped expressions on the faces of both Hopkins and Keep.

Henry Hopkins wasted no time in enlightening them. He was forthright and brutally frank. All four of them, it was now known, had been taking money from the bank and investing it in the stock market. They were, so to speak, all in the same boat. And since this was true, they had to be careful to protect themselves. If any one of them carelessly let this secret slip, then all of them were in jeopardy.

Hannah Winthrop and Freddie Mayhew listened to all this, unable to believe what they were hearing. Hannah already knew about Keep, but was shocked and stunned to find that Hopkins, too, was involved. Freddie and Hannah could conceive of themselves being embezzlers. They were, after all, little people and needed money desperately. But these two men, Hopkins and Keep, were the chief executives of the Puritan, their superiors. It was almost impossible to believe that the president of the bank and its treasurer could be embezzling money. These men were supposed to be models of propriety, men you looked up to, paragons of virtue, and by definition, completely honest.

It took a while for Freddie and Hannah to adjust themselves to this new situation. They were shaken, true, but they also felt a certain sense of relief. Neither was alone now in this business. There were others to keep them company, people far more important than they. They began to feel a certain sense of community. Almost of false security.

Hopkins embellished this point in his talk.

"Like it or not," he said, "we're all in this together, and we must act together. One for all, and all for one, so to speak. Whatever action we take now must be a common action, agreed by all of us."

Freddie shuddered. "I'd hate to think what would happen if they caught us. They'd have us up as embezzlers, and that would mean jail . . ."

"You're wrong, my boy," said Hopkins smoothly. "I mean, in your choice of words. We are not—I repeat, are not —embezzlers."

"No?" said Freddie. "Then what are we?"

"We're investors. Investors in the stock market. Which is another way of saying we're investors in American business. You see, the difference is this, my boy. Embezzlers steal money from a bank and have no intention of paying it back. We didn't steal any money. We simply borrowed it."

"Borrowed it?" said Hannah.

"Of course. I assume that in due course we all intend to repay the money we took."

His eyes challenged the other three. They all nodded vigorously in agreement. Then Keep chimed in, for the benefit of Freddie and Hannah.

"Mr. Hopkins is right. All we did was to make some unsecured loans." He hesitated for a moment. "So to speak."

Hannah and Freddie were silent for a moment. They were trying to digest this convoluted code of ethics. They were being conned, to use the slang, by both Hopkins and Keep. But the president and treasurer were also conning themselves.

"Mr. Keep here is right," said Hopkins. "After all, the business of a bank is to lend money." He paused for a moment, looking for exactly the right words, knowing that Hannah and Freddie were still not one hundred percent converted. "Of course, these loans we made were—well, somewhat irregular. But all of us here are decent, honest people. You might say our collateral is our character." He liked the expression so much that he rolled it around and then repeated it. "Yes, let us all look at it that way. Our collateral is our character." Then he looked at each investor benevolently. "Again, we must promise ourselves and assure each other that we intend to pay our, er—loans at the earliest opportunity."

The others assured Hopkins again that this was a matter of honor, and then Hannah said:

"What do we do now, Mr. Hopkins?"

"Yes," asked Freddie. "Where do we go from here?"

Hopkins thought for a moment. "Under the circumstances, I think we'd be wise to cash in our stocks by the end of this week and return the exact amount we borrowed from the bank. After that, we can readjust our books to conform, and we'll all be in the clear."

There was a long silence, and then Freddie Mayhew came up with the question that lay heavy on their minds. As already stated, all of them had lost heavily in the plunge the market had taken during the past week. That is to say, they had lost heavily in their profits. But they still had their original "investment" money and more. Each could still boast of some profit. And it was on this point that Freddie spoke:

"What about the profits we've made?"

Of all the embezzlers, Henry Hopkins showed the most chicanery. He was cleverer than the other three. His greed ran the deepest, and it was this trait, probably built into his genes ever since Increase Hopkins had cheated the Indians, that got him and the others, as we shall see, in deep trouble later on. In reply to Freddie Mayhew's question, he said:

"As to the profits, we keep them. Naturally." He shrugged. "As investors, we've taken a risk and we're entitled to some reward. Moreover, we couldn't return the profits to the bank. That wouldn't make any sense. How could we justify them as entries? How could we explain about the bank's coming into this extra money, without accounting for it? So the obvious thing is to keep what we've made." He looked around the table. "Agreed?"

In this he found no dissenting voice.

*

At this point, it all seemed simple enough.

But the conspirators did not know, and could not have possibly known, what lay in store for them.

Had they had a crystal ball on the center of the Board Room table, and had they been clairvoyant enough to read it, they would have seen four luminous and trembling images staring up at them from the sparkling limbo. All the faces were familiar, and all were famous, and all belonged to men whom the four embezzlers normally would never hope to meet in a lifetime. Yet, in one way or the other, the people who bore these faces were destined to affect the destiny and careers of the employees of the Puritan Bank and Trust.

The first was a famous Wall Street plunger, one of the biggest of the Big Boys; the second was a vicious and merciless criminal, already known as one of the country's most wanted public enemies; the third was a former President of the United States; and the fourth was an unidentified and faceless man, famous—or infamous—in his own right.

And if they had been *really* clairvoyant, they might have detected a dark shadow, still very faint, beginning to cloud the clear crystal and slowly but surely growing and spreading, like some malicious infection.

16

On THE MORNING of the next day, Tuesday, October first, C. F. Bennett sat slumped in the rear seat of his yellow Rolls-Royce as his chauffeur slowly piloted the car through the thick traffic of Broad Street. He was on his way to his office on the seventeenth floor of the Bankers Trust Company, located on "The Corner," at the intersection of Broad, Wall, and Nassau streets.

His wife was away again, visiting her widowed sister, Mary Haggett, in Riverside. He had spent most of the evening with Dixie Day in the expensive apartment he had rented for her on Fifth Avenue. In recent weeks, their relationship had begun to disintegrate. She had nagged him lately for a bigger living allowance, much bigger than he thought was generous. She wanted to go on a Grand Tour of Europe with him, and he could not possibly get away for any length of time. Up to a month ago, she had made certain demands on him, sexual demands he could not possibly fulfill at his age. And in subtle and oblique ways, the bitch had constantly reminded him of his inadequacy. He had, of course, found this humiliating.

Then suddenly she had ceased to be interested. Each time,

when *he* was ready, she pleaded a headache or told him she simply was not in the mood. He suspected that she had a young lover on the side and hired a private detective to watch her. His suspicion was confirmed.

Last night he had been furious at Dixie for his being cuckolded in this way. They had quarreled bitterly, and he had told her they were finished and to get out of the apartment within the month. She not only wearied him now; he could not stand the sight of her. She threatened to sue for alienation of affections, but since he was already a married man, she did not have much of a case. He decided to do the usual thing. He would stop by at Tiffany's sometime later this week and buy her a bauble expensive enough for her to walk out of his life without protest. Or, if this were not enough to really get her off his back, he would buy her an apartment building somewhere, as he had done for some of the others.

His limousine was equipped with one of those newfangled auto radios that were just coming out. A news broadcast was on at the moment, and he listened wearily.

There were conflicting reports on the state of the market and why it had gone down so far last week. C. F. Bennett was uneasy about it and, at this moment, wasn't sure which way to jump. According to the news announcer, Alexander Dana Noyes, financial editor of the *New York Times,* the market was too high and was adjusting downward to reality. But John Pierpont Morgan, Jr., who controlled the huge investment trusts of both the United and the Allegheny corporations, inferred that it was only a technical correction and the market would go higher. Any statement out of the House of Morgan had to be taken seriously. On its preferred list in Allegheny Corporation, for example, were such names as General Pershing; Charles Lindbergh; John J. Raskob; Charles Adams, Hoover's secretary of the navy; Richard

Whitney; and many other notables—not to mention practically every banker of any clout in New York City.

Morgan's opinion was backed by the famous astrologer
and seer Evangeline Adams. She had, it was said, forecast
Lindbergh's time in crossing the Atlantic within twenty minutes of his actual landing; she had predicted the death of the
great movie lover, Rudolf Valentino, within just a few hours;
and in 1923, she predicted that Tokyo would suffer a great
earthquake in a few days, an event which actually happened.

Now, in her studio over Carnegie Hall, she had sat down
and calculated the position of the various planets, their in-
teraction and relationships, not forgetting the signs of the
zodiac, the cusps and the positions of the solar second and
fourth houses, the transit of the sun, and the slow transit of
Uranus and Pluto. To the thousands of her newsletter sub-
scribers and the long line of clients waiting for her counsel,
she had predicted the market would swing back upward and
hit dizzy heights to come. She had thousands of fanatical
followers all over the country who religiously followed her
forecasts. No one noted, however, that she made this particular forecast on the day *after* J. P. Morgan had made his. She
usually went with the power, wherever it was.

Still, C. F. Bennett knew that certain of the Big Boys were
quietly selling. He knew that Joseph P. Kennedy had gotten
out of the market and was relaxing in Florida with his wife,
Rose, and the children. He knew that Bernard Baruch and
his son were gradually liquidating their extensive holdings.

He knew also that Jack Bouvier, a specialist at post 11 in
the stock exchange, had converted most of his securities into
cash. Only two months ago, Bouvier had passed out cigars
at the birth of a daughter, Jacqueline, and almost at the same
time had gradually and quietly begun to reduce his portfolio.
It was rumored that Albert H. Wiggin, chairman of the
board of directors of the Chase National Bank and one of the

really Big Boys, was selling short in shares in the giant bank of which he himself was the head. If true, it was a very pretty ploy.

But C. F. Bennett knew that the bears were only a handful, even among the insiders. Most of the investors—or more truly to the mark, speculators—were bulls, and getting fatter and more numerous every day. And now the radio commentator, in a bit of whimsy, added that Winston Churchill, the British chancellor of the exchequer, had made a neat profit by finally deciding to sell his stock in Simmons Company. He had bought the stock because he had been intrigued by its advertising theme: "You Can't Go Wrong on a Simmons Mattress."

C. F. Bennett told his chauffeur to turn off the radio. Then: "Let me off here, Harry. I'll walk the rest of the way. Need a little fresh air."

He got out of the car and walked briskly toward Wall Street, his limousine shadowing him. When he reached the Corner, he paused for a moment to watch the familiar scene. Crowds jammed the sidewalks or hurried back and forth across the Street. There were guards, peddlers, bankers, secretaries, clerks, pages, bankers, brokers, and just plain tourists and gawkers. There were messenger boys lined up together, as though marching lock-step in some penitentiary, with an armed guard leading them and another bringing up the rear. They carried precious burdens, steel boxes tightly locked and filled with securities. Sometimes this human chain had as many as twenty boys moving between the banks and brokerage houses.

There were always itinerant preachers on or near the corner of Broad and Wall, and this morning was no exception. What better place to preach their hellfire and damnation than in the heart of Mammon itself? Two of these lay preachers had already set up their sidewalk pulpits, soapbox podiums draped with the American flag and vividly illustrated Bible texts. Hour after hour, they would harangue the crowds until they were hoarse, providing a certain amount of diversion and entertainment, especially for the lunchtime crowds. But in this location, they garnered few converts, due to the character of the crowd. Each, however, had a collection box plainly in view. Now and then, a Salvation Army Band would show up and deliver a serenade or two. Standing where he was, C. F. Bennett could even hear the organ music wafting from the doors of Trinity Church, at the juncture of Wall and Broadway. The pews of the church were always crowded with people of many denominations, some who came just to hear the music recital, and others who came to pray, not for their restless souls, or those of loved ones, now deceased, but for the health and welfare of American Tel and Tel, Curtiss-Wright, and General Asphalt.

Suddenly a line of shiny black chauffeured limousines turned off Broadway and entered Wall. It looked, at first glance, like a funeral cortege. Each limousine stopped for a moment at 23 Wall, the fortresslike building which was the House of Morgan, and each discharged a Morgan partner.

The line of huge shining black cars made an impressive show, and each morning crowds came to gawk, just as tourists came to watch the changing of the guard at Buckingham Palace. Two doormen rushed forward as each Morgan partner, serene in his majesty and with grave face, left his car and climbed the stone steps into the citadel. Each carried a bulging attaché case.

First, as always, was Charles Steele. He was a pale man and wore a black suit, and he had a hard stare that had intimidated many a board room meeting. The next limousine discharged Frank Barrow. The third, George Whitney; the fourth, Russell C. Leffingwell. Then came the imposing Parker Whitney, a dandy in a black topcoat, gray hat, and gloves. E. T. Stotesbury came next, the feisty banker whom even his partners simply called E. T. After him came Thomas Lamont, wearing a black pinstripe, tall and aristocratic, fifty-nine years old and still handsome. It was said that J. P. Morgan spoke only to Thomas Lamont, and Lamont passed his pronouncements along to the various partners.

And in the last car, of course, was Jack Morgan himself, wearing his usual wing collar, gray tie and pearl stickpin, and shining lace-tied black boots.

"Look at those sons of bitches."

C. F. Bennett turned, startled at the voice over his shoulder.

It was Joseph P. Kennedy, who had been a friend of Bennett's for a number of years.

"Hello, Joe," said Bennett as they shook hands. "Thought you were taking it easy in Florida with Rose and the kids. Just sitting on your money. What are you doing back here in the salt mines?"

"Oh," said Kennedy vaguely. "Just looking around. Just looking around." He kept staring at the doorway through which the Morgan entourage had just passed. "Those Episcopalian bastards. Think they own the world."

Kennedy spoke bitterly, and with good reason. He had once sought an interview with J. P. Morgan, and he had been rudely snubbed. At this time, Wall Street was still three-quarters Protestant—what is now called WASP—in a city where the great majority of people were Catholic, Jewish, or Black. Wall Street was an island, or enclave, of the old-school tie. To be one of the chosen, one of the "in" people, you had to come from the right family, the right university, the right church. And the House of Morgan, on the executive level, was very clannish in this respect.

Joe Kennedy hated the Morgans, and they thought of him as a "pick-and-shovel Paddy." But he was a lot more than that. He was a handsome, tanned six-footer, bursting with vitality and charm, when he wanted to turn it on. He liked to make deals using his own rules, and he could be tough and ruthless. He had a razor-sharp mind, a hot temper, and blue eyes which could turn icicle at any insult, real or fancied, he thought directed at his heritage.

The two men had a mutual bond in the sense that both of them were outside the Establishment and had been born poor. Joe Kennedy's father had been a docker. C. F. Bennett had been born the son of an Arkansas sharecropper. If the Morgans rejected Kennedy because he was a Catholic, they had no use for indiscriminate plungers like Bennett, either. They considered him a kind of outlaw, a wildcatter. In their view, he did not act like a gentleman. He gave the market a bad name.

After Joe Kennedy had gotten out of the market and liquidated his holdings, he had gone to Hollywood, bought movie studios, and manipulated others into a huge fortune for himself. Now that he was back on the Street, C. F. Bennett was curious.

"Joe, tell me the truth."

"Yes?"

"What are you really doing here?"

"I'm an old firehorse, I guess," said Kennedy. "Anytime I see a fire, I can't help running toward it."

"Then you think the market's still going up."

"No," said Kennedy. "I still don't like the smell of it."

"But everybody's buying."

"More power to them. I figure on selling short when this market takes a bath."

"But the word is that this recent drop is just a technical setback."

"Depends on whose word you listen to. But I'll take the word of God anytime."

Bennett stared at him, puzzled. "The word of God?"

Joe Kennedy grinned. "I asked the bishop of my diocese which way he thought the market would go. He's a hell of a lot closer to God than I am. Anyway, he passed the Word on to me. Straight from upstairs. One of these days, there'll be a break. A big one."

That was Joe Kennedy, Bennett thought. One moment, he could be as hard as steel, absolutely ruthless. The next moment, he could give you a warm smile, crack a joke, slap you on the back, invite you for a drink. At any rate, Bennett was a little disturbed. He believed—as much as any speculator could believe—that the market had not yet shown its true strength. With a few notable exceptions, like Noyes of the *Times* and Roger Babson, the perennial voice of doom, almost everybody else who counted believed it, too. But Bennett respected Kennedy. The Irishman was smart. He had proved a Midas before when it came to the golden touch.

"One thing," said Bennett, "this goddam market is a roller coaster. Up and down, up and down. I'd feel better if it lay on its side for a while, just went to sleep for a few days and stopped giving everybody heart failure."

"You're right, Charlie. All we can do is roll with the punches. But there's one rule I've always followed."

"Yes?"

"Do just the opposite of what the crowd is doing. I'm talking about the little guys, the elevator boys and the taxi drivers, and the barbers of the country. They've gone into the market up to their butts, buying on margin with every dime they have. They don't have cast-iron stomachs, and they scare easily. Give them a little bad news, and they'll sell like mad. When that happens, I buy. Or, if it goes the other way, and they're buying—then I sell."

Bennett invited Kennedy up to his office for coffee and further conversation. But Kennedy declined. He had many things to do this morning. They shook hands, and Kennedy crossed the street and entered the Bank of Manhattan Building.

*

The C. F. Bennett suite in the Bankers Trust Building was not even listed in the directory on the ground floor. It was protected by the doorman of the building, who had been bribed into denying its actual existence. Only those with approved appointments were allowed past this guard, and they were then whisked by express elevator to the seventeenth floor.

In the vast outer office worked some seventy people, picked personally by the chief executive of Sunrise Investment Trust. They were warned to keep their mouths shut, or get fired. Among them were market and trend analysts, statisticians, secretaries, tipsters, and people who answered the dozens of telephones, or watched the quotation board or ticker tapes. C. F. Bennett also employed a certain amount of outside help. The financial analysts of two prominent financial publications were secretly in his pay, and they gave glowing analyses of SIT, whenever possible.

Sitting now at his huge desk, Bennett surveyed the up-to-the-minute reports on his desk wearily. He phoned one of his spies on the floor of the exchange. He was told that the word was "buy," that the market was on its way up again and there were crowds at every post trying to get in their orders. He wondered why he had let Joe Kennedy shake him at all. He, C. F. Bennett, trusted his own gut reactions. And why shouldn't he? Through them he had become a multimillionaire. Normally he was not a man to listen to other opinions, and he told himself he must be getting tired.

And he *was* tired. Tired of Dixie Day and New York. He knew he needed a rest. Some kind of short vacation. He thought of his wife, staying with her sister up in Riverside. For the moment, he thought of her affectionately. He always did, after he had broken up with some woman and before encountering someone new. Edna Bennett was a little on the stout side, and she had not aroused him sexually for years. But there was something warm and comfortable and loyal about her.

It struck him now that it might be a good idea to run up to Riverside for a few days. He had never been to that city, although he had met Edna's sister in New York. It occurred to him that he could relax in Riverside for a little while and let the rest of the world go by. He believed in George M. Cohan's famous line: "Everything outside of New York is Bridgeport." Yet he was sure he would find Riverside refreshing. In addition, it would be valuable to know what the investors there were doing and thinking. They would be representative of heartland America. Being here, in the center of the financial district, sometimes warped your point of view. It was *they* who had sent this market skyrocketing. And it was they who could bring it down.

He called his wife and told her he was coming up for a few days. She was delighted, and so was her sister.

Then he buzzed his secretary and asked when the next train would be leaving Grand Central for Riverside.

*

When it came to the social scene in Riverside, Mary Haggett was no slouch. To have C. F. Bennett stay at her house was news. She immediately telephoned the social and personal editors of both the Riverside newspapers. The story got into the evening editions, and C. F. Bennett was met at Union Station by a battery of newsmen and photographers. He gave them a short interview and proceeded by limousine to Mary Haggett's big Colonial house.

Shortly after dinner, he received a phone call from a Henry Hopkins who, it seemed, was the president of one of Riverside's more important banks. There was to be a chamber of commerce luncheon the next day, and they needed a speaker desperately, and would C. F. Bennett attend and favor the most prominent businessmen in the city with a few words?

Bennett was about to refuse, when Hopkins mentioned casually that among those who had accepted an invitation and would attend was Calvin Coolidge.

After this, Bennett accepted.

This luncheon, he decided, might give him a good perspective on how the smaller cities were currently feeling about the market. More than this, he had never met the ex-President before.

He was curious about Silent Cal, and always had been. After all, it was Coolidge Prosperity that had put him, C. F. Bennett, at the top of the heap.

17

THE MONTHLY MEETING of the Riverside Chamber of Commerce was held in a private dining room in the Highland Hotel. The Highland was famous throughout the area for its lobster dinners. The lobsters, trucked in from Maine in the early morning, were fresh and succulent. They were boiled in the classic New England manner, not broiled, and served with melted butter, and with sweet corn during the season. Boston clam chowder began the lunch, and dessert was always deep-dish apple or blueberry pie.

Henry Hopkins sat at the head of the table. Coolidge sat on his right and C. F. Bennett on his left. Hopkins had pulled a coup. It was seldom the chamber could honor two great men like this. Every member of the chamber was present, and the occasion was fully covered by the press.

C. F. Bennett, sitting directly opposite the ex-President, was fascinated by Coolidge. This was the recent chief executive who made out his own income tax, who had taken two naps a day in the White House, come hell or high water, who looked so ordinary, so self-effacing, with a personality so dry and nonmagnetic that he immediately aroused a special kind of interest. To C. F. Bennett, Calvin Coolidge looked like any junior clerk in his office back on Wall Street. He saw now that the newspaper photographers, throughout Coolidge's term, had worked hard to soften the lines of the man's face. These were a kind of Coolidge trademark. The mouth was tight-lipped, so much so that it appeared to be a thin gash across the face. The corners of the mouth dipped in sharp creases. Between the sandy eyebrows were other lines, which seemed to indicate concentration, and crow's-feet spread out from the corners of his eyes. He had been an easy subject for the cartoonists of the time to caricature because of these lines. A few key strokes, and you had Calvin Coolidge. He was neatly dressed in a gray suit and blue polka dot tie, but still wore the detachable collar which was fast losing ground at this time to the new style of shirts. Bennett had seen Coolidge as he walked in, wearing the severe high-crowned derby which, it was said, he even wore on the golf links. And of course, the high shoes.

In twelve years, Bennett knew, Calvin Coolidge had never been seen in his shirtsleeves. No one ever called him Cal, and no one ever slapped him on the back. Now that Coolidge had retired, he did not hesitate to smoke in public. Bennett watched him as he meticulously clipped a big Perfecto, then rolled between thumb and index finger the famous paper holder into which he carefully inserted the cigar.

All in all, thought Bennett, he was the very picture still of the shy and introverted Yankee. All during the lunch, Calvin Coolidge had never initiated a conversation, and he was miserly in his responses. Bennett could not believe that this small man had headed a great nation, the most prosperous nation in the world, and had made the expression "Coolidge Prosperity" a permanent fixture in American history.

Henry Hopkins rose and introduced C. F. Bennett to the assembly as "one of our great financial geniuses," a leader in his field, a staunch disciple of private enterprise, and a living example of the kind of success story that could happen only in America.

C. F. Bennett started his talk by telling the chamber that he found their city not only beautiful, but refreshing. But more to the point, Riverside to him represented heartland America. Wall Street was not the place to feel and diagnose the national heartbeat. The marketplace was too self-centered, too beset by rumors, too hypertense, too frenetic, to listen to what the *real* people of the country were saying and doing. A town like Riverside was the place to keep your ear to the ground, to listen to the opinions of solid businessmen, and get the feel of the real situation in the nation.

"Gentlemen," he went on, "America is now a nation of consumers. If a man wishes to keep his position in this society, he now needs a car, radio, and refrigerator. His wife needs a washing machine, an automatic furnace so that she no longer has to shovel coal herself, and the latest in bathroom plumbing. She wants new clothes, a trip to the beauty parlor, and she wants to redecorate her home every five years. Yesterday all this was beyond her wildest dreams. Today they are all realities. Yesterday very few had the money to buy these things. But today we have the installment plan . . .

"Yes, gentlemen, the installment plan. The greatest boon to American business in our history. Buy now, pay later. And people are buying till it hurts. All of which keeps our industry booming. We have had Coolidge Prosperity—" here he nodded toward the ex-President, who showed no change of expression—"and now we have its extension in Hoover Prosperity.

"Which brings me to my own terrain—the stock market. There are those who are showing some timidity. Others are prophets of gloom and doom who think the market is too high. There are those who call people who invest in the market speculators. Gamblers. But in my opinion, nothing is further from the truth. The people who are getting into the market all over the country are investors in American business. The companies listed on the exchange are precisely those companies engaged in satisfying the limitless demand of the American people for more of everything. My view is that the bulls are going to run rampant. That the stock market has not as yet shown its real strength, that there are many securities, those of great American companies, which are deeply underpriced, and that the direction of the future is UP.

"Gentlemen, I know all of you here work hard for your money. But why not turn it around? Let your money work for you. All that is required is faith. Faith in our system of government, faith in the industry and hard common sense of the people in this great country, faith in our great President, Mr. Hoover, and our other leaders, faith in the golden future of America and its shining destiny."

C. F. Bennett finished to a standing ovation. He smilingly accepted it and then raised his hands for silence. Then he smiled at Coolidge.

"Now, perhaps the President would like to honor us with a few words . . ."

"I did not come here to speak," snapped Coolidge. "I came to listen." At this, Bennett's smile faded. He had sensed, all through his talk, that Coolidge had been cool, withdrawn, and subtly hostile. Now the others in the dining room became aware that the vibrations between the two men were not sympathetic. Here was Calvin Coolidge, the frugal, thrifty, down-to-earth Vermont Yankee who actually believed the old adage that a penny saved was a penny earned; and here was C. F. Bennett, the plunger and speculator, profligate and luxury-loving spendthrift, with his houses, yachts, and mistresses, the ultimate consumer. It was hard to imagine two men more different.

"I'm sorry, Mr. President," said Bennett. "I just thought it would be appropriate . . ."

"Thank you, sir," said Coolidge, frostily. "I do not, and will not, choose to make a speech. I have had enough of that. But I should like to venture one opinion."

There was complete silence as Coolidge continued: "I do not refer to you gentlemen here, who obviously are in good circumstance. Or to myself. But any ordinary working man who mortgages his future by borrowing from his broker, taking loans on margin, is not only a gambler. If he cannot afford to lose, he is a fool. But the country seems full of fools. However, if a ditch digger or elevator boy can be persuaded that he can get rich quick by speculating in the market, I suppose there is no one on this earth, or heaven above, with the power to stop him."

From Silent Cal, it turned out to be quite a speech, after all.

*

After the luncheon, Henry Hopkins drove C. F. Bennett to Charlie Lothrop's brokerage office so that Bennett could see what the market was doing. Both men were pleased to see that most of the stocks were on the rise again and selling briskly.

Then Hopkins drove Bennett to his sister-in-law's house. And as Bennett got out of the car, Henry said:

"Oh, Mr. Bennett."

"Yes?"

"I'd appreciate a little advice on the market, if you don't mind my asking . . ."

"Not at all, Mr. Hopkins. If there's any way I can help . . ."

Hopkins explained that he had a portfolio of stocks, and he enumerated them. C. F. Bennett listened without comment. Then, when Henry had finished, he said:

"Well, sir, you have some good solid securities there. But there's not enough action to them. Why don't you let *me* make your investments for you."

"You?"

"Why not? Through SIT—Sunrise Investment Trust. I pick the securities I like and put them into one package. I'm a professional and an expert—you're not. And our performance record—well, you read the financial pages. We've doubled and tripled in a year. So I have no modesty about recommending my own investment trust. As to safety, well I'll tell you this, Mr. Hopkins—I have ten million dollars of my own money in it. That's confidence. And the fund is growing by leaps and bounds every day. We can't even process the applications fast enough."

"SIT," murmured Henry. He seemed hypnotized by the name. "SIT."

"Exactly." Then C. F. Bennett looked around him, and then, in what was almost a whisper:

"You've been very kind to me here, Mr. Hopkins. Inviting me to the luncheon, chauffeuring me around. And so I'll give you a little tip."

"Yes, sir?"

"What you're hearing is straight from the horse's mouth. Mine. I expect SIT to double by the first of December. No, I don't just expect it. I happen to know it."

And with that, C. F. said good afternoon, and strode toward the house.

Henry Hopkins sat at his wheel for a full minute. He sat very still. Then, stirring himself, he went into action. He drove swiftly to the Puritan Bank and Trust. He reached it shortly before closing time.

There he informed Freddie Mayhew, Hannah Winthrop, and Jonathan Keep that there was to be a special meeting that evening. It would be held, not in the Board Room this time, but at his residence. He knew Tuesday night was his wife's night at her bridge club, and they would not be interrupted.

Both Mayhew and Keep began to object. Freddie had a date to take Ellie to a dance, and Keep had some other matter to attend to. But Hopkins would take no excuse.

This, he snapped, was an order. They were all to be at his house at eight o'clock sharp.

Something extraordinary had happened, he said, something unexpected, and they were all involved.

He put on his coat and left the bank, leaving the others not only confused, but extremely fearful.

And Henry Hopkins let them sweat, on the theory that later, in their relief, they would be more amenable to what he had to say.

18

THE FOUR "INVESTORS" met at Henry Hopkins' house promptly at eight that night, as ordered.

Only Jonathan Keep had been inside the Hopkins residence before. Normally, Freddie Mayhew and Hannah Winthrop would have been awed by its magnificence, the deep Persian rug in the living room, the Tiffany lamps, the overstuffed furniture, and the new love seats. But now they were too tense and too worried to take more than cursory note of their surroundings.

Henry Hopkins, wearing a velvet smoking jacket, welcomed them all with a benevolent smile. He stood before the fireplace, in which a bright log fire crackled, and asked them all to sit down and make themselves comfortable. His manner was relaxed, he was every inch the solid squire. He offered both Keep and Mayhew a Havana cigar, which they accepted. His three guests were somewhat mollified by Henry's unworried attitude, yet they were still uneasy. Keep said:

"What's this all about, Mr. Hopkins?"

And Hannah Winthrop blurted: "Has anyone found out?"

Hopkins smiled and reassured them.

"Everything's fine. Just fine. Nobody knows anything."

They all sat back and relaxed. They watched Hopkins curiously. He took his time dramatically, blowing a cloud of tobacco smoke toward the ceiling. Then:

"What if I told you that if we wait a couple of months, say into December, before we return the money to the bank, we can double the profit we already have."

They all sat upright and stared at Hopkins.

"Double it, did you say?" said Freddie.

"Possibly triple it."

After a long silence, Keep finally asked:

"How?"

"By selling our stocks and putting all the cash in a single security." Henry took a beat, and then: "To be exact, into Sunrise Investment Trust."

Keep stared at Hopkins, skeptically. "That's big talk, Mr. Hopkins. You hear it all over town. This stock is going to double. That stock's going to double. It's always a sure thing . . . What makes you think Sunrise Investment Trust is going to hit the sky? Remember, all of us here are in a very risky business right now. We're playing with other people's money. Frankly, I'm getting pretty nervous about it. Can't sleep nights. I thought we all agreed . . ."

"We did. But this was just too good to pass up."

"I still don't understand what makes you think it's going to double," said Keep. "It's probably just another one of those damned rumors that keep flying around."

"No. Not this one, Jonathan. I got it straight from the horse's mouth, you might say."

"Really?" said Keep sarcastically. "And what is the name of this particular animal?"

"From C. F. Bennett himself."

There was a long, stunned silence.

"From C. F. Bennett himself?" whispered Freddie.

"Exactly. Told me himself when I was driving him home from the chamber of commerce meeting. Took a liking to me, I guess. Told me it was confidential—but of course, we're all one here. And don't forget, he runs Sunrise. He *is* Sunrise. And he ought to know."

"I still don't believe it," said Keep stubbornly. "He could tell you anything. After all, he's playing with other people's money."

"Not exactly."

"No?"

"He's got ten million of his own invested in SIT. That's putting your money where your mouth is." He looked at the others, one by one. "Am I right? And I don't have to tell you, he's one of the biggest of the Big Boys. And they *never* lose."

There was a long silence. These were decent people, truly brought up in a moral way, and it had been drummed into their heads that Honesty is always the best Policy. All of them were in inner conflict now. They had been infected with a new devil. This devil did not wear horns or a tail, or carry a pitchfork, and its name was not Satan or Beelzebub.

Its name was Greed.

Before it had been only a whisper in their ears. Now it was a loud word. Yet, two of the group put up some semblance of resistance.

"I don't know," said Hannah. "You can never tell about the market, or these people—the ones you call the Big Boys. Maybe we still ought to return the money to the bank."

"I'm inclined to go along with Miss Winthrop here," said Freddie. "I mean, Mr. Hopkins—you're sure this isn't— well, a little dangerous?"

Hopkins smiled at Freddie reassuringly.

"There's absolutely nothing to worry about, my boy. No one here is going to tell anyone. And the bank examiner never shows up until after Christmas. You all know that.

We'll replace the seed money we took from the bank long before then. Why should we be hasty, when we have this inside information? Why should we say no to a sure bonanza?" He looked around at the other three conspirators. "Any further questions?"

There were none. They all looked a little worried, but they all shook their heads. Keep looked unhappy, but finally went along. He wanted that new bank in Westfield badly.

"Very well," said Hopkins. "You deliver your securities, or any money you've derived from them, to me. I'll take charge and handle the investment for all of us. Agreed?"

They all nodded, and suddenly there was a nervous, half-hysterical giggle from Hannah.

"My goodness," she said. "That makes us a syndicate, doesn't it?"

"You might say that," said Hopkins.

She giggled again and looked at the others.

"I mean, just like the gangsters have."

The others could not help smiling at this suggestion, coming as it did from Hannah Winthrop, of all people. Hopkins said:

"In a sense, Miss Winthrop, that's true. We are a kind of syndicate now, in that we're pooling our efforts toward a common goal. But of course, we're not gangsters. Nor are we embezzlers, as I have said before. Real embezzlers actually steal money and have no intention of returning it. We intend to return every cent, at the right time. And again, to repeat something I've said before, if you come right down to a fine point, we are doing nothing illegal. Absolutely nothing. The business of a bank like the Puritan is to lend money to borrowers. We're simply borrowers, investing, as I have said before, in the future of this country. True, the loans we have made are unsecured. But again, as I have said, our collateral is our character. And our loyalty. As president of the Puritan

Bank and Trust, it is my duty to assess the risks in lending money to borrowers. And I consider you all—including myself—the finest kind of risk."

After this, any lingering doubts vanished. Henry Hopkins, when he wanted to, could be very persuasive. He could even make you feel virtuous.

*

The following day, Freddie Mayhew was missing from the bank.

And Ellie Hopkins had left the house very early that morning. She carried a traveling bag and a hatbox. She wore a stylish new going-away outfit—Patou satin cloche hat, a smart new sheer tweed, and over this a moulded silhouette coat. Her whole manner was watchful and surreptitious, and she walked on tiptoe so as not to wake her parents.

Just around the corner, Freddie Mayhew was waiting for her in a new roadster. He was dressed in his usual Sunday suit, and he smiled as Ellie looked wide-eyed at the car. Then she said breathlessly:

"Oh, Freddie. A Stutz Bearcat!"

"Pretty snazzy, huh?"

"Where did you get it?"

"Borrowed it from a friend of mine. Just for our honeymoon. Hop in, Ellie."

For a moment, they sat there soberly, saying nothing. Then Freddie turned toward her:

"Ellie."

"Yes?"

"You're sure? You really want to go through with this?"

"Of course. I wouldn't be here if I wasn't."

"You're not scared."

"No." A pause. "And you?"

"No. I love you, Ellie."

"And I love you, Freddie."

They embraced and kissed each other, and then Ellie warned Freddie that they had better get started. It was early in the morning, but still this was her neighborhood, and if someone saw them and notified her father . . .

"All right," yelled Freddie exultantly. "Let's go, Mrs. Mayhew!"

He started the car with a leap, put it in high gear, and raced down the road, south toward Connecticut. They stopped in at a justice of the peace and were married, and he slipped a ring on her finger. Now man and wife, the two headed for their honeymoon retreat, the Surf Hotel, overlooking Ocean Beach at New London, Connecticut.

*

That night, after dinner, Mr. and Mrs. Freddie Mayhew sat on the rail of the terrace overlooking the ocean. A full moon cut a yellow path across the rolling, shimmering surface, and gentle waves sighed a little as they expired on the white beach. Freddie was wearing white flannels and a smart double-breasted blue blazer jacket. His new bride looked ravishing in an evening gown of princess transparent velvet. From the dance floor inside, they could hear Bunny Bixby and his Melody Boys play "Embraceable You."

Now Freddie Mayhew leaned over and kissed his wife tenderly on the lips. Then he took out a small flask from his pocket, unscrewed two small cups from the end of it, and poured a drink for each. They never stopped looking at each other. They both raised their little silver cups in a toast.

"To us," said Freddie.

"To us."

They drank, and then Freddie raised his glass again and said:

"*And* to Sunrise Investment Trust."

Ellie looked at him puzzled. "Sunrise Inv—what's that?"

"Oh," he said, airily. "Just one of my investments. Tell you all about it, one of these days."

Now, Bunny Bixby and his Melody Boys segued into another number, this one "Body and Soul." Freddie took his wife's hand, and they both danced through the French windows and into the hotel ballroom itself. To the wailing of the saxophones and the seductive singing of Bunny himself, Freddie and Ellie continued to dance for a while, cheek to cheek, oblivious to the rest of the world. Then she pulled back suddenly, her brow in a frown.

"What's the matter, Ellie?"

"Freddie. We'll have to tell them."

"I know."

"Daddy's going to be terribly upset. And Mummy, too."

"Don't worry. I'll take care of your father."

Ellie was impressed with her new husband. Suddenly he had become strong, confident. He showed absolutely no fear of her father. It was wonderful how transformed he had become. And now he was saying, gently and tenderly:

"Darling, are you ready?"

"Oh, yes, darling," she breathed, into his ear. "Yes. *Yes.*"

"So am I. Let's go."

He put his arm around her waist. He asked the room clerk for key number 422, and together they walked toward the elevator.

*

They undressed and snuggled together in the huge double bed. This was their honeymoon night, and for a moment they savored the joy of simply lying close to each other. Each room at the Surf had been equipped with the latest Atwater Kent superheterodyne radio, and now, at the moment, an announcer was saying that that sensational young singer,

Bing Crosby, with Paul Whiteman and his Rhythm Boys, was about to sing a solo rendition of the new hit song—"I Surrender, Dear."

To Freddie Mayhew, in bed with his beloved, it seemed the perfect song for such an intimate occasion, and he put his arm around his bride and cupped one of her cool breasts in one of his hot hands. He felt her nipple stiffen, and his penis shot up, and he released it from his pajamas and then began to kiss her on the cheek and mouth. But curiously, she held back. There was something on her mind, and he asked her what it was.

"Freddie, it's my parents. Maybe we'd better call them now."

"Later."

"No. Now." He squeezed her breast a little harder and threw his leg across her thigh, but she repelled him.

"No, darling. Not now. In a minute. But we just have to tell them. I wouldn't feel right unless we did."

"All right," he said. He spoke with some irritation, the unrequited lover. Women, he decided, were crazy. The sensation in his groin was driving him crazy. He threw off the covers so that she could see his magnificent tool, gorged with blood and standing straight up. Then he reached for the telephone and asked the switchboard operator to put in a long-distance call to the Hopkins house.

"Freddie, Daddy's going to be awful upset."

"I know."

"Try to be calm."

"Don't worry," he said, with airy confidence. "I told you. I'll take care of your father."

Ellie couldn't believe her new husband. Again, what she saw was the new Freddie Mayhew. She looked at the clock. It was five after two. She shivered a little and clung to Freddie's arm. Maybe they *should* have waited till morning. She put her ear next to Freddie's, close to the receiver.

They heard the phone ring in the Hopkins house, again and again. Finally Mrs. Hopkins answered in a sleepy voice: "Hello?"

Then Hopkins' voice, a few feet away, angrily: "Now who in the hell is *that,* calling at this time in the morning?"

Ellie spoke into the mouthpiece. "Mother, it's Ellie."

"Ellie? Where have you been? We've been sitting up all night, wondering where you—"

"We're at the Surf Hotel at Ocean Beach . . ."

"Give me that goddam phone," said Hopkins. "Now look here, Ellie . . ."

"This isn't Ellie, Mr. Hopkins," said Freddie calmly, taking the phone. "This is your new son-in-law."

"My *what?*"

"Your new son-in-law. Freddie Mayhew."

There was a long silence at the other end. Then the sound of apoplectic choking. Then, sudden yelling:

"Why you miserable little pipsqueak! You no good little skunk! Where do *you* get off marrying *my* daughter? I'll be damned if you're going to get away with it, do you hear? I'll have this thing annulled if it's the last thing I do . . ."

Ellie Hopkins Mayhew was horrified and frightened. She knew the parameters of her father's wrath, and they were limitless. But she was amazed how composed Freddie was, listening quietly, smiling quietly at her father's diatribe. Hopkins continued to rave without a stop. Finally, Freddie Mayhew administered the coup de grâce.

"Let's talk about it when we get back—*partner.*"

The angry gabble in Hopkins' voice stopped abruptly. There was a long silence. Freddie waited a moment or two for Hopkins to say something more. But Hopkins, caught in shock, was silent. Freddie hung up and smiled at Ellie. She stared at him, puzzled.

"Partner? You and my father . . ."

"Tell you about it later."

Freddie reached over, put his arm around her, and kissed her. She asked him no more questions. Together, they slid from their sitting positions to under the sheets. Freddie's arm reached out, fumbled for the light switch on the bed-table lamp, finally found it, and put out the light.

He caressed her a moment, kissed her breast and stomach and then entered her. She started to moan, "Oh, baby, you're so marvelous, so BIG," and he said, breathlessly, "Am I hurting you, baby?" and she answered, "Oh, no, baby, oh, no, go deeper, you're so wonderful, so marvelous," and he kept on pumping away, and she kept rising to meet him, and the climax, while some distance away, was coming up swiftly to meet them when—the phone rang.

It rang again and again.

Ellie cried out: "Don't answer it, darling, don't answer it . . ."

But it kept ringing and ringing, and finally Freddie Mayhew could stand it no more. Ellie lay supine, and he was still in her, and he muttered, "God damn, God damn" and lifted the receiver and shouted:

"Hello."

It was Henry Hopkins. "Freddie, I forgot to tell you. There's a special meeting tomorrow for all four of us at the bank. And you'd better be there."

"To hell with that," said Freddie. "We're here for a week."

"You young idiot," said Hopkins, incensed. "Have you seen this morning's paper?"

"No."

"Then you better damned well get dressed and drive back here and right away, or you may find you may have to wash dishes to pay your way out of the hotel. The market's taken a nose dive, and we're all in trouble. Real trouble."

"You're lying, Dad."

"Damn you, don't call me 'Dad'! And don't call me a liar. Read the paper, you damned gigolo, and then apologize to me later. And you'd better be back here in Riverside by noon tomorrow. *If* you value what's left of your investment."

At that, Hopkins hung up. Freddie's erection inside Ellie suddenly went limp. Try as he might, he could not get it up again. All of which made Ellie very unhappy. She had been gung-ho and ready to go when that phone call came. She started to cry a little. It was a terrible way to start a honeymoon. Freddie banged his fists on the pillow in frustration. He cursed his penis. Why didn't the damned thing do what he told it to do? He had always admired it, but now, in his humiliation, he hated it.

He put in a call to the night bellboy. Was there a morning *New York Times* available? The bellboy said the lobby shop was closed, but he kept a few in the elevator for sale, and Freddie told him to bring one up. The bellboy shoved a copy through the door. Freddie gave him a quarter and then spread the *Times* to the front page. And he read, in bold headlines:

YEAR'S WORST BREAK
HITS STOCK MARKET

Trading of 1,500,000 Shares
in Final Hours Swamps the
Whole List

STEEL DROPS TEN POINTS

Freddie's eye ran down the list. Everything had dropped. Sunrise Investment Trust, selling at 25 yesterday, had lost 5 points overnight. One-fifth of its entire value.

Ellie Mayhew was even unhappier when her husband soberly announced that they had to cut the honeymoon short. Somehow, this first night seemed to her to be of special significance, to be binding, because it was the first time they had copulated as man and wife, and in her imagination she would have always remembered the baby had been conceived tonight, and not before.

But now, because of Freddie's flaccid penis she could not enjoy even this fantasy.

Disappointed and aggrieved, she pressed and nagged him for an explanation. Why had he called her father "partner"? Were they actually in business together? This was something she could not conceive of in a hundred years. But still Freddie Mayhew would not tell his bride. She would know all about it in good time.

19

IN EARLY OCTOBER, the price of many good securities had dropped to what seemed to be good "buy" levels. A large number of small investors, fear clutching at their bellies, had sold out for what they could get. Steel, for example, after being quoted at 262 a few weeks earlier, had dropped as low as 204. American Can, at the closing on the fourth, was nearly 20 points below its high for the year; General Electric was 50 points below its top quotation; and Radio had gone down from 114¼ to 82½.

A kind of national fright gripped the ordinary people of the country. Thousands, buying on margin, had been unable to meet their brokers' demands and had been wiped out. There was talk of impending disaster. Or recession. Or depression. Of the country itself going down the drain, or the government helpless to stop the sudden selling. There was a story that Herbert Hoover was suffering from acute indigestion; that he had developed an ulcer; that he called in financial delegation after financial delegation, wringing his hands constantly.

Yet the Big Boys, especially the ones with the iron stomachs, continued to buy. They usually did, when there was a break in the market. In fact, in the face of all this tremendous liquidation, brokers' loans, as calculated by the Federal Reserve Bank of New York, mounted to a new high record on the second of October—a sure sign that the real investors, the Big Boys, the insiders, were not deserting the market, but coming in heavier than ever.

In his office, C. F. Bennett was constantly on the phone. SIT had bought heavily at what it considered bargain prices. This recent drop was merely a "technical shakeout," and the market would take off again like Lindbergh's *Spirit of St. Louis.* In short, the word was buy. Buy. Take something to settle the butterflies in your stomach and buy.

One of his callers was Henry Hopkins. For a moment, C. F. Bennett did not remember him. Then it came to him —that banker from Riverside. And he gave the same word.

Buy SIT. Or simply sit with it. What else?

*

Now Henry Hopkins held a special and emergency meeting of the syndicate immediately after banking hours.

The meeting place itself was rather exotic. He could not hold it at the bank. Twice with the same group would be suspicious. The other employees might ask some embarrassing questions. Why the same four people? Why should they, the other employees, be excluded?

Hopkins could not hold the meeting at home. His wife had big ears, and so did the two servants they maintained.

Finally, in desperation, he picked a deserted cold-storage plant, located on a street off Hungry Hill. The bank itself had foreclosed the plant two days ago, and Hopkins had the only keys.

The conspirators sat on the huge chopping-block tables, all of them freezing with the cold, even though they wore coats, hats, and ear muffs. All around them huge carcasses of frozen cows and beef quarters were hanging on hooks. The windows of the cold-storage plant were thick with frost, so that no one could look in. Occasionally, the members of the syndicate would cough or sneeze, and their teeth chattered when they spoke.

"Mr. Hopkins, you could have found a better place than this," said Keep.

"Like to get my death of cold," sniffled Miss Winthrop.

"Let's get this over with," said Freddie. "The faster we get out of here, the better."

Henry Hopkins now went over the syndicate's resources. They had melted down to a point where they had just about enough to replace the money they had taken from the bank. They now owed the Puritan Bank and Trust, in order to cover their depredations, about $200,000. The true value of their securities in SIT amounted to approximately $225,000. In short, the syndicate still had a meager profit. The question now before them was this: whether to sell now, replace the money "borrowed" from the bank, and walk away with a small profit, or hold out, wait for the market to shoot up as all the bulls had predicted, sit tight, and do nothing.

Freddie was the first to speak. "I vote to sell and get out."

"He's right," chimed in Hannah. "Let's put the money back, and then we can all sleep soundly."

Keep took the same position as the other two. They began to babble among themselves. *"It's a bear market," "I don't believe these bulls," "A bird in the hand," "We'd be crazy to hold on . . ."*

"Wait a minute," said Hopkins, holding up his arms. Frosty vapor sprang from his nostrils. "Now hold on. Hold on, all of you." Gradually their babble subsided as they watched him. "I talked to C. F. Bennett just before we got here."

"You did?" said Freddie.

"Personally."

"And?"

"The word is that this move on the downside was manipulated."

"Manipulated?"

Henry nodded. "By Rockefeller, Morgan, Albert Wiggin of Chase National, and the others. It's a move to shake out the suckers and the small fry—I suppose people like us. Except we're not in that category. We're part of Sunrise Investment Trust—playing ball with C. F. Bennett. He's on our side. And as you know, nobody fools Bennett."

"And he says hang on?" Keep wanted to know.

"He's saying the same thing to all his clients. The market's going to boom."

Keep's brow furrowed. "You're *positive* about this?"

"I *told* you, Jonathan. We have the best kind of inside information. All we have to do is sit tight and follow the smart money. The rest of the idiots are scaring off. But the smart money says buy. Not sell."

The syndicate took a vote. It was three to one, Freddie Mayhew casting the only dissenting ballot. Then they left the cold-storage plant, each hoping that they hadn't caught a hard cold, let alone pneumonia.

*

Suddenly, the market shook off its fetters, pumped up its adrenalin, and rampaged on more strongly than ever. The bulls roared through the Street.

On the New York Stock Exchange on Saturday, U.S. Steel leaped ahead almost eight dollars a share. General Electric's surge was even more spectacular; it went up 10 points. American Tobacco stunned everybody by making one of the most fabulous rises of all. It shot upward to an unbelievable thirty-eight dollars a share. Sunrise Investment Trust rose 7 points. And the Dow Jones Industrial Average regained more than 16 points during the dramatic turnabout.

At noon on Sunday, Bernard Baruch's private railroad car, hooked to the Twentieth Century out of Chicago, slid into Grand Central Station. With him were his guests, the sun-tanned Winston Churchills, who had stayed in California as guests of William Randall Hearst. An enterprising reporter (one paid by one of the Big Boys) reported that he had heard Baruch express regret that he hadn't stayed in the market instead of selling out. But sometimes even the best of them missed the boat.

A wave of buying euphoria hit the country. Call money hit the 6 percent mark. San Francisco was breaking down the walls, waving buy orders for Transamerica. It was said that in St. Louis some brokers were sending out employees to buy throat gargles to ease their throats, made hoarse from yelling.

The story was the same. The Big Boys had now stepped in and they were buying.

On the steamship *Berengaria,* as it crossed the Atlantic, passengers lined up before the wireless room to put in their bids to buy. It was said that Helena Rubinstein, that arbiter of fashion, had calmly and regally put in buy orders for a cool million dollars.

*

Naturally the syndicate was delighted.

For the moment, Henry Hopkins was the hero. He had had the courage to hold on when others had faltered. The president of the Puritan Bank and Trust could not help strutting a little. The syndicate was now back into a modest profit position, and the way things were going, no one could tell how high it would go.

But the euphoria was short-lived. On October 16th, the

Committee of Investment Bankers Association in New York stunned the financial community by making a special announcement. It believed that "speculation in public service stocks has reached a danger point and many stocks are now selling far above their intrinsic value."

In the next few days, the market took a dive. General Electric fell 12 points, Westinghouse over 11, U.S. Steel nearly 10.

By Saturday, October 19th, the syndicate was thoroughly alarmed. The agate type on the financial pages told the real story. Another meeting of the syndicate was urgent and mandatory.

The alarm came to them in different ways. In Freddie and Ellie's room, at the Hopkins' house, Ellie was lying on top of Freddie, teasing him by squirming her body, kissing him, giggling. They had had two rum and colas apiece—two young marrieds enjoying each other, when an all too familiar voice came over the radio:

"This is WBZA . . . for your listening pleasure. And now . . . the five o'clock news. Your commentator: Gabriel Heatter." Heatter's voice of doom came on: "This is Gabriel Heatter. There is bad news today. The market dropped another four points, and a wave of selling continues . . ."

At this, Freddie sat up abruptly, throwing Ellie over so that she fell on the floor. He listened intently, his face tense . . .

*

Henry Hopkins was just finishing a poker game in the locker room of the club. He was in high bad humor. He had just lost fifty dollars, and had been outbluffed time and again. The radio was turned on. And what he heard now made him sit up straight . . .

"According to all indications, and to reliable sources, there will be a large correction on the downside. The big investors are said to be unloading large blocks of stocks . . ."

*

Hannah Winthrop was at the bathroom sink, studying her face in the mirror. Time and again, she pushed her harelip in a straight position, trying to picture how her mouth would look after Dr. James Ricardi had finished his surgery. She tried to conjecture how Edgar Morton, the hardware man, would look at her then. She might, or might not, give him the time of day after that. She did not know . . .

Suddenly her ear caught the sonorous voice of Gabriel Heatter on the radio in her living room . . .

"It may be that the market is overbought. That the fever of speculation has reached a point where it has ballooned out of sight. Certainly, the tremendous plunge of the market today would indicate that . . ."

Hannah Winthrop stood staring in the mirror, her eyes widening in sudden fear.

*

The parlor of the Sans Souci, in a street adjacent to the paper mills in Holyoke, about eight miles from Riverside, was filled on this night. It was a rather large and elaborate place, with the traditional red velvet decor, rococo Tiffany lamps, and chandeliers. A number of "the girls" were sitting around, scantily clad and heavily made up. They were laughing and drinking it up with their "gentlemen callers." The madam, whose real name was Stella DuBois, was moving around, seeing that everyone was having a good time. In one end of the parlor, a man wearing a brown derby was playing a tinny piano and singing the lyrics in a cracked and husky voice: "I Wanna Be Loved by You."

Madame DuBois took great care that her establishment be thoroughly traditional. She found that her clients liked it that way. She had just told her piano player to step it up a bit when she saw one of her regulars come in.

It was Jonathan Keep. He wore his same battered hat and the same black suit. The madam hurried forward to greet him. He was clearly an old and steady client.

"Good evening, Mr. Keep."

"Good evening, Stella."

"Would you like Cecilia again?"

Keep nodded. "If she's available."

The madam nodded. She went to a doorway which led away from the parlor to the bar area. Cecilia was there, and she came quickly to the madam's summons. When she saw Keep, she smiled at him, patted him on the cheek, and with her eyes promised him everything. Jonathan Keep was not a man who looked for variety. When he found something he liked, he stayed with it.

They moved to the stairway, leading to the upper, or boudoir, floor. Cecilia preceded Keep, shaking her derrière in his face as he followed.

They entered one of the rooms. Cecilia closed the door. She took off her robe, revealing her naked body. Then she started to peel off her stockings. Meanwhile, gravely and deliberately, Keep took off his hat and jacket, and then stripped down to his long johns, or what were then called "union suits."

It was a ritual they had been through many times, and no word was needed or spoken. Already there was a slight hardening in Jonathan Keep's crotch.

Cecilia was lying on the bed now, flat on her back, legs slightly spread, smiling seductively at Keep. She knew this would not take long, not with Keep. He was impatient with any kind of foreplay. There were plenty of customers waiting in the downstairs parlor, and this promised to be a profitable evening. With a man like Keep, the quicker the better.

Now Keep stripped off his union suit. He stood there naked, his scrawny body trembling a little, his penis half-erect. It was here that Cecilia made her mistake. There was a small Atwater Kent radio on the bureau. It was playing organ music, not calculated to put Keep in a proper frame of mind. She turned the dial and came to a news commentator. It was Gabriel Heatter, and this was toward the end of his broadcast. She started to turn the dial again, when Keep held up his hand. This was something he apparently wanted to hear, and Cecilia was in the business of pleasing her customers any way she could.

Gabriel Heatter had turned on his usual prophetic voice, his trademark voice of doom, and he was now saying:

". . . No one knows what this tremendous drop in the market today portends. Even our pundits and experts profess to be baffled. Already many of our small investors have been wiped out. The ticker is a half-hour late, and roaring crowds around the posts in the stock market are screaming to sell. Perhaps this is only temporary. Perhaps it is simply a mote in the sky. Or perhaps it is some kind of dark omen. Again, rumors are rife. Rumors that the so-called Big Boys are running like animals before a forest fire, trying to get out quickly. Perhaps they know something we do not know. If a disaster is imminent, the insiders always know it first." Heatter took a long breath. "And now, a message from our sponsor."

Throughout all this, Jonathan Keep stood silent as a statue. His face was impassive. His half erection went totally limp.

Cecilia saw that he was disturbed. Slowly, she wiggled her body, did a few bumps and grinds lying in the bed, opened her legs wider to give him a better view of the dark mystery located there.

But she might as well have been appealing to a stone

statue; Jonathan Keep paid no attention to her. Slowly he drew on his union suit, buttoned it up from crotch to neck, slipped on his trousers and shirt, and put on his shoes and socks. Then with slow deliberation, he buttoned his jacket and placed his hat firmly on his head. Then he reached into his pocket, put a crumpled five-dollar bill on the bureau, and took his leave of Cecilia and the Sans Souci.

*

When he got home, there was an urgent message waiting for him. It was from Henry Hopkins and was marked *Emergency* in red pencil.

There was to be a special meeting of the syndicate at four in the afternoon on Monday, shortly after banking hours. The place was to be the Board Room, and everybody in the syndicate was expected to be there.

Everybody.

*

Henry Hopkins, his face grave, came right to the point. The syndicate's investment in SIT had been hard hit. They had just enough in the kitty now to pay back the bank its $200,000 and come out clean. Their profits had vanished like a puff of wind in the debacle of the last few days.

"The question is," said Hopkins, "what do we do now? Which way do we go?"

Jonathan Keep was emphatic.

"As far as I'm concerned, Mr. Hopkins—sell. Let's get out!"

"Let's not jump to hasty conclusions, Jonathan. The market may shoot up today. Let's give this some thought . . ."

"Damn it, Henry," said Keep, red-faced. It was the first time he had ever called Hopkins by his first name. "I say, sell!" He turned to the others. "Freddie. Miss Winthrop. What do you say?"

"Sell," said Miss Winthrop.

"Sell," said Freddie. "Let's come out of this clean."

"There you are, Henry," said Keep. "We're all agreed. We say *sell.*"

"All right," said Henry, his own face red. "You don't have to yell, Jonathan. I hear you. But I don't agree with you. I think we'd be fools to sell now."

"Do you?" said Keep. "Why?"

"I say *hold.* And wait for the upturn."

Now Freddie Mayhew spoke up. *"What* upturn?"

Hopkins gave his new son-in-law a contemptuous look. "There's always an upturn after a break like this. You saw it happen before. We'll be back in a profit position in a week."

"You don't have a crystal ball, Henry. How the hell would you know that?"

Subtly, the relationship between Keep and Hopkins had changed since the syndicate was formed. At this meeting, at least, they were no longer employer-employee. They were partners. And Jonathan Keep, in his own way, was enjoying this new relationship. He could be insolent to his boss, even arrogant now, without fear of dismissal.

"I still say we hold," said Henry Hopkins stubbornly.

Hannah Winthrop had been twisting her handkerchief in her hands. She seemed close to hysteria.

"Mr. Hopkins, I just can't stand this anymore. I needed the money for something important, very important to me. But I just can't stand this anymore. The market going up, the market going down, never knowing what's going to happen until you open the paper next morning. I'm so nervous, I can't eat, I can't sleep. I just keep thinking that if we go on like this, we could all end up in jail." Her voice ended in a wail; she was close to tears. "I'm just sorry I ever got into this."

"That goes for me, too," said Freddie. "I've had enough."

"All you've got is nothing," said Henry Hopkins tartly. "You have the nerve to marry my daughter, *my* daughter, without even asking me or her mother . . ."

"All right, Henry," said Keep. "Let's keep out the personalities and get on with it. You've heard the consensus here. Get out while the getting is good . . ."

"All of you, listen to me . . ."

"No," interrupted Keep, sharply. "You'd better listen to us. We've had our bellies full, Henry, and that's for sure. If we hang on, like you suggest, we'll only be throwing good money after bad. As you've just told us, if we sell Sunrise Investment Trust in the morning, we'll have just enough to replace the cash we took from the bank. And that'll take a little doing. We'll have to doctor some documents, some books, Henry. We'll need the time before the bank examiner gets here . . ."

Henry Hopkins studied them all defiantly. And with a certain contempt. Of them all, he was the true speculator, the only one with any real courage. He had told his wife that he would soon repay the money she had lent him, which he had lost in Florida. He had been absolutely confident about it. He hadn't told her *how* he was going to do this; it was a secret, a business secret. But the thing was, he had *convinced* her. He could not bear the idea of backtracking now, and he pictured her nagging him on a whole new level, as a boaster, an empty braggart, and a liar. And so, with a certain desperation, he tried the old argument again, shaking his head sadly at them, as though in despair at their stupidity.

"Listen to me. All we need is a little nerve. And patience. Don't you understand what the Big Boys do? When everybody else is selling, they *buy* . . ."

"You know what, Henry?" said Keep.

"What?"

"I'm a little tired of the Big Boys. And this theory of

selling when everyone else is buying. I don't think they know what the hell *they're* doing, either."

"I agree with Mr. Keep," said Freddie. "They don't know their ass from a hole in the wall." He blushed suddenly. "Oh, I'm sorry, Miss Winthrop. I didn't mean . . ."

"That's all right, Freddie," said Hannah. "We've all been under such terrible strain. I think we're all agreed here, except for Mr. Hopkins. We want to get out now, before it's too late. I call for a vote."

"Vote, vote!" said Freddie.

Now Keep took over. "All those in favor of selling Sunrise Investment Trust today and putting the cash back where we found it—raise their hands."

Three hands shot upward.

"All those opposed," said Keep.

Henry Hopkins did not even bother to raise his hand. Keep said:

"All right, Henry. Sell us out at the market, first thing tomorrow morning. Then we'll *all* get some sleep!"

*

Over coffee the following morning, Henry Hopkins studied the financial page.

The big front page story was that Bunny and Clive had hit another bank, this one in Old Orchard, Maine, and that the Bankers' Association of Massachusetts had offered a reward of $10,000 for information leading to their capture and arrest. But Henry Hopkins hardly gave it a glance.

Of late, the market had held fairly steady. Professor Irving Fisher, the darling of the bulls, stated in an article that the recent drop meant only a "shaking out of the lunatic fringe." Furthermore, he was of the opinion that "even in the present market, the prices of stocks have not caught up with their 'real values.' " In a speech to the Purchasing Agents' Association, he insisted that stocks had reached "what looks like a permanently high plateau" and said that he expected stock prices, within a few months, to be much higher than they were today.

On this day, Tuesday, October 22nd, there was another item of interest in the *Riverside Union.* Charles Edwin Mitchell, president of the National City Bank, had just arrived from an Atlantic crossing. He was tanned, fit, and almost bouncy with optimism. Surrounded by reporters, he stated unequivocally that the sagging market had overreacted and that "the fall had gone too far, carrying many issues below their true values." In short, he agreed with Professor Fisher. His implication was plain. The suckers had been shaken out. Now was the time to buy.

More than this, Colonel Leonard Ayres of the Cleveland Trust Company stated that basically the decline was due to the fact that stocks had been passing not so much from the strong to the weak as from the smart to the dumb. R. W. McNeel, director of the highly respected McNeel Financial Service, stated that "some pretty intelligent people are now buying stocks. Unless we have a panic, which no one seriously believes—stocks have hit bottom." The *Boston News Bureau,* in its financial column called "Broad Street Gossip," stated that inside opinion on the Street was almost uniform. "The recent break makes a firm foundation for the big bull market in the last quarter of the year." In other words, the deflation had ended, and a great many investors were ready to buy again. And in its editorial opinion, the *News Bureau* said that "whatever recessions are noted are those of the runner catching his breath . . . the general condition is satisfactory and fundamentally sound."

The financial news, on this morning, was definitely upbeat.

Henry Hopkins slammed down his newspaper, refused a second cup of coffee, and decided he was associated with a pack of lily-livered, gutless fools. He had hoped they would go along with him. Counted on them. Stay in the market instead of cut and run. But they were who they were, and nothing could change that. Little people, scared people. People like Freddie Mayhew, he reflected bitterly, whom his daughter had, in an act of juvenile insanity, married and brought into the family.

*

Shortly after the bank opened, Henry Hopkins left his desk, put on his topcoat, and walked to the brokerage house of Charles Lothrop and Company on State Street.

He did not want to discuss the transaction he had been ordered to make that day. At least not over the telephone at the bank, where he might possibly be overheard. He wanted to talk to Charlie Lothrop personally about this matter.

When he walked into Lothrop's, he found the place in bedlam. Four or five brokers, sweating in their shirtsleeves, were at their desks, their ears cradled to telephones, taking orders. The place was crowded with investors, speculators, and citizens who knew where the excitement in town would be that day. They were all watching a big raised blackboard at one end of the boardroom. On it were listed the latest stock market quotations. An employee stood on a raised platform erasing old quotations and chalking in new ones as they came over the ticker. Over the blackboard was a panel on which the Dow Jones average for the day was indicated. At this moment, it was moving back up again.

As Henry stood there, an office boy came out from the inner office and handed a message to the employee on the platform. The man glanced at it, erased the previous Dow Jones figure, and put in another one.

The Dow Jones was now up 4 points and still climbing. There was a spontaneous cheer from everyone in the boardroom. They laughed, yelled, shook hands, and slapped each other on the shoulders. It was clear that the market had simply shaken out the timid bears, and now the bulls were on the rampage again, nostrils snorting, horns low, and running for the horizon.

Charlie Lothrop's private office was separated from the rest of the boardroom by a big glass partition through which he could see what was going on in the boardroom at all times. Lothrop was excited, sweating. His shirt collar was open, his tie awry. At the moment he had the phone cradled between shoulder and ear and was studying the ticker tape coming out of the glass-bowled machine standing on a table next to his desk.

He caught sight of Henry Hopkins standing just outside his office. He waved Henry in, asked him to close the door, finished his phone conversation, a sizable buy order. Then he leaned back, and said:

"My God, Henry, what a day! You see the way the market's kicking back? Hell bent for election. I think the DJ's going to ten, maybe fifteen, before they ring the bell for the day." Then, almost abruptly: "What can I do for you, Henry?"

"I came in to sell my SIT."

Charlie Lothrop sat upright in his chair. He stared at Henry:

"Sell Sunrise Investment? Are you crazy? It's just gone up two points, Henry. TWO points. And still going. Speaking as old friends, why the hell would you want to sell a fine security like that? C. F. Bennett's right on top of it, and he's squeezing the juice out of it. And if I know anything about the old bastard, he's just beginning to ride it up. I'll lay odds that SIT will be selling for twenty-five before the week is out."

"You really think . . ."

"I'm buying it for my private account. That's what I think. And if you've got any money, buy, for Christ's sake. Now's the time. You must have read the morning papers."

"I still can't understand why the market did this kind of turnaround. There has to be a reason."

"There is. It's called 'organized buying support.' The Big Boys have all gotten together and decided that they'd pool their buying power. Keep the bull market alive and never let it fall too far back. I'm talking about Arthur Cutten, John Raskob, Percy Rockefeller, Billy Durant, the DuPont brothers—people like that. People like that, guaranteeing the market. How can you lose if you stay in there, Henry?"

"Then you really think I shouldn't sell . . ."

"I *told* you. I think you're crazy for even entertaining the idea."

Henry Hopkins walked out of Lothrop's office. He was perspiring, in a weird state of excitement. He looked up at the board. He saw the familiar symbol, SIT.

In the short time he had been in Lothrop's office, Sunrise Investment Trust had jumped another point.

Now, he stood there indecisively. He knew he had been ordered to sell that day. The syndicate had made that plain enough. But still—suppose he decided to take matters in his own hands. Wait another day—maybe two. If the bull market continued, he could show the others decisive results. He could show them that by using his own good judgment and ignoring their fears, he had increased their equity and could still build it higher and higher.

It was tempting. Very tempting. Give it another day. One day at a time. He decided to wait. He could always sell tomorrow. Or the day after. None of the others would really know the difference. If there was a profit, he could pocket it himself, and they would never know the difference. They would assume he had sold at the break-even price. But of course, he would never do that. He was not that kind of a man. But he could be the kind who could make them all rich —in spite of themselves.

Yet he was uneasy about his decision. More than that— a little queasy. A lot depended on where the people thought the country was headed. That was the emotional factor that made the market rise or fall. The question was—how did they see the future of the country?

What Henry Hopkins needed was some sound advice, and there was one man who could give it to him. An old friend, a friend of hard-headed common sense whose opinion Henry would really respect. The old friend was a busy man, but he might, just might, give Henry a little time.

A few minutes later, Henry Hopkins went to the telephone and asked the operator to get him a number in Northampton.

20

OVER A BREAKFAST of pancakes and maple syrup at his home, Calvin Coolidge rattled a copy of the *American Mercury* and swore:

"That son of a bitch," he said.

"Who?" asked his wife, Grace.

"H. L. Mencken. Still after me in that damned column of his. Doesn't he realize I'm not in office anymore?"

"Now, Calvin, all you have to do is ignore him. You know you'll get one of your asthma attacks if you don't."

"What I *should* do is sue old Mencken for libel, or slander!"

"But why? What did he say?"

"What did he say? Says that I fed at the public trough for almost thirty years, and retired with three or four hundred thousand dollars in my tight jeans. Calls me a darling of the gods, lucky to be governor, lucky to get in the White House just by doing nothing. And listen to this, Grace. Let me read it to you. 'Here was Cal's really notable talent. He slept more than any other President, whether by day or night. Nero fiddled, but Coolidge only snored.' Said I knew exactly when to get out and let Hoover get stuck with all the problems the country has now. Says I must be laughing now, while old

Herbert is struggling to keep the market from blowing up in his face."

Calvin Coolidge flung down the periodical, almost spilling his coffee cup. He began to wheeze, and Grace Coolidge gave him the atomizer he always carried. Finally, gently, she simmered down his anger and told him it was time to go to the office. He left the half of the small duplex in which they lived and was driven to his office by his hired man, who doubled as chauffeur. Already Massasoit Street was lined with cars carrying sightseers, staring at the duplex or hoping to catch a sight of the ex-President himself.

His office was in the old Masonic Building, which contained a rickety elevator which was out of service on Saturdays and Sundays. He had five rooms which he shared with his old law partner, Ralph Hemenway. There, usually with one of his feet propped on an open drawer of his desk, Coolidge dictated replies to the many letters he received from friends, well-wishers, and people seeking advice. In this service, he had recruited one of his former secretaries, Edward T. Clark, to act as literary intermediary between himself and Washington.

There is always the question of how ex-Presidents newly out of office will spend their retirement. It did not take Calvin Coolidge long to make up his mind. The pressures upon him to adopt a literary career were great, and he accepted. He had put notes together on his personal and private experiences in public office for the autobiography he had contracted to write. Later, the critics pronounced it dull, unrevealing, and full of platitudes. Still, the canny Yankee made a fortune on it. The ordinary American, each a kind of clone of Calvin Coolidge, understood and appreciated it. Coolidge further fattened his pockets by writing articles for the *Ladies' Home Journal, Collier's,* and the *Saturday Evening Post.*

More than this, the McClure Syndicate, despite the President's obvious lack of literary talent, had persuaded him to write a couple of paragraphs of daily newspaper commentary. His column appeared in almost 100 papers, and in the year it ran, it earned over $200,000, a large percentage of which went to Coolidge himself.

It can then be said that Coolidge Prosperity went right on —even through the Depression—on a personal level.

He was in the midst of dictating one of his articles when the phone rang. Edward Clark answered it:

"It's Henry Hopkins, sir."

"Old Henry?" Coolidge reached for the phone. "I'll talk to him."

Coolidge never answered the phone while he was busy, unless it was from one of his old Amherst classmates.

"Morning, Henry. What can I do for you?"

"I need a little advice, Calvin."

"Well," said Coolidge, grinning, "as long as it's not money."

"If you could give me just a few minutes later this afternoon."

"Of course, Henry. You'll be coming alone?"

"Yes."

"See you then. Say four o'clock. How's Helen?"

"She's fine. Sends her love to Grace."

"Fine. See you then, at four?"

"At your office?"

"No. I'll be home by then. Come right on up to the house."

*

They sat on the Coolidge porch for a while, and then Coolidge said:

"You'll stay for supper, Henry?"

"Well, I don't know . . ."

Coolidge turned and shouted into the kitchen. "Grace, old Henry's going to stay for supper. That is, if we have enough."

"There's plenty," said Grace.

"Fine," said Coolidge. He turned to Hopkins with a grin. "Something's wrong with our refrigerator. Don't know what it is. But rather have you eat what's left than see it spoil."

The front porch and the back steps were important details in most of the homes of New England during the period. The steps of the front porch at 21 Massasoit were no more than about twenty-five feet from the sidewalk. Crowds walked the street to catch a glimpse of Mr. Coolidge as he smoked his cigar. He was an inveterate porch sitter, both before and after supper, and he tried to ignore them. Several people among the crowd paused and lifted their cameras to take pictures. Others, bolder, tried to enter the gate and get the former President's autograph, but the gate was locked and guarded by a Secret Service man.

It was the traffic on Massasoit Street, however, that annoyed Coolidge. He turned to Henry and said:

"You know how many cars pass on the street and gawk at me? And if not me, at the house. Ten cars a minute. About one out of every six seconds. Smell up the whole neighborhood with their gas fumes. Lot of the people jump over the fence and trample my lawn. Had a lot more privacy in the White House." Coolidge grinned. "Only reason I wish I was back."

Henry Hopkins looked at the crowds and the cars. "Don't see how you can stand it."

"Can't. Got my belly full of it. That's why I bought this new place. The Beeches."

"The Beeches?"

"Big place. Set back from the road. Nine acres and sixteen rooms. Grace is going to go crazy trying to clean all those rooms. Can you imagine it, Henry? I pay forty dollars a month rental for this little place. I'm buying the Beeches for forty thousand dollars. That's quite a difference."

"I would say so."

"Makes me feel guilty."

"Guilty, Calvin? Why?"

Coolidge snuffed out his cigar. His face suddenly turned grave. "I'll be living high, while a lot of people, ordinary folk I mean, are going to have trouble paying their mortgages."

"Then you believe the country's headed for a downspin?"

"Don't know for sure. But I feel it in my bones."

"In a way, that's the advice I came to hear, Calvin."

"Yes?"

"I mean, the market. We all know it reflects the condition of the country. It seems to have gone crazy. Up and down. Up and down. Like one of these roller coasters."

Coolidge looked at Hopkins sharply. "Are you in the market personally, Henry?"

"Me? Of course not, Calvin," he said hastily. "I'm a respectable banker. Wouldn't do for my clients to know I was gambling like everyone else. Maybe they do it in New York, but not in a place like Riverside."

"I'm glad to hear that, Henry," said Coolidge. "Don't forget I've got some money tied up in the Puritan Bank and Trust. Like to feel it's safe there at all times."

"Of course."

"The reason I came to ask your advice is this, Calvin. *I'm* not in the market, as I said, but a lot of my clients, my borrowers, are. People who do business with the Puritan. They're always asking me for my opinion. I tell them I don't have a crystal ball. I don't know where the market is going, any more than anyone else. But they don't believe me. I'm a banker—supposed to be a financial expert. Supposed to have inside information of what the Federal Reserve is doing. You know, that sort of thing."

Calvin Coolidge lit another cigar. He sat for a few minutes, deliberating. Then he said:

"Tell you, Henry. This reminds me of an old country doctor we had up in Plymouth. Used to tell my father that when people were sick in the stomach, he gave them advice. And when they were sick in the head, he gave them advice as well." Coolidge chuckled. "Charged them the same either way, he said." He thought for a moment, then added: "In my opinion, the American people are sick both in the stomach *and* the head. There is nothing wrong with American business. But you can always abuse a good thing. You take a boy with a piece of Christmas candy. He bites off one end of it. He chews it and swallows it, and it tastes good. He does the same again. And again. And then he can't stop until he's eaten the whole candy cane. Then comes the stomachache."

"You mean, things are moving too fast."

"Too many people boiling too many kettles. I don't mean the rich people, I mean the poor. They've gotten it into their heads there's a way to get rich quick. Maybe there is, if you find oil or a gold mine on your land, but ordinarily there's no other way than hard work and an eye for an opportunity. People expect to bury their money in the dirt of a flower pot and just watch it grow. Can't be done. There's got to be a disaster somewhere—and soon."

"But the government is aware of the problem."

"The government is a little late, Henry. And it can't deal with fools. Trouble is, a good part of the American public insists on playing the fool. I can't criticize old Herbert. This thing's gotten beyond his ability to stop it. He might as well try to stop a runaway train with his bare hands. In my opinion, he should have cracked down on the Federal Reserve. He should have raised cash requirements for stock purchases and reduced margin credit. But he's the President, not I. Thank God, Henry, not I. Personally, I never knew much about the national financial situation when I was in office. I listened to old Andy Mellon and took his advice most of the time."

"Then, in essence, Calvin, you see trouble coming."

"Big trouble. If I were you, I'd advise anyone to sell their stock for a while and keep their money high and dry, in the bank, or in their britches. I can't tell you exactly why, Henry. It's a feeling I have in the pit of my stomach."

"Something I'm curious about, Calvin. It's a little personal, and you don't have to answer, of course."

"Yes?"

"When you said you didn't choose to run, did you do so because you saw what was coming?"

"I didn't see it, Henry. But I sort of smelled it."

"Then you're lucky."

"That's what that son of a bitch Mencken says. That's what a lot of people say. To tell you the truth, Henry, I think that way myself. I'm the luckiest ex-President that America will have. What will happen to old Herbert Hoover and his administration, I don't know. But they'll always remember me in terms of Coolidge Prosperity, and that's something that'll go down in history—Coolidge Prosperity."

*

After supper it had begun to rain. On his way home, Henry Hopkins now made a clear and definite decision. He would call Charlie Lothrop first thing in the morning and sell at the market, regardless of whether it had gone up or down.

As he approached the Agawam Bridge, crossing the Connecticut, a big Graham-Paige with bright headlights came down the hill on his right. There was a stop sign, but the driver, probably drunk, ignored it. He went right through the sign and smashed into the side of Henry Hopkins' Pierce Arrow. The Pierce Arrow skidded to the left, smashing into the railing that guarded the river bank.

Henry Hopkins sat where he was. He sat perfectly still, with his head lying on the wheel.

When he was rushed to Riverside Hospital, it was found that he was suffering from multiple cuts and bruises, none of them of a particularly serious nature.

But there was one injury that worried the doctors. He had been struck in the head and was now in a coma. He was unconscious and remained so, despite all efforts to revive him.

*

On this Wednesday, the bulls and Charlie Lothrop all seemed to be right.

The rally seemed solid. By the close of trading that Tuesday, Western Union was up eighteen dollars a share, Columbia Carbon almost seventeen dollars, and Hershey Chocolate almost ten dollars.

Many were convinced that blue skies had started to smile again, and that it was turnaround time. One of these was Richard Whitney, acting president of the New York Stock Exchange. He felt so relaxed and confident that he decided to take the next day off, get away from Wall Street, and participate in his favorite sport—horse racing.

On this particular Wednesday, he was one of the two stewards in charge of the races at the Essex Fox Hounds track in Far Hills, New Jersey. He was, of course, in touch with Wall Street via the telephone, or the radio that had been installed in the clubhouse.

Shortly after noon, the market began to plunge downward.

No one knew what caused the suddenness of this drop. It seemed to be a kind of simultaneous knee jerk of investors and speculators both.

*

But this was only the beginning. The worst was yet to come.

The next day, Thursday, October 24th, was not just a disaster. It was a debacle.

Stocks plummeted downward. Great blocks in tens of thousands of shares were put up for sale. Clerks were smothered in selling orders. In the offices of brokers everywhere in the country, the tape watchers were stunned. Where was this selling deluge coming from? Why was it happening?

No one could answer this question in definitive terms. Some historians say the cause was not actually fear. Not in the first or second hour of trading, at least. Neither was it short selling. It was caused by people with their backs to the wall who were *forced* to sell. By the small investors and speculators whose margins were growing thin and about to run out and who were dumping hundreds and thousands of shares on the market in the desperate hope of saving something, anything. The huge price pyramid had become overloaded with speculative credit and now was falling apart of its own weight.

After the first few hours, fear made its entrance and multiplied the carnage. There was a wild stampede to get out at any cost, and traders at the various posts in the exchange were almost swarmed under with shouting, screaming investors to "sell at the market." The roar of the crowds on the floor of the exchange became a roar of fear and panic.

A few still clung to the usual shibboleths. The bargain hunters would come to the rescue. The Big Boys would now move in and buy the stocks dirt cheap. The bankers who only a few days ago had supported the market on their shoulders would come back in and get prices moving again.

Where was Charles Mitchell? Where were all the bulls? The Big Boys? Where were Albert Wiggin, head of Chase, Thomas Lamont of the House of Morgan, William Potter, George F. Baker?

They were in the offices of J. P. Morgan and Company, holding an emergency meeting. There they guaranteed $40 million each to form a pool to shore up the market.

This was the historic day when Richard Whitney, acting as floor broker for the Morgan interests, and backed by the pool, strode through the market buying this stock and that, and . . . especially Steel. He bought 20 or 30 million dollars' worth of shares, and for a while prices held steady.

But he was only a poodle trying to stop the onrush of the huge, shaggy bear.

*

Hannah Winthrop, Jonathan Keep, and Freddie Mayhew were quite relaxed about the debacle. They watched it with almost detached amusement. And why not? They were out of the market now. And with a handsome profit. Henry Hopkins, on their instructions, had sold them out on Tuesday, two days before. They had been smart, or just lucky. They had gotten out just in time, and secretly they congratulated each other.

From the hospital they received the report that Henry Hopkins was still unconscious, but that there seemed to be no skull fracture or other signs which seemed critical. He had awakened once or twice and then become unconscious again. As of now, it appeared to be simply a concussion of some sort.

The calm of the other three members of the syndicate proved to be short-lived, however.

At two o'clock, the phone rang. Jonathan Keep answered. It was from Charlie Lothrop. His voice was raspy and hoarse. He had, of course, read about the accident.

"How's Mr. Hopkins?"

"He's still in a coma."

"I'm sorry to hear that, Mr. Keep. But you'd better find

some way to bring him to. SIT has gone from 30 to 24. My advice is for him to sell so that he can still come out with something."

There was a long pause. Then Keep said:

"But you're wrong, Lothrop."

"Wrong about what?"

"Henry Hopkins sold out all his Sunrise Investment Trust day before yesterday. Every share of it."

"Did he? That's news to me."

Suddenly, Jonathan Keep felt a chill. "But he went there to sell . . ."

"He was here all right. But he decided to hold it another day or two. No transaction was made. He still owns SIT. And it's dropping like a stone."

"Then sell it, Lothrop," said Keep desperately. "Sell the whole damned thing right now."

"I can't."

"But why not?"

"The stock's in *his* name. Not yours. For the record, *he* owns those securities. He's the only one who has the authority to buy or sell. I've got to get the order directly from him."

"But he's in the hospital. In a coma. Unconscious."

"I'm sorry to have to say this. But that's *his* problem. Pretty soon, if this market keeps up, I'm going to have to ask for more margin."

Keep was desperate. "But dammit, there must be a way . . ."

"There is. If you can get power of attorney. But you can't do that when Hopkins can't even swing a pen, let alone talk." There was a pause. Then Lothrop said: "Why are you so interested, Keep? You sold out Baldwin Locomotive months ago. You're out of the market. It's just Henry Hopkins' tough luck that he's still in. But as I said, he won't be in much longer if he doesn't come up with some more margin money. We're getting pretty close now."

*

Now there was panic among the partners.

A few minutes after the bank closed, they rushed up to Riverside Hospital to see Hopkins.

He lay in the bed, very still, his face waxen, his eyes closed, his hands folded across his chest. To Freddie, Hannah, and Jonathan he looked exactly like a corpse, except for the fact that he was breathing gently, very gently. The three did their best.

"Wake up, Mr. Hopkins," said Hannah Winthrop, speaking close into his ear.

"Open your eyes, Dad," said Freddie Mayhew. "Try to listen. We're in trouble. You've got to make a telephone call."

Jonathan Keep was less patient and gentle. "Damn you, Henry," he said. "You got us into this. If you don't come out of this, we're all ruined."

But Henry Hopkins slept on peacefully. The trio cornered a Doctor John Wickes, who had charge of Hopkins' case. Desperately, they asked him when Hopkins would become conscious again. Wickes shrugged his shoulders.

"There's no way of telling," Dr. Wickes shrugged. "Might be in the next hour. Might not be for days. We don't think there's any serious cranial damage, but we still can't be sure. We'll just have to wait."

When Wickes left, the three stood in the corridor. All caught in despair. Helpless.

"What do we do now, Mr. Keep?" asked Hannah.

"I don't know what *you're* going to do, Miss Winthrop. But I'm going down to the Barrel and get me a drink."

"I'll join you," said Freddie.

"You know," said Hannah Winthrop, beginning to weep softly. "We could all go to prison for this."

"Exactly," said Keep. "Which gives me an idea. I'm going to order a double."

"Jesus," said Freddie, "when I tell Ellie, she'll divorce me. Even if she's beginning to show . . ."

"That son of a bitch Hopkins," said Keep. "Get-rich-quick Hopkins. If it weren't for him, I'd have my own bank now."

"And I'd have a new face."

"We told him to sell," said Freddie passionately. "We ordered him to sell. He promised to sell. Why didn't he?"

"Ask him when he wakes up," snapped Keep. "He's your father-in-law. Maybe he'll tell you. As far as I'm concerned, I don't give a damn whether he wakes up or not!"

*

The fatal phone call came the next day, Friday, October 25th.

And still Henry slept.

It was another terrible day on the exchange. SIT, like many of the investment trusts, was particularly hard hit. It dropped like a stone. Quoted on the morning line at 10, it dropped to 6 by early afternoon.

At two o'clock, Charles Lothrop phoned. His message was to Jonathan Keep, who was next in command. He asked for more margin, and Keep said there was none. At this Lothrop sighed reluctantly:

"Keep, when Henry Hopkins awakes, *if* he awakes, tell him that as far as Sunrise Investment Trust is concerned, he's totally wiped out, to the last dime. All he can do with the certificates he has now is paper the wall with them. I'm sorry you have to convey this bad news to Henry. He's always been a good friend of mine. But he just stayed in a day too long

—didn't know when to quit. Not that he's alone. You should see this place down here. People tearing their hair out. Some of them crying, right out loud." There was the sudden sound of breaking glass. "Got to hang up and call the police. Somebody just threw a rock through my front window. God, there's hell to pay down here. And it looks as though it's going to get worse."

In this, Lothrop was right. The worst was yet to come.

21

At twelve o'clock on the morning of Tuesday, October 29th, C. F. Bennett walked into a broker's branch office on Broadway, knowing what was happening, yet unable to believe it.

He seemed a little unsteady on his feet, and his eyes were glazed.

An hour ago, the big gong had sounded at the exchange, and the trading day had begun.

First C. F. Bennett studied the broker's big board, which completely covered one side of the room. On this board the prices of the leading stocks were normally recorded. He was startled at the LOW and LAST figures written there. Then he realized they were wrong. The young men who slapped into place the cards which showed the latest prices coming out of the ticker just could not keep up with the changes, so rapidly did they come. They ran wildly from here to there, pinpointing a card there, another there, but fighting a losing battle. The changes just came too fast.

Realizing there was nothing reliable he could read here, C. F. Bennett turned to study the shining screen across which ran an endless marching parade of figures hot from the clicking ticker. Even the experienced tape watchers—and Bennett was one of them—could hardly interpret the readings. No wonder. The ticker itself was running an hour late. The figures it recorded had been history for that long now. The question was—what was happening at this moment? At high noon on October 29th, 1929?

Every ten minutes the ticker in the corner clicked off a list of prices direct from the floor. A clerk would pull out the long, thin ribbon of paper uncoiling from the ticker like some snake and shear it off with a pair of huge scissors. Then, as the crowd quieted to a dead silence, he would read the figures aloud, or rather, mumble them in a monotone, to the men occupying every seat in the room and standing packed close together along every wall. All of them were white-faced, unbelieving, as they heard their investments wither away or go down the drain entirely. Some bit their nails. Others wiped the sweat from their foreheads, their eyes reflecting their agony.

The clerk, among other quotations, read off the price for C. F. Bennett's fund. SIT. Down to 3. And its top price had been ten times that.

C. F. Bennett began to walk slowly up and down. He was unaware that he had a piece of paper in his hand and was tearing it to small pieces. He was unaware that it was a twenty-dollar bill he had taken from his pocket. Next to him, a man was grinning and chuckling like some small boy watching a movie as he heard the quotation on a security, which actually was an obituary for his lifetime savings. Phones rang incessantly. Men screamed at the clerks for the latest news on Westinghouse or American Sugar Refining . . .

C. F. Bennett walked out of the office. He had a strange, empty, light-headed feeling. As though he were standing on some other planet, in some other space and time.

The Sunrise Investment Trust, he knew, no longer existed. It had been his creation, and now it had ended as a horrible dream. He had sold all his assets, begged and borrowed, to keep it alive. But the bankers were screaming for margin and closing him out when he could not produce enough money to cover the loans. Not enough of his own money, nor of that of the clients who had put their faith in him.

He found himself walking onto the floor of the stock exchange itself without having the slightest idea of how he got there. Had he walked or taken a cab? He could not remember, and it wasn't important.

The storm in the exchange was now at its highest fury. Great blocks of stock, issued by the most famous of American companies, were thrown on the floor for what they could bring. Five thousand shares of Radio sold at the market—except that there was no buyers' market to speak of. Ten thousand shares of Beacon Oil. Twenty thousand of Curtiss-Wright. And still no takers. Now the big traders, the Big Boys, were being sold out as well as the little ones, the end result of the panic that had begun on Thursday.

The scene on the floor, as C. F. Bennett saw it, was chaos. Again and again some specialist at one of the pillars would be surrounded by brokers shouting themselves hoarse, elbowing each other, fighting to sell even though there were no buyers. Bankers, brokers, clerks, messengers were red-eyed from lack of sleep over the past few days. They were now almost at the end of their endurance. Day and night, they had been trying to keep up with the most tremendous torrent of paper that had ever descended upon them.

Every stock took a savage beating as all of America watched, horrified. The ticker continued to fall far behind the actual transactions. As the afternoon wore on, the pandemonium increased. Traders, clerks, messengers, and page boys ran like headless chickens around the perimeter of the mob and then plunged in, trying to deliver some message to a specialist. When Steel collapsed at post 2, dropping to 179, the crowd turned ugly in its panic. Men swore at each other, shoved and mauled the specialists, clawed at each other's collars, wept and screamed and shouted to the gods in their madness. Several men fainted. Two or three ran around the floor tearing at their hair, completely deranged.

In just thirty minutes, over three and a quarter million shares had been sold for a combined loss of over $2 billion.

*

C. F. Bennett walked out of the exchange and onto the Street.

Nothing unusual about SIT, he thought. There were some 750 so-called investment trusts, and hundreds of them were already wiped out. Bennett remembered one financial critic who had been very sour on the trusts. He had compared them to scientists of ancient times trying to turn base metal into gold. The critic declared that the trusts were really designed to suck in the spare dollars poor people had saved.

Well, the man, in a sense, had been right. Now he, C. F. Bennett, one of the Big Boys, had become a Little Boy. All in the space of just a few days. His lifetime savings were gone, and he had been just as badly hurt as his smallest subscriber. Suddenly he was a poor man. He had known poverty, and known what it was like. It was something he hated as much as everybody else. Poverty was the essence of inconvenience.

Wall Street, by this time, was a crowded mass of humanity, blocked from Broadway to the river. Police estimated the crowd on the Corner as between ten and fifteen thousand people. Among the crowd, men wept openly. Others raised their fists in frustration in the direction of the exchange, shouting obscenities. Police sensed incipient violence. They formed phalanxes before the House of Morgan and the various banks. Many people looked upstairs for help. They crowded Trinity Church. It was jammed for the thirty-minute service that started at noon and would continue for the rest of the day. It was filled with Catholics, Protestants, and Jews, all uncaring about denomination. Some sat in the pews, their heads bowed, covering their faces with their hands. Others knelt, praying in supplication.

But C. F. Bennett could see no comfort in this. Even God in all His might would not bring SIT back, would not resurrect a corpse. He had too many other things to do. One of the itinerant preachers set up his soapbox, pinned the American flag on it, and began to preach on the wages of sin. Now, he said, God had finally vented His wrath upon the Philistines as he, the preacher, had warned. He exhorted the crowd to purify their spirits in the name of the Lord, although their purses might be empty.

At this, an angry crowd knocked the man off his perch, upset his soapbox, and was about to trample him to death, when the police intervened.

At noon, the selling on the stock exchange continued to swamp the sweating specialists and clerks. The paper blizzard kept on and on.

Officially, at one o'clock, 12,632,000 shares had been sold on the exchange, and the selling kept right on going, never stopping to catch its breath.

Tuesday, October 29th, 1929.

This was the day they called "Black Tuesday."

This was the day of the Crash.

*

From the street, C. F. Bennett entered the Bankers Trust Building. The doorman at the elevator, who usually gave him a cheery "Good morning, Mr. Bennett" or "Good afternoon, Mr. Bennett," was silent now. Apparently he had heard the news about SIT. The face was still respectful, but the man's eyes seemed to say, "You're one of us now." There was nothing like a disaster to create a common denominator.

The express elevator whisked him to the seventeenth floor. He walked quickly through the huge outer office, looking neither left nor right. He saw pale faces around him. Some voices offered sympathy. Some people were still on the telephone, explaining that SIT was finished. But the whole feeling of the place was that of a great locker room where a team had lost some championship and was now sadly gathering together its belongings. Or perhaps it was more like a morgue. Dead was dead, but there were still a few who could not believe it, would not believe it.

C. F. Bennett walked into his office, divested himself of hat and coat, and then sat at his desk. He continued to sit awhile, in meditation. Actually he felt quite calm. He put in two phone calls. The first was to his wife, Edna. He heard her anxious voice:

"Charles, are you all right?"

"I'm fine, Edna. Just fine."

"But the market. I heard about what happened to . . ."

"Forget it, Edna. Nothing happened."

There was a long pause. Then Edna, in a quavering voice: "Charles, tell me the truth."

"Yes?"

"What really happened?"

"I told you, darling. We're doing fine. We're richer than before."

"But I heard reports on the radio . . ."

"Forget them. They think I sold long. But I sold short. Made a few millions, Edna."

"Oh," she said. "I'm so relieved."

"Fine. Go out and buy yourself a new dress. Ten new dresses, if you like."

"You're sweet, Charles."

"Oh, Edna. One thing."

"Yes?"

"I won't be home for dinner tonight."

"Oh, darling. I've had Hilda make such a lovely roast."

"I'm sorry, Edna. Got a business appointment. With a very important client. It may run rather late. So don't wait up for me."

"Then I'll see you later this evening."

"Yes. You'll see me then. I promise you that." A pause, and then: "Edna, something I forgot to tell you."

"Yes?"

"I love you. And I always have . . ."

"Why, Charles . . ." she began. But before she could finish, he hung up.

Next he called the Hotel Savoy Plaza. He asked for a Miss Nora Haley, room 810.

"Oh. Charlie. I didn't expect your call till much later."

"Had to call early this time, honey. The evening's off. I can't possibly make it."

"Oh, damn." She sounded disappointed. And even when she swore, she sounded much more refined than had Dixie Day. More class, he liked to think. He wondered how she would have been in bed. He had expected to reach that stage tonight. But now he wasn't really interested. He wasn't really interested in anything anymore.

"Look," he said. "I'm sorry. But you know. Business is business. Tell you what, Nora. Why don't you go down to Tiffany's and buy a little something for yourself? Tell them to put it on my account."

"Oh," she squealed. "Charlie, do you really mean it?"

"Of course I mean it."

"You darling." He heard her smacking kisses on the phone. "Wait till I get hold of *you!*"

C. F. Bennett left orders that he was not to be disturbed under any circumstances. He had an important decision to make, and he needed time to think. He sat at his great desk, musing, for at least half an hour. The only sound in his huge office was that of the stock ticker, clattering and stopping, clattering and stopping, jerkily. It built a pile of curling white tape on the floor near his feet. He did not even bother to look at the ticker.

Finally he took a large Perfecto from a cigar box on his desk, lit it, and leaned back, savoring its aroma. At this moment it tasted delicious. The blue smoke eddied up around his mouth and nostrils, and he wondered why he had never appreciated the aroma half as much as he did now.

He went to the bar, found his favorite bottle of bourbon, and poured it to the brim in a drinking glass of expensive crystal. It was inscribed with the letters C.F.B. He forgot where he had gotten the crystal. Perhaps it was a gift from Edna, from Germany or Sweden, picked up on one of her Grand Tours through Europe. Strange. He thought of her affectionately now. He felt sad for her now, very sad. She had been damned good to him, and for him.

Hell, he told himself. All of a sudden I'm getting sentimental. Me. C. F. Bennett.

He drank the bourbon, filled the glass to the rim, and emptied it again. He felt the warmth creep up inside him; he felt afraid of nothing. He was C. F. Bennett, and they would hear from him yet.

The clatter of the ticker tape annoyed him now. It did more than that. It angered him. It was no longer his old friend. It was no longer his personal crystal ball, which had made him so many millions. It just went on clattering in its stupid way, like some gabbling old woman, discharging yard after yard of paper tape.

He raised his fist and smashed the glass globe protecting

the tape roller and the machinery. It shattered into shards, tinkling to the floor. Still it would not stop. C. F. Bennett, now thoroughly angered, took a heavy paperweight from his desk, and smashed again and again at the inner machinery of the ticker tape. Finally it stopped. He was unaware that he had cut his hand and that it was bleeding.

He took another drink. Everything seemed so right now, so much in place. He noted the huge pile of used ticker tape on the floor. It reminded him of something they used to do at Christmas when he was a boy. He took the long streamers of tape and hung them from the great chandelier over his desk. He draped other strips across the bar, the easy chairs, and his own desk. He wished he had grown a Christmas tree in his office. That would have made it perfect.

He looked at his handiwork and smiled. Everything was done that could be done. It was time to go.

He took off his jacket and loosened his tie. For reasons he did not understand, he took off both shoes. He went to the window, opened it, and heaved out the shoes. He saw them dropping until they became invisible against the teeming street scene below.

Now he stood on the windowsill.

From this vantage point seventeen floors up, he could see the ships sailing up and down New York Harbor. It seemed strange to him that they would be going about their daily business on a day like this, as though nothing had happened. Perhaps it was because they were moving about on water and therefore could not feel the shaking and trembling of the earth on the Street just below.

His eyes strayed back to the upper sections of the buildings along Wall Street, from which protruded graceful sculptures of stone and brass, the weathered heads and necks of stone lions and wolverines and horses, and large, grotesque gargoyles cut deeply in the stone, their ugly faces and angry tongues jeering at the world at large. From this window, also, he could see ten of America's largest banks, so close at this height that they seemed to lean into each other.

Far down below, on the sidewalk and street, crowds of tiny people teemed like ants, vehicles jammed the Street. Dimly, he heard the bells of an ambulance, like some ghostly echo coming from a distant hell. The crowds seemed to surge in one direction, then the other, aimlessly. These were the little people with the big dream. Their dream had made him a fortune. But now it was all gone.

C. F. Bennett felt at peace now. Strangely unafraid. He looked up at the overcast autumn sky. He took a long, last, deep breath of the sharp, clear October air.

Then he jumped.

$$22$$

WHEN FREDDIE MAYHEW'S lunch hour began on this, the 29th day of October, he went directly to Lothrop's brokerage firm. He had no appetite for food. He knew he had already been wiped out. Now he visited the brokerage house out of morbid curiosity.

A few minutes later he walked out of the boardroom like a sleepwalker under the influence of some nightmarish dream.

The story had come in over the news ticker that the founder and godfather of the now defunct Sunrise Investment Trust, C. F. Bennett, had jumped out the window of his office and had plunged seventeen floors to his death.

Freddie Mayhew went immediately to the Worthy Hotel and saw his prospective partners in the radio station, Carl Maynard and Sam Ellinson. The station was already in the process of construction, and Freddie asked them if he could withdraw from his agreement and get his money back. He still had $2000 invested in the project. The two partners told him there was no way they could return his money. It was all in the contract. In fact, they explained that they were in deep trouble themselves. Both had been investing heavily in the market, and both had been badly hurt. The problem now was whether they would be able to complete the building of the radio station itself. Unless they were able to get outside financing from somewhere, the whole project could fold up and die. And the chances of getting a hard cash loan, after what had happened today, would be pretty grim.

After that, Freddie Mayhew walked to Court Square and sat on a bench for a while. He stared at the statue of the Civil War soldier leaning forward and holding his bayoneted gun atop a polished stone pedestal honoring the names of the Riverside men who had fought in that war. Beyond that and across the street stood the First Congregational Church of Riverside. Traditionally, its door was always open to those who wished to stop in for a moment and pray. But right now he didn't believe in a god who could cause such a terrible crash in the market and ruin his, Freddie Mayhew's, life in just a day or two.

He noted that, strangely, the world seemed to go on. The grounds keeper raked leaves near him as though nothing had happened. People were still on the streets; cars, buses, and trolleys still ran. It seemed impossible to him that this could be just one more Tuesday like any other. There should be a mood of national mourning—people wearing black, stores, banks, and offices closed, flags flying at half-mast. Perhaps, he thought, people were not yet aware of the debacle.

But when he returned to the Puritan, he saw his first real proof that people *knew.* They had heard the news over the radio. Now a line of people had already formed in front of the bank entrance, and it was getting longer all the time. And of course, Freddie Mayhew knew why.

He went back to his cage at the Puritan. Nobody was depositing any money at his window. They were all making withdrawals. Afraid of losing their life savings. After the market had taken the big plunge on the previous Thursday,

a couple of small banks in upstate New England were reported to be in trouble. Their canny Yankee depositors came
in droves to withdraw their funds. It was rumored that the
bank examiners were already there, auditing and probing the
situation.

Freddie had been at his window for about an hour, when
Jonathan Keep approached him. Freddie drew down the
curtain over the window of his cage, and he and Keep went
into the men's room. Hannah Winthrop, stricken, watched
them go. She would have dearly loved to attend this conference, but of course, that was impossible.

"How's it look, Freddie?" Keep wanted to know.

"They're still withdrawing. Some of them are closing their
accounts."

"That figures," said Keep.

"What about our cash on hand, Mr. Keep? I mean, how
long can we hold out if they keep withdrawing?"

"Hard to tell. But I'd better alert the Atlantic Trust in
Boston to send us more cash to keep on reserve." The Atlantic Trust was a kind of central, or "mother," bank to a
number of smaller banks throughout Massachusetts. It could
be called on for cash or other services when needed. "They
don't have to know we're a couple of hundred thousand short
—at least, not now."

"Mr. Keep," said Freddie Mayhew suddenly, and in despair, "what are we going to do?"

"Damned if I know," said Keep. Then softly: "That son
of a bitch Hopkins. May he rot in hell. He got us all into this,
and it's up to him to get us out."

"But he's still in a coma. Suppose he never—comes out of
it."

"Then we'll all go to his funeral—and spit on his grave,
before they take us away."

After the bank had closed, Freddie Mayhew again counted

his misfortunes. At this moment he was dead broke. He, Freddie Mayhew, was an embezzler. A thief. Even now, the syndicate could be in imminent danger of discovery.

He would of course be tried and sentenced, and go to jail with the others. The Puritan had been around a long time. It was an institution highly revered in Riverside, a model of good, conservative banking procedures, highly community-minded, and a generous contributor to all charity drives. They might be hard on himself and the others for violating the trust given to them. He had no idea how many years he would have to serve. But he would be behind bars, like any common criminal, when his baby, his little son or daughter, would be born. He would be unemployable after he finally got out of jail. There would always be some police record to haunt him, and his reputation would taint the life of his child forever.

He thought of Ellie. It was probable, after this, that she would divorce him, perhaps change her name, move to some strange place, and start a new life.

He contemplated running away. He imagined the head-lines in the local papers. FRED MAYHEW, EMBEZZLER, FUGITIVE FROM JUSTICE.

But where could he run? He had no money. He considered the idea of suicide. He decided he was too young to die. All he could do now was pray that some miracle might happen.

He decided to have a couple of drinks at the Barrel and try to forget his misery for a while.

It seemed, at the moment, the most sensible thing to do.

*

When Hannah Winthrop got home, the first thing she did was feed her cats.

After that, she sat down and wrote a letter to Dr. Ricardi, cancelling the appointment she had made for the plastic surgery on her lip.

Then she went to the top drawer of her bureau and took out the drawing of the new face Dr. Ricardi had promised to create for her. Bit by bit, she tore it into tiny pieces and threw them on the floor.

In the same drawer, lying under where the letter had been, was a newspaper photograph of Edgar Morton. He had been photographed in a group attending a hardware convention at the Highland Hotel. She had very carefully scissored out the other men, leaving Edgar Morton alone. She picked up the clipping, looked at it for a moment, and then tore it to tiny bits as well.

It was late afternoon now, and she was tired, deadly tired. She decided that what she needed was a warm bath, and then a good sleep.

In the bath, she wondered what women's jail was like. She wondered how many years she and the others in the syndicate would get. She wondered whether, once she was behind bars, the other inmates would laugh at her, jeer at her distorted mouth, make her the butt of all their jokes, give her some awful nickname, the way they did in some of those prison movies she had seen. She would die if that happened.

She dried herself after her bath and stared at her face in the long door mirror. It fascinated her. Especially the way her mouth slanted so crookedly. It was really unique for anyone to have a mouth like that, especially a woman. How many women in this world could boast that their mouths were unkissable?

Suddenly she felt light-headed, giddy. She wanted to laugh —she wanted to cry—she didn't know quite which. She picked up a lipstick from her dressing table. She thought of Edgar Morton again and wrote his name across the mirror with the lipstick in big red letters. She didn't know why; it was just something she felt like doing. Then she ran the lipstick over her mouth, again and again, until it became a grotesque exaggeration. The kind of mouths worn by clowns in circuses. Then she colored the end of her nose red and drew large red eyebrows, and now she actually looked like a clown. She stared at her reflection in the mirror and laughed aloud. She wondered whether circuses used female clowns.

The name "Edgar Morton" in the crooked letters of lipstick she had on the mirror seemed to be laughing at her. She saw his face behind the letters, smiling broadly. She took the rest of the lipstick out of the tube, rolled it in the palm of her hand, and smeared the letters over until they were indecipherable.

She took a double dose of Dr. Argyle's nerve tonic. Then she lay down on the bed and wept herself to sleep. Her cats leaped on her bed, licked the lipstick still on her face, and decided they did not like it.

Hannah Winthrop never noticed them.

*

At midnight on this same evening, something unprecedented had happened at Madame DuBois' establishment.

The girls were all there and ready, and so was the bar. But not one gentleman caller had shown up. Not one single client. It was almost eerie, there in the bordello. By this time, the madam would ordinarily be moving about, making sure the gentlemen were making contact with the girls they liked and buying drinks—the expensive champagne cocktails the establishment featured.

Upstairs not a blanket was turned back, not a sheet ruffled.

The madam was puzzled. She went to the piano player, who bore the curious name of Johnny Chicago. He was bored by the lack of action, softly tapping out with one finger the theme song of the place, "I Wanna Be Loved by You."

"Johnny," she asked, "what do you think has happened? To our customers, I mean."

"They're in no mood for the ladies tonight, Stella."

"But why not?"

"You read the papers today? Listen to the radio?"

"Yes."

"Then you know what happened on Wall Street—the Crash."

"Yes. But why should that make any difference?"

"Most of the trade who came here were in the market, Stella. They all got hit hard—some of them wiped out. They're probably home now, figuring how much they lost, or getting drunk somewhere—something like that. But they're in no mood for girls. Girls are for fun time, and tonight ain't fun time for these guys. A lot of 'em probably feel they couldn't get it up, even if they did come in tonight . . ."

They were interrupted by the ring of the outside bell. The madam opened the slot in the door and then opened the door herself to admit the visitor.

It was Jonathan Keep.

"Well! Jonathan. Good to see you here again."

"Evening, Stella."

The madam studied Keep for a moment. Keep was now suffering from a kind of aftershock. His face was haggard; there was something strange in his eyes. He did not appear as though he was a man looking for a good time.

"Cecilia's available," she began. "If you . . ."

"Later," said Keep. "First, drinks for everybody in the house."

The madam stared at him. This wasn't the Jonathan Keep she had known at all. And this wasn't like Keep. He had never ordered a drink before. He came in, did his business, paid the fee, and quietly went home.

"Mr. Keep," she said, "you don't mean that . . ."

"I said it once, and I'll say it again. Champagne cocktails. For everyone in the house."

The madam snapped her fingers at the bartender, and he went to work. The girls all crowded around Keep. He took a cocktail himself and drank it. Then he had another. The madam almost had to rub her eyes, knowing Jonathan Keep was a teetotaler. He called for music and more music. He swayed unsteadily, toasting all the girls. By the third cocktail, he was drunk.

Finally, the madam said:

"Do you still want Cecilia?"

"Love Cecilia," he said thickly.

"Cecilia," said the madam, "Mr. Keep would like to go upstairs for a little while."

"Not a little while," slurred Keep. "All night."

Both the madam and Cecilia stared at each other. Then the madam said, "Mr. Keep, as you know, an all-night companionship with one of our girls is quite expensive. And you've spent enough already. You don't realize your bill . . ."

"All night," said Keep, swaying. He took a wad of bills from his pocket and thrust them into the madam's hand. He did not even bother to count them. "All night," he repeated. "With my loving Cecilia."

Halfway up the stairs, he fell flat on his face. He was stone drunk, and out. The two women undressed him and put him to bed.

He stayed in a deep sleep all night long, and never really got his money's worth.

23

SHORTLY BEFORE MIDNIGHT on this same Tuesday, Henry Hopkins came out of his coma.

He was allowed no visitors until noon of the next day. The doctors told him he was a very lucky man. He had been in a coma for a long time. There was no fracture of the skull, no brain damage. He had suffered a concussion, true, but fortunately there were no complications, and with a few days' rest, he could leave the hospital.

His first visitor was his wife, Helen.

She was allowed only a few minutes with him. She kissed him and held his hand and said how thankful they both could be that the accident hadn't led to more serious consequences. The driver of the other car, a mechanic from Westfield, *had* been drunk. After running into Henry, his car had swerved into oncoming traffic and smashed into a fast-moving truck, and the driver had been killed.

She found Henry weak but lucid.

She had something to ask him, but she decided that she had better wait until he was a little stronger. The fact was that she herself had taken heavy losses in the market. After buying Seaboard, she had really become infected by the fever itself and had invested heavily in a number of other stocks, on the advice of that nice young man, Mr. Curtis, in the Lothrop office. Now that same nice man was calling her constantly, asking for more margin to cover her losses.

In fact, she needed over $100,000.

She was a Clement, a member of the wealthy Clement family, which owned a paper and pulp mill in Holyoke. Her father had died and left her an inheritance somewhere in the neighborhood of a half million dollars. Of this, she had lent Henry the two hundred thousand which he had lost in Florida. On her own, she had invested in the market part of what she had left. The rest of her inheritance, which she kept in her safe deposit box, had, almost overnight, shrunken way down in value. This was because her father had left her legacy in the form of solid and conservative stocks, like U.S. Steel and American Tel & Tel, which were called by some "widows' stocks," because they were absolutely safe and always paid dividends.

Of course, Henry did not know she was in the market. He would be furious when he found out. But she was in trouble now, and she would have to face it out. She would request —no, demand—that her husband pay back part of her loan to him. So far she had managed to hold on, but it was getting very tight. Her husband was a banker, a financial man, and surely he could arrange to find $100,000 somewhere. Perhaps he could borrow it from his own bank, the Puritan. She did not know where he would get it, and she really didn't care. But she would take no more excuses from him. She needed that money, and she needed it desperately.

But of course, now was not the time to ask him.

She kissed her husband goodbye and told him she would be in to see him tomorrow and that she would bring him a few personal effects he would need while he was still in the hospital. Then she left.

As for Hopkins, he could not wait for his wife to leave. As soon as he heard her footsteps echoing down the corridor, he rang for a nurse. When the nurse came in, he asked her for a newspaper. The nurse demurred. He was supposed to rest and forget about everything else. He told her he had to see a newspaper. It was urgent. When she again refused, he tried to sit up and made his demand again, this time in a loud voice. She saw that he was becoming agitated, which clearly was bad for a man who had just recently come out of a coma. She decided to do as he asked, if only to keep him quiet.

She found a copy of the *Riverside Union* at the nurses' station and brought it to him.

This time Henry Hopkins did not have to turn to the financial section to see what had happened.

It was right there in big headlines on the front page.

*

The moment the bank closed, the other members of the syndicate headed immediately for Riverside Memorial Hospital.

They had been calling every hour on the hour, inquiring as to the state of Henry Hopkins' health. They had been informed that morning that Henry had come out of his coma. And when told, finally, that he could receive visitors for only a few minutes at a time, it was hard for all of them to wait until closing time at the bank. They were busy servicing depositors, who continued to wait in line to make withdrawals. For the time being, Jonathan Keep was in nominal charge of the bank.

Keep, Freddie, and Hannah Winthrop almost charged into Henry's room. They did not even bother to ask Henry how he felt. They spewed out their anger and bitterness. He had gotten them into this mess by touting them onto Sunrise Investment Trust. He had blown their entire investment by failing to sell their holdings the day *before* the Crash, as he had been instructed to do, as the members had duly voted him to do. He had betrayed their trust in him.

They held him personally responsible. Jail was staring them all in the face. Jail and disgrace. They were sure to be exposed as soon as the bank examiner made his usual audit in December. But now, under the circumstances, he might not even wait until December. He might show up at the Puritan at any time now.

Henry Hopkins listened to them all, dumbly. He wished he were in a coma again. He almost wished he were dead. Anything to escape the wrath of his fellow conspirators. He knew they were right and was tormented by his own guilt. He shouldn't have listened to that damned fool, Charlie Lothrop. All that crap he had given him about the Big Boys. Cutten, Raskob, Rockefeller, Billy Durant, the DuPont brothers. Just shaking out the suckers and then hitting the upturn. The same old baloney. Damn Lothrop, he thought. It was *his* fault, when you came right down to it.

"All right, Henry," said Keep. "Face it. It's your fault, and we expect you to get us out of it. Now—what are you going to do about it?"

"Look," said Henry. "There's nothing I *can* do about it. Where the hell do you think I could get two hundred thousand?"

"Why not ask your wife?" said Keep.

Hopkins stared at Keep.

"Helen?"

"She's a rich woman. Her father left her well off, we all know that. Why don't you just tell her the truth and ask her . . . ?"

"You're crazy, Jonathan."

"Am I? Why?"

Henry desperately searched for an out. There was no way

he was going to ask Helen for the money. He already owed her $200,000. To ask her to lend him the same sum all over again to cover his losses in new speculation was a little too much. He'd die before he would go to her. He stared at the expectant faces that were looking down at him, waiting for his answer. He had only recently received a hard blow to the head, but it had not affected the sharpness of his mind. He had to worm his way out of this. And he did.

"First, my wife's father left her the money in trust. She can only draw so much a year. Second, the money he left her wasn't in cash. It was in stocks. And you know what happened to *them.* I would imagine they're not worth a hell of a lot right now. I'm not sure she's even *got* two hundred thousand left right now. In fact, I seriously doubt it. And there's something else you haven't thought about, Jonathan."

"Well?"

"My wife will want to know *why* I need all that money. I'll have to tell her the truth. That'll implicate all of you. I mean, we'll be letting an outside party know what we've done, and that's dangerous. Helen happens to be the kind of woman who can't keep her mouth shut. She never *thinks* while she talks. Sooner or later, she'll blab it out to someone, somewhere. We'd be crazy to even take the risk."

The others listened silently, dejected. Keep pointed out that there were other problems to face, besides. There was a run on the bank because of the Panic. Cash on hand was running low, and Keep had made a request from the Atlantic for more money. The collateral held by the bank, much of it in securities, had melted away to a fraction of what it was worth, and a lot of their borrowers were bound to forfeit on their loans. The board of directors, naturally, was very upset. And its members would be more so when they found out the bank did not have certain assets it was supposed to have.

It was then, while Keep was droning on, that Hopkins remembered. Pat Nolan, the bootlegger. He had offered Hopkins—or the bank—a blank check, fill in your own amount, for a seat on the board. He told the others of Nolan's offer. Now, he said, was the time to take advantage of it. Nolan, they all knew, was a rich man. Henry again emphasized that Nolan would put up any amount for the prestige he wanted.

His visitors were dubious. Would the proud Yankee members of the board accept an Irishman, much less a bootlegger, on the board?

"They've already rejected him once," said Keep. "Why would they accept him now?"

Henry pointed out that overnight, times had changed. He knew that the other members of the board had been in the market up to their necks and had probably lost heavily. If you came right down to it, they would consider money for the board fund, fresh new cash, more important now than prestige. He, Henry Hopkins, would push for Nolan's membership heavily. Usually the board went along with him on almost anything. He was its undisputed leader. Anyway, the important thing was to get the money *now;* they could worry about everything else later.

He proposed to get in touch with Nolan at once. But unfortunately, this particular room had no telephone. This, of course, presented a problem. There was a public pay telephone in the corridor just outside Hopkins' room. The question was, how could they get him out in the corridor so that he could call Nolan? At this point, Hopkins was too weak to walk. And he had, of course, been forbidden to leave his bed.

Freddie Mayhew solved the problem by going out into the corridor and finding an empty patient conveyor, one of those beds on rollers used to transport patients to and from the operating room. He waited until the corridor was empty of anyone else, then wheeled the conveyor into Hopkins' room.

Carefully they rolled Henry Hopkins from his bed and onto the conveyor. They watched the corridor and waited till it was deserted once again. Then quickly they wheeled Hopkins to the public telephone. Jonathan Keep quickly looked up Nolan's phone number, dropped a nickel in the slot, gave the operator Nolan's number, and handed the telephone to Hopkins, who was lying prone.

When Nolan answered, Henry Hopkins made his pitch. Nolan was still interested. He had made the offer, and the offer still held, within reason. Henry told Nolan the magic number. Two hundred thousand. Nolan calmly said he had the money Hopkins needed. In cash. And it was available immediately.

At this point, Henry Hopkins instructed Nolan to bring the money to the bank the next morning and deliver it personally to Jonathan Keep in a sealed package. Keep would hold it in escrow. He, Henry Hopkins, would be out of the hospital in time to chair the next meeting of the board, ten days from now. And he personally would guarantee that Nolan would be approved. Henry Hopkins was a shrewd salesman when he wanted to be. As a sweetener, he also offered to put up Nolan's name for membership at the Longmeadow Country Club. Nolan seemed pleased at this. He asked no questions as to why Henry wanted the money delivered in such a bizarre fashion. But he was in the kind of business where very few questions of this kind were ever asked.

Henry's face was covered with sweat when he laid his head back upon the pillow. He told the others that the $200,000 would be forthcoming, and from the gist of the conversation at his end, they already knew it.

"By God, Henry," said Keep, exultantly, "you've done it. You've really done it."

Hannah Winthrop was almost crying with relief. She wanted to lean forward and kiss Henry for what he had done. But at the last moment she remembered and held herself in check. Freddie Mayhew was trembling now that the tension was over. He lit a cigarette, put it out, lit another. He felt the terrible need for a drink.

At this point, the head nurse of the floor appeared in the corridor. She was stunned, then outraged, at what she saw. She upbraided Hopkins for his stupidity, wheeled him back into his room, and then angrily ordered the others to leave the hospital at once.

*

The next morning, Pat Nolan ate a solitary breakfast. His wife had gone to Boston to spend a few days with her mother, who was ailing.

After he had finished, still in pajamas and robe, he went down into the cellar of his house. His cash was hidden in a cache behind some loose bricks in the cellar wall. This particular wall was located just behind the coal bin. The bin was always filled with coal, and because of this, the section of wall behind it was not only hidden, but difficult to get to. Burglars might reason that Nolan's money was hidden somewhere in the house, and, in fact, had broken in twice looking for it. But they had never found it.

Nolan picked up a shovel and pushed enough coal to one side that he could crawl over the top of the bin to the wall. He reached down, took away the loose bricks, and took out $200,000. Whenever he needed to get cash, he always wore his pajamas or old clothes, rather than crawl over the coal in a business suit, which obviously would show the dirt.

Since 1919, when Prohibition became law, Pat Nolan had

amassed a considerable fortune. The $200,000 was going to put a considerable nick in it, but he figured it was not really a loss, since, as he would be a member of the board, the money would be used to buy shares in the Puritan. Thus, as Nolan saw it, this was really an investment.

He got dressed and then wrapped the money in a package, the way Henry Hopkins had requested. It was a bulky package consisting of $100 bills, 2000 of them. He wondered why Hopkins needed the money so urgently. He suspected that it had something to do with Black Tuesday. Almost everybody had been hit by the Crash. He made a shrewd guess that a number of members of the board had been hurt badly in the market, that they now needed their shares in the board fund to meet margins. And that fresh money, even from an Irishman, would be welcome to add to the fund. But this was pure conjecture on his part. He didn't give a damn why Hopkins wanted the money, as long as Hopkins delivered. Even if it were a straight payoff to Hopkins and did not go to the board fund at all, Pat Nolan was willing.

He wanted a seat on that board, and he wanted it badly. He would be the first Irishman to make it, and it would be the first big breakthrough. He did not doubt that Henry Hopkins could arrange it. The name Hopkins was very big in Riverside, socially and politically. It was he who really ran the Puritan and dominated the board.

He got into the Marmon, put the package on the seat next to him, and started off for the Puritan.

As he drove down Sumner toward Fort Pleasant, his mind turned toward business. And about this, he was disturbed.

A few days ago, he had received a visit from the legendary Legs Diamond, and he had been told to buy his liquor from the Coll-Diamond combination—or else. He had looked into Diamond's cold eyes and agreed. He did not want someone, on some dark night, to throw a bomb into his house, blowing it to hell. Diamond had been very subtle. He had only hinted at such a consequence, but Pat Nolan had gotten the point. He had pointed out to Diamond that if he made this deal, he would need some kind of protection. Diamond had told him not to worry. The Schultz-Madden suppliers had already been forced out of the New England territory, and he would not be bothered.

He could still see Diamond's hard face, and it haunted him.

Nolan was very uneasy. His regular suppliers had been very unhappy at the change and did not hesitate to tell him so. They hinted darkly that they still controlled the New England territory and told him to think it over.

Now, he had been put squarely in the middle. No man could ride two horses, and the strain was beginning to get to him. After some soul-searching, he had decided to go along with the Diamond-Coll suppliers. They seemed the worse of two evils, more prone to violence. And violence was one thing Pat Nolan hated.

Now he began to contemplate getting out of bootlegging altogether. He was tired of always being threatened. He had made his pile and could go into some respectable business. Politics, for instance. He was well known and liked everywhere. If he ran for alderman of Riverside, he would get the entire Irish Catholic vote, he was sure. A seat on the board of the Puritan would certainly enhance his clout around Riverside. It would give him the prestige and respectability he would need in a political campaign.

As he turned down Fort Pleasant Avenue, he did not notice the big black Packard limousine behind him, or if he did notice it in his rearview mirror, he saw nothing unusual about it. But suddenly the Packard pulled out and drew alongside of him. It held four men. One of them had a rapid-fire rifle pointed toward his head. Pat Nolan tried to swerve his car, but he was too late. The last thing he saw on this earth was the glint of the sun on the killer's gun barrel.

The man in the Packard fired six shots in rapid succession directly at Pat Nolan's head. The big black car then drove rapidly away. Pat Nolan's head slumped against the steering wheel of the Marmon, dripping blood. His car, now out of control, swerved and hit a tree.

*

Naturally his original suppliers were very upset at Nolan's disloyalty, and they felt they had to set an example for all the dealers in the entire New England territory.

When the police found Nolan, they also found a big package sealed in plain brown paper, which was lying on the car floor. When they unwrapped it, they found $200,000 in $100 bills.

The police held the money, pending further investigation. They had no idea where Pat Nolan was headed for with that kind of money or what it was for. But it was the first incident of real gangland violence in Riverside, and for days it was a big story in the *Riverside Union* and the other local papers. It also made the wire services and even rated a composograph in Bernarr McFadden's sensational tabloid, the *New York Graphic.* McFadden was known as the high priest of physical culture in the twenties, but he was also the originator of this new form of photojournalism called the composograph. This was the technique of composing a fake picture to highlight some ghoulish occasion. He had first used it in 1926, just after Rudolph Valentino had died. The body was hardly cold before the *Graphic* had sent two photographers to Frank E. Campbell's Funeral Church on Broadway—one to actually take pictures and the other to pose in an empty casket. A headshot of Valentino was superimposed on the figure in the casket. Thus the tabloid was able to hit the streets an hour or so later with an eerie front-page shot of the Great Lover "lying in state," before the body had even reached the undertaking parlor. It was a sensation. The *Graphic* ran its presses all night to meet the demand of thousands who wanted to see the photo.

A *Union* reporter had taken a photo of Nolan dead at the wheel. The *New York Graphic,* intrigued by the fact that Nolan had $200,000 in the seat beside him and that this seemed to signal the first shot and beginning of a gangster war in New England, bought the picture and made a composograph of it. The fake photo showed Nolan slumped, head on the wheel, and in the background a big car filled with men, their guns blazing away. The flame and smoke of the gunfire partly obscured the faces of the men. But two of them looked remarkably like those of Dutch Schultz and Owney Madden.

The Riverside papers used the composograph, with permission from the *Graphic.* And the killing was an event talked about for many weeks later.

But for the syndicate at the Puritan, it was a disaster. More than that. It was a deathblow.

24

THE SITUATION in which the embezzlers found themselves now was not just critical. It was hopeless. Their last
chance lay riddled with bullets on a marble slab at the city
morgue. They could only wait helplessly until the state auditors came to the Puritan. The auditors would, of course,
quickly discover a cash arrears of some $200,000. There
would be an investigation, and then, inevitably, arrest and
punishment.

Henry Hopkins was released from the hospital five days
later. He had doctor's instructions to remain at home and
rest quietly for at least two weeks before resuming work at
the bank. This was fine with Hopkins. He did not want to go
to the bank at all. He knew he would have to endure the
anger and the bitterness of his fellow conspirators. They still
pointed their fingers at him. He was the cause of their misery
and their ultimate ruin. And Freddie Mayhew, who now
lived in his, Hopkins', own house with his daughter Ellie,
would not even speak to him. Ellie and Helen Hopkins, of
course, noted this hostility. It bewildered them, but neither
Hopkins nor Freddie would make any explanation. The
women finally decided that Hopkins still resented Freddie's

spiriting away his daughter, marrying her, and then becoming a boarder. And that, naturally, Henry's new son-in-law responded in kind to this hostility. In time, the women decided, Henry would feel differently about his son-in-law, especially when the baby came.

The tension in this unhappy household was further increased when Helen Hopkins finally asked her husband for the $100,000 she needed to hold on to her diminished securities in the market. It was only half of the debt he had owed her for years, and she considered the request reasonable. But Hopkins turned her down. He would like to oblige her, he said. But he did not have that kind of money, and there was no way he could borrow it. Not in these times. She had assumed he had personal investments and resources she did not know about. He then confessed that, like almost everyone else, he had been in the market and had been wiped out. He did not, of course, tell her where or how he had obtained these resources.

As a result, Helen Hopkins was unable to come up with enough money to meet the margins on her investments, and was informed by the Lothrop office that she herself was wiped out. Her bitterness toward her husband was tinged with something else he found very hard to take—contempt. She regarded him as a fool, and she made no secret of it. First, he had lost a large sum of her money in the Florida disaster, and now he had lost everything he had in the market. As a speculator, he was a dud. She herself had been burned in the same way. But as she rationalized it, that was different. She was a woman and wasn't supposed to know anything about these matters. Henry was a banker and was considered an expert when it came to financial affairs.

This did nothing but compound Henry's misery. He went into a deep depression. He had one visit from Jonathan Keep, who had a desperate suggestion to make—one last chance. He suggested that Henry go to see his wife's brother, Jonas

Clement, who now ran the Clement Paper and Pulp Prod-
ucts Company in Holyoke. Clement was a wealthy man.
"Why not go see him, Henry?" said Keep. "Make a clean
breast of things. Tell him the truth about taking the bank's
money, everything. Put it right on the table. Tell him you'll
go to jail if you don't get the money you need. Ask him for
a personal loan of two hundred thousand dollars to cover
your embezzlement."

Henry stared at Keep. "What makes you think Jonas
Clement would lend me that kind of money?"

"Because," said Keep, "you're married to his sister. If you
go to jail, she'll be disgraced. You know, wife of a jailbird.
There'll be big publicity, Henry, and it'll be ugly. If you shut
your eyes, you can see the headlines. The Hopkins family
name dragged in the mud, and indirectly, the Clement name.
Old Jonas might want to avoid that, at any cost."

"You don't know Jonas Clement, Jonathan."

"What do you mean?"

"He's a skinflint. He wouldn't give me a dime."

"Try," said Keep. "It's worth a chance. And I disagree
with you. The Clements are pretty proud of their name and
reputation up in Holyoke. They wouldn't want it dirtied in
any way. I think Old Man Clement might, just *might,* pay
off."

Henry thought for a moment. Then he said:

"What you're suggesting, Jonathan, is a kind of black-
mail."

"Call it anything you like," snapped Keep. "But it's the
only chance I can think of right now to stay out of jail. I don't
want to go to prison, Henry. Neither do the others. Just
because you stupidly waited that extra day, instead of selling
when we—"

"All right, Jonathan," said Henry. "All right. I'll think it
over."

"The hell with that, Henry. We don't have the time. *Do*

it. We can't be sure when the auditors will come around, the way we used to."

Reluctantly, Henry agreed. Keep discussed a few routine matters with him about bank business. There had been a big run on the bank's cash. Keep had made one request of the Atlantic for more cash, and this had been delivered. But the Puritan needed more, and Keep had made a second request.

The Puritan, unlike some of the other banks in the region, had to have very large reserves of cash on hand. Riverside was the biggest industrial center in the Connecticut Valley, and there were many huge company payrolls to meet, companies that employed hundreds and even thousands of workers. Now the tellers at the windows needed extra cash to pay off the many depositors who were withdrawing their money, and, out of fear, closing their accounts. It was important that the Puritan keep the confidence of the Riverside community, and it could only do this by having enough cash on hand for every emergency.

Henry Hopkins listened in a perfunctory way, agreed that Keep was handling the bank's affairs very well, and again, pressed by Keep, said he would talk to Jonas Clement.

What Keep did not know, when he left, was that Henry had already made his decision.

Old Jonas Clement was a hard and crusty businessman. There was bad blood between Clement and Henry, on certain family matters. He pictured himself squirming in Clement's office, admitting he was a thief, begging for money. The very thought filled him with nausea.

There was no way he was going to suffer this humiliation. He would go to jail first.

*

In the waning months of 1929, the movies were the prime source of entertainment in America. It was almost a ritual for husbands and wives to pick out at least one night of the week as "movie night," and Henry and Helen Hopkins were no different from anyone else. The talkies, now fully developed, attracted big audiences. And they became bigger almost immediately after the Crash. People swarmed into the big rococo palaces and lost themselves in fantasy, just to escape the ugly reality of what was now going on outside— factories closing, workers being laid off, homes foreclosed, and the general sickness of the economy.

Thursday night of each week was movie night for Henry and Helen Hopkins. This was maid's night off, and they usually went out for dinner beforehand. On this particular Thursday in mid-December, they had the usual argument about which movie to see. Henry wanted to go to the Capitol to see a new Western movie called *The Virginian*. It starred Richard Arlen, supported by Gary Cooper and Walter Huston. Henry liked westerns, and he was also interested in seeing Cooper, whom the movie magazines billed as a rising young star, after he had made his mark in *Wings*. The Capitol was also playing *Broadway Melody,* and Henry was in the mood for something lighthearted to take him away from his troubles for just a little while.

But Helen Hopkins had different ideas.

She wanted to go to the Bijou to see the sensational young actress Joan Crawford in *Our Dancing Daughters.* The other feature on the double bill at the Bijou was a new silent movie called *The Great Bank Robbery.* At this particular time it was easy to see why this program did not appeal to Henry Hopkins.

But it was Helen who finally won out. As she said:

"Tonight's dish night at the Bijou, Henry. They're giving out gravy boats with each ticket. I've already got the other dishes—my meats, and salads, and soups—but I'm missing the gravy boat, and this is my one chance to get it."

These dishes, of course, were used in her home as an ordinary, everyday set. For company, she used her fine bone china and crystal.

Henry protested, but finally went along.

And, as it turned out, he was glad he had.

*

When Henry Hopkins and his wife walked out of the Bijou, his mind was racing. His heart was beating high in excitement. During the program, it had come to him.

The Big Idea.

It was breathtaking in its daring and its magnitude. His mind raced with its possibilities. The more he thought about it, the better it seemed. Properly executed, it could get the whole syndicate off the hook on which it was now impaled.

That night he twisted and turned in his bed, unable to sleep. He rose, went to his study, and made several notes. He deliberately looked for bugs in the plan, for flaws that might be dangerous. There were some, to be sure, but they were worth the risk. Charles Lindbergh had flown the Atlantic, knowing the risks. Nothing ventured, nothing gained. And the prize in this case was to stay out of jail.

Finally he fell into an uneasy sleep.

*

The next morning, only a few minutes after the bank opened, Henry Hopkins called a special meeting of the syndicate in the Board Room.

He was aware of the curiosity of the other bank employees as to why these particular four were holding another one of their special meetings. But this time, Henry ignored this. He hadn't time to set up a special location.

He locked the door of the Board Room and then turned to address the others:

"Gentlemen . . ." he bowed toward Hannah . . . "and ladies. I think I have it."

"You have what?" said Keep.

"The way out of our predicament. I've spent day and night trying to think of a way to get us out of this mess. Then, suddenly, it came to me. The answer . . ."

They leaned forward to listen, eagerly. They saw that Hopkins was transformed. He was smiling, quietly confident. He waited for a few moments, enjoying their suspense. Finally Hannah Winthrop could wait no more, and she said:

"What's happened, Mr. Hopkins? Did you talk to Jonas Clement?"

"I did," lied Hopkins. "And, as I suspected, he turned me down. But now I have a much better idea."

"Yes? And what is that?"

"Simply this. All we have to do—is rob our own bank."

There was a long moment of stunned silence. They were all staring at him, astounded. Their mouths had dropped open. Finally Freddie Mayhew said incredulously:

"*Rob our own bank?*"

"Exactly."

"You're crazy," said Keep.

"Absolutely mad, Mr. Hopkins. I never heard of such a thing."

"You're hearing it now," said Henry.

"I'll say it again," said Keep. "You're crazy."

"Am I? Figure it out, Jonathan. We arrange it from the inside. How much cash do we have in the vault now? Just give me a rough figure."

"With that last delivery from Boston, about two hundred and fifty thousand. But what—"

"All right. As I said, this is an inside job. All we have to do is perform a fake robbery, empty the vault of all its cash, and walk away with it. The important thing is to make the robbery look real."

"Go on," said Keep. He continued to stare at Hopkins, fascinated.

"That way, everybody will think the bank was really robbed—by professional bank robbers. They'll be blamed for the missing money—not us. That will explain the shortage of two hundred thousand, when the auditors come. And no one will know the difference, which means we'll be out of it, once and for all."

There was a long silence. Then Keep said:

"By God, Henry, maybe you've got something there."

Both Hannah and Freddie Mayhew dissented. They could not digest the enormity of Henry's suggestion.

"Mr. Hopkins, we'd be crazy to even think of trying something like this. I mean, we just couldn't get away with it."

"Why not?"

"Because none of us have ever robbed a bank before. We wouldn't have the slightest idea of how to go about it."

"Freddie's right," said Hannah. "And there's another thing. We'd be real thieves then. We'd be stealing money that didn't belong to us. We'd be committing a real crime."

"Miss Winthrop," said Henry, quietly, "may I remind you that we have already committed a crime."

"I know," she said stoutly. "But you're singing a different tune now, Mr. Hopkins. When we—er—borrowed from the bank, we intended to pay the bank back—every cent. But if we did an insane thing like this—we'd actually be stealing a quarter of a million dollars in cash. And the question is . . ."

She hesitated, biting her lip. Henry Hopkins spoke gently to her.

"Yes, Miss Winthrop. What is the question?"

"What happens to all the money we take? What on earth will we do with it?"

"Well, we obviously can't return the money to the bank. *That* would be pretty hard to explain, you'll agree, and there's no point in burning it. So the only thing left to do is keep it ourselves."

"You're talking about more than two hundred thousand dollars," said Keep softly. "You're saying that since we're stuck with this cash we steal, we *have* to keep it. Is that what it amounts to, Henry?"

"Exactly. As you neatly put it, we're stuck with a quarter of a million dollars, more or less. So, we'll just have to divide it up among us all—according to the percentages of our investment." He looked at Hannah. "I see you still don't like the idea, Miss Winthrop."

"I'd never dreamed I'd ever be involved in stealing other people's money. That was not the way I was brought up. The whole idea revolts me. I just can't go along . . ."

"Miss Winthrop, let me remind you that none of our depositors will lose one cent they have placed in trust with the Puritan. The bank is insured for robbery to the extent of that amount. It will be obligated to replace the cash at once so that the bank can continue to function. In a very real sense, only the insurance company will lose. And they've got all the money in the world. Speaking of robbery, they're the biggest robbers of them all. They're big and impersonal, and they've got millions—money they squeezed out of people like us. In a sense, Miss Winthrop, we're not really stealing money from the bank. It's from the insurance companies."

"But it's still stealing," said Freddie.

"Look, son, as far as the Puritan is concerned, I disagree. We've paid these insurance companies high premiums for God knows how many years and never collected a cent in claims. When you look at it a certain way, it's about time we did. We're only collecting back what we paid them."

They thought over this convoluted argument, trying hard

to make it compatible with their personal moral values. Finally Hannah said:

"Mr. Hopkins, you will have to count me out. I can't do it."

"Why not?"

"Because it's wrong. And we all *know* it's wrong. No matter what you say."

"I go along with Miss Winthrop," said Freddie. "And I'll be honest with you. This thing scares the living hell out of me. I mean, robbing a bank, for God's sake. *Our* bank . . ."

"All right," said Henry. "Nobody *wants* to do a thing like this. I don't want to, any more than anyone else, but we have no option, no alternative. We're in this deep, and we might as well go all the way. What can we lose? Let's say, just for the sake of argument, we don't bring it off and we get caught. If we don't go through with this, we're all going to jail anyway. And so what's the difference? But if we get away with it, we're home free."

"With two hundred fifty thousand dollars in our jeans," said Keep softly. "Money we couldn't report on our taxes. Money for ourselves, to spend any way we like."

"I wasn't thinking of the money, Jonathan," said Henry. "I was thinking only of getting out of this terrible situation we're in and staying out of jail. But of course, you're right. Like it or not, we'd have to keep the money."

There was a long silence. As always, Henry Hopkins was a persuasive salesman when he wanted to be, and this time he had exceeded himself. In the minds of the others, another element crept in subtly to blunt the edges of revulsion or fear. To be charitable, it could only be said that this new element was intensely human, and universal in man. There was a name for it.

Greed.

In the mind of Jonathan Keep, if the plan worked, he could still fulfill his life's dream—to be the president of his own bank.

In the mind of Freddie Mayhew, the money would be ample to reopen his partnership at the radio station—and to buy a new home so that he and Ellie could move out of the Hopkins' house and live in a place of their own.

In the mind of Hannah Winthrop, she could reschedule her appointment with Dr. Ricardi in Boston and get herself a new mouth.

And in the mind of Henry Hopkins, he could pay off most, if not all, of that damned debt he owed his wife.

In the minds of all of them, Henry's statement had struck home. The insurance company would foot the bill. But to them this kind of claim would be peanuts, when you looked at the overall picture.

Finally Jonathan Keep said:

"There's only one big question, Henry. After we burgle the bank, there'll be a police investigation, of course. None of us here, as Freddie pointed out, have any experience in robbing a bank. We're rank amateurs. We're sure to make mistakes. How do you think we're going to make them believe this was a professional job done by real burglars?"

"Because by the time we're ready, we'll all be professionals. We'll learn the way it's done."

"But how?"

"By *seeing* one done. And I mean step by step."

They stared at Hopkins, bewildered. And finally Hannah Winthrop said:

"Mr. Hopkins, I'm sure I speak for the others, as well, when I say that I simply don't understand . . ."

"I'll clear it up for you soon. I want you all to meet me in the balcony of the Bijou Theater tonight, just before the show goes on. In the *balcony*—not on the main floor or mezzanine. Miss Winthrop, I'll want you to bring a note-book. You'll have to take certain notes."

"For God's sake, Henry," said Keep, "what's all this about?"

"There's a movie I want you all to see," said Henry.

25

A T SEVEN O'CLOCK that night, the four embezzlers sat
high in the balcony of the Bijou just under the projection
room. Freddie and Hannah were dipping into bags of popcorn. Keep and Hopkins sat tensely, waiting for the picture
to begin.

The Bijou's lights went down and then out, and the beam
from the projector appeared just above their heads, hitting
the screen. At this point, Henry told Hannah Winthrop
sharply to put away her popcorn, pick up her pencil and
dictation pad, and pay strict attention.

The organist began to play a sinister theme, misterioso,
and the title of the first picture came on.

The Great Bank Robbery.

As it did, Henry Hopkins hissed to the others. "Watch
closely. You, Miss Winthrop, take as many notes as you
can."

The movie opened on an empty street. Across the street
stood a building with a sign reading THE MERCHANTS NA-
TIONAL BANK. Now they saw a big black car come in. It
parked a few feet down the street from the entrance of the
bank itself.

Inside the car are five men. They study the bank carefully. They see a lone policeman, walking his beat, twirling his nightstick. The leader of the burglars nods to the others, points to his watch, and grins. The implication here is that the burglars have previously checked the timing of the lone policeman on his beat and knew exactly when he would check the bank.

They watch the officer as he stops at the bank, checks the doors and windows to see that they are locked. They are. They watch as the patrolman turns the corner, still swinging his nightstick.

The street is deserted again.

Now the burglars hastily put on eye masks, pull on their gloves, and check their guns. The organist in the Bijou steps up the music, heightening its sinister motif. Now the hood next to the man at the wheel signals the driver to move up. The car moves slowly past the entrance to the bank. Four burglars leap from the car, which parks a few feet farther down the street. The lookout stays at the wheel.

The burglars run to the door of the bank, hiding in the shadows of the entrance, looking up and down the deserted street. They are carrying bags and what appears to be a small tool kit. One of the burglars is boosted up on the shoulders of a companion, who, with a wire cutter, snaps a wire— presumably the main wire connected to the alarm system and located above the entrance. The man standing on his companion's shoulders snips the wire. Meanwhile, the man at the door is expertly jimmying the lock. The door opens and they all rush in, closing the door behind them. The lookout waits nervously at the wheel of the car outside.

"You see they're wearing gloves," whispered Henry. "Make a note of the tools they use, Miss Winthrop."

Hannah Winthrop scribbled furiously in the dark.

The interior of the Merchants National Bank now flashes

on the screen. It is semidark, but it resembles the interior of the Puritan. The same lineup of cages, the same vault setup in the rear. The burglars spread out, each doing a particular job. One runs around to each window of the bank, pulling down the shades so that no one can see inside. Another heads for the vaults in the rear. He picks the lock of the protecting gate quickly with his jimmy. He turns on a pencil flashlight, enters the vault itself. Putting his ear close to the dials, he turns them expertly this way and that. It is clear that he is an expert safecracker. The third burglar carefully cuts other wires, especially the telephone wires, and then joins the fourth. They begin to rip papers and ledgers from tables. They go behind the tellers' cages, rip open the drawers, and hurl out the contents all over the floor, looking for money. In a few moments, the bank is a shambles.

"Make a particular note of *that,*" whispered Henry to Hannah.

Now the other three burglars gather around the man, who is kneeling, manipulating the dials. By their actions, we see that they are impatient; they are telling their companion to hurry up. Calmly, he keeps his ear pressed against the dials, turning them gently, listening to the fall of the tumblers. Then he finds the right combination and flings open the big safe door leading into the vault. He has been working with bare hands. Now he puts his gloves back on his hands and carefully wipes the fingerprints from the dial.

"No fingerprints. A special note on that, Miss Winthrop," hissed Hopkins.

Now they see the burglars rush into the vault. They find the cash drawers. They are filled to the brim with money. The burglars pull folded bags from inside their shirts. They resemble large shopping bags, each with a drawstring. They start to stuff the cash into the bags.

The film now cuts to the outside of the bank. The cop on

the beat is seen coming around the corner. He saunters toward the bank. This is clearly a surprise to the man at the wheel of the getaway car. He reacts, disturbed, and watches the patrolman. The patrolman turns his head suddenly and notices the waiting getaway car as the robber at the wheel ducks out of sight. The police officer becomes a little suspicious. He turns to look at the bank door. He walks up to the door and finds it open. He stands there a moment and draws his gun. At this moment, the robber in the getaway car shoots at the patrolman. He falls, wounded, clutching his shoulder. The four burglars come rushing out, leaping over the body of the fallen patrolman. They race across the street and into the getaway car. It starts to move. The wounded cop lying in front of the bank door takes out his whistle and blows a few blasts on it. Suddenly a police siren sounds, and a police car comes around the corner on two wheels. It sets out in pursuit of the robbers. The robbers fire at the cops, and the cops fire back . . .

At this point, Henry Hopkins rose. For him, and for the others, the important part of the film was over. At any rate, he had seen it before. The others stayed.

But before Henry Hopkins left, he told the others that the present program would be on for three more nights, and that they would all go to the Bijou to see the picture over again on each of those three nights. Just to absorb every detail of the bank robbery itself over and over, so that they would act like professionals when the time came.

*

Now, under the leadership of Henry Hopkins, the syndicate made preparations to rob the Puritan.

Freddie Mayhew bought gloves for the entire group, and the tools needed to jimmy the door and the cash drawers. Hannah Winthrop contributed the drawstring bags. Jonathan Keep phoned the burglar alarm service the bank used and asked them to send a man up to examine their alarm system. His pretext was that the bank was considering a new and more modern alarm system. In this way he learned every detail of the bank's alarm system, including just where professional burglars would cut the wires to make the system inoperative. They decided that under the circumstances, it would be better to enter the bank without masks.

For two days, after the bank had closed and the innocent employees had left, the members of the syndicate returned to conduct mock rehearsals of the robbery as they had seen it done in the movie. Henry Hopkins supervised every phase of the operation, in minute detail. He pointed out the importance, for example, of destroying all the records and ledgers, which itemized cash on hand and any cash transactions. This would be during the period when they trashed the bank, just as the burglars had done in the movie when they were looking for money. Thus the police or the auditors, in their investigation later, would have no information on any discrepancies that might have been discovered *before* the planned robbery.

Actually, as Hopkins saw it, the whole operation should be simple and carried off swiftly. After all, they had immediate entry to the bank and to the vault. They had only to make the whole thing *look* professional.

Hopkins was still not satisfied that everyone was ready and trained to do the particular job assigned to each. He felt he needed more time. As a target date, he picked the night of November 25th to do the job. There were still a few rough spots in the operation to be smoothed out.

Later, and for very good reason, he would be forced to act sooner than he had planned.

*

On the twenty-third, two days before what would now be called D Day, an armored car pulled up in front of the Puritan Bank.

Two uniformed armed guards opened the rear door and jumped out. Supervised by a captain, they hauled a couple of big metal cases from the truck and carried them into the bank. Once inside, they carried them toward the vault area and set them down before the gate.

Both Henry Hopkins and Jonathan Keep stared at them in complete surprise. So did Freddie and Hannah Winthrop. Keep and Hopkins came out from behind the executive area and addressed the captain.

"What's all this?" Hopkins wanted to know.

"A fresh shipment of cash, Mr. Hopkins. We just brought it in from the Atlantic Bank in Boston."

"But this wasn't due until the first week in December," said Keep.

"Yes, sir. But the people at the main branch knew you were still having heavy withdrawals. And they decided to ship it out a little ahead of time. Just to make sure you didn't run out. Didn't even want to bother with a formal notification." Then: "Would you mind opening the vault, gentlemen? As you know, we can't leave until it's safely delivered to the vault area. Inside."

"How much is there?" asked Hopkins.

"Two hundred thousand," said the captain.

Keep gaped at Hopkins, who gaped back at him. Stunned, they opened the vault area. They watched the captain unlock the covers to the cases with two sets of keys. Both of the steel cases were loaded to the brim with packages of money. They put the cash in one of the huge cash drawers, which happened to be empty. Keep carefully locked the drawer. The captain asked Hopkins to sign a receipt for delivery. Hopkins did so, barely aware of what he was doing. The captain remarked that this extra shipment should keep the depositors at the bank happy for a while. Then he and his men left.

"My God, Jonathan," said Hopkins. "What do we do about *this?*"

"There's nothing to do except steal it along with the rest. If you're a professional burglar, you're obviously going to take all the cash you find. You wouldn't just leave part of it. It wouldn't make sense, and obviously it would raise suspicion."

"How much did we have in cash, before this?"

"With all those withdrawals, we're down to a hundred and fifty."

Henry took a long breath. It was, of course, a matter of simple addition. The syndicate was now "stuck" with $350,000.

*

The next day, the syndicate was hit with another surprise. This one far more unpleasant.

At the Worthy Hotel, a few blocks from the Puritan itself, a middle-aged man with an unsmiling, hawklike face checked in. He wore an overcoat against the winter cold, and he looked tired. He declined giving his bag to the bellhop, indicating he would carry it himself. He was on the government payroll, and his travel allowance was sparse. And so he avoided tipping whenever possible.

The desk clerk was surprised to see him.

"Well, Mr. Benziger. We expected you after Christmas, as usual. You're early this year."

He shoved the register to Benziger, who replied, as he signed in:

"I know. But these are strange times. Banks closing, going down the drain—it's been playing hell with my normal schedule."

"I suppose you'll be looking at the Puritan first."

"Usually do. It's the biggest in town."

"Will you be going right over there?"

Benziger reached into his vest pocket and took out his watch. It was quarter of three.

"No. It's almost closing time. Besides, I'm too damned tired. I've been traveling up and down New England the last couple of weeks and working late hours." He smiled in a wintry way. "I'll try to catch the boys at the Puritan with their books down—in the morning. Not that I expect anything. Tell you one thing about the Puritan. I've been auditing them for over twenty years and never found one thing wrong. It's as solid a bank as you'll ever find in the whole country. And confidentially, even in times like this, I wouldn't hesitate to put my own money in the Puritan."

"Yes, sir," said the desk clerk. "I'm glad to hear that. Because my money's in that bank."

He gave Benziger the key to room 423. The moment Benziger took the elevator, the desk clerk—whose name, for the record, was Herbert Ely—put in a quick telephone call to Jonathan Keep at the Puritan.

*

Naturally this news came as a tremendous shock to the members of the syndicate.

They had half expected that the bank examiner might be a little ahead of time this year, but they hadn't expected him *this* early. And it meant, of course, that they had no more time for preparations. The job would have to be done tonight.

Immediately after bank hours, the four conspirators gathered at Hannah Winthrop's place. The syndicate had been meeting there lately, and it was there that the burglary equipment was stowed away.

Freddie Mayhew, Hannah Winthrop, and Jonathan Keep

were under great tension. They realized they were only a few hours away from robbing the bank, and now they really were shaken by the enormity of what they were about to do. Embezzlement was one thing. It was a quiet kind of theft, and they had always intended to replace the money. This had enabled them to soothe their consciences.

But this was something else. They were actually going to rob a bank, like professional crooks, and keep the money for themselves. Before, they had had some rationale. They could still maintain the illusion, at least, that they were decent and honest people.

Now they were about to become criminals—breaking and entering—this time, deliberately keeping the money. Protecting themselves from jail. Piling one crime upon the other. And this one far more serious.

Only Henry Hopkins seemed calm. His eyes were abnormally bright, his face flushed. Hannah Winthrop was visibly on the edge of hysteria. First she served them coffee. Her hands were trembling. She spilled half a cup of hot coffee in Keep's lap. He jumped up, hopped around, swearing, and glared at Hannah.

"Godammit, Miss Winthrop," he said, "will you watch what you're doing?"

"I'm sorry, Mr. Keep." Her mouth was trembling. She looked ready to cry. "I'm so nervous. I don't know what to do." She turned to Henry Hopkins. "Mr. Hopkins, I really don't think I can go through with this. I really don't want to go through with it. I mean, it's not just wrong—it's insane."

"Calm down, Miss Winthrop," said Henry. "Nobody here *wants* to do this. It's just that we *have* to."

She started to cry. "No," she said. "I won't do it. I just can't. You three go ahead. I'm going to stay right here . . ."

"You can't, Miss Winthrop. Remember? We're all in this together."

"I can't consent to become a common criminal. I can't imagine myself as one. I can't imagine how we ever even *dreamed* of doing this terrible thing." She was near hysteria now. "I won't go, Mr. Hopkins! I'm very sorry, but I just won't go!"

"Miss Winthrop," said Hopkins, "you forget something. We're only doing this to protect ourselves. You don't want to go to jail, do you?"

"No."

"Well, if we don't do this, we will."

"I—suppose we get caught?"

"That's a chance we've got to take, Miss Winthrop. But the way we planned it, we won't."

"But suppose we *do!* I mean, if we go to jail, we'll be sentenced for many more years."

Now Freddie Mayhew began to waver.

"She's right, Mr. Hopkins. Embezzlement's one thing, but bank robbery's another. It's a lot more serious. We may go to prison for twenty years, not just five . . ."

"Shut up, Freddie. Nobody here is going to jail. Not if I can help it. I know this is a damned crazy thing we're going to do, but I'll put it to all of you for the last time. We have no option. If any of you have a better idea for keeping iron doors from slamming against our faces, then now's the time. Let's hear it."

There was silence. Hannah Winthrop gradually calmed down and finally agreed to go along. Especially when Henry Hopkins pointed out to her that if they were caught, she would be an accessory even if she stayed home, since she had been involved in planning the robbery. Finally, when the table had been cleared, Henry Hopkins took charge.

"All right. Tonight's the night, as we all know. I'd rather

we had more time, but it can't be helped. If each of us does his job, there should be no hitch." Then he turned to Freddie. "You double-checked the night patrolman on the beat?"

"Yes, sir. He always comes by the bank at midnight, give or take a minute or two."

"You're sure?"

"Every time I've watched him, he's always been right on the dot—a minute or two before twelve, or after."

"Where does he go after that?"

"He keeps on going down Main Street, turns left on Liberty, and then starts to patrol Columbus Avenue."

Then, for the last time, Henry Hopkins reviewed the procedure. He looked at Hannah.

"Miss Winthrop?"

"I stay in the car. Act as a lookout."

"And if anything suspicious happens while we're inside?"

"I blow the horn twice."

Hopkins nodded. "Good, Miss Winthrop. Very good." Now he turned to Freddie.

"Freddie?"

"First, I cut the alarm wire, earlier in the evening. Same with the main circuit wire. Then when we get into the bank, I run around and draw the shades. Then, with Mr. Keep here, and yourself, we throw things around, break up the cash drawers, take whatever money there is in them. Just the way they did it in that movie."

"Right. Now Jonathan?"

"I open the door to the bank, and we all go in. Then I jimmy the door lock to make it look real."

Hopkins watched Keep, his eyes narrowed.

"And after that?"

"Help Freddie open the cash drawers and throw the ledgers and papers around while you open the vault. Then Freddie and I run into the vault and we open the cash compartment. We load the bags, run out through the door, load the car. Then you move Miss Winthrop over, take the wheel, and get us the hell out of there."

"All right," said Hopkins. "Then we'll go in about twelve-thirty. That patrolman should be some distance away by then."

After that, Hopkins conducted an equipment check. They had stored what they needed in Hannah Winthrop's kitchen cabinets: a wire cutter, a screwdriver, a chisel and a special ratchet for jimmying the door, gloves for each, so as not to leave fingerprints, and the bags with which to carry out the cash. Hopkins estimated that the whole thing should not take more than fifteen minutes at the most.

Everybody was to return to Hannah Winthrop's house at twelve sharp. There, he, Henry Hopkins, would pick up the others, plus the equipment, in his own car. Later, after they had done the job, they would return to Hannah's place, divide the money, and then go to their homes. Nervously they wished each other good luck and left.

This was a night the amateur bank robbers would remember for the rest of their lives. Actually, the plan seemed a good one, and despite their tension and insecurity, they expected it to succeed. But they did not know, and they could not anticipate, the strange circumstances, the bizarre turn of events that would make this night so memorable.

26

At twelve-thirty sharp, Henry Hopkins parked his big Pierce Arrow across the street from the Puritan Bank and Trust.

Riverside was an early-to-bed town, and after the movie houses closed at ten-thirty, the entire downtown area was deserted. There was one all-night restaurant open, but that was on a side street, near the railroad arch, and nowhere near the bank. Main Street was empty of pedestrians. Henry Hopkins shut off the ignition. According to plan, Hannah Winthrop would take his place in the driver's seat and act as a lookout. If anything looked suspicious, or if the night patrolman in the area suddenly reversed his daily routine and came back in the area, Hopkins reminded her once again, she was to blow two sharp blasts on the horn as a warning to those inside.

It was a cold night, and Hopkins, Keep, and Freddie Mayhew all wore heavy sweaters. They stuffed the money bags under their sweaters and drew on their gloves. Then, carrying their tools, they left the car and hurried across the street. Keep quickly unlocked the door, and they entered.

They did not notice the big black Peerless sedan, its curtains drawn, parked a block away, near the corner of Bridge Street.

They did not have to worry about any alarm going off, since Freddie had returned to the bank earlier that evening, as planned, and had cut both the alarm and the main circuit wires. These particular wires monitored all the entrances and windows and would go off with a fearful blast of sound if these were opened or tampered with.

Once inside, according to plan, Keep jimmied the lock. He tried to make it look as professional as he could. Meanwhile, Freddie Mayhew raced around the bank, pulling the curtains down in all the windows. Then he cut all the telephone wires. The trio then started to trash the bank, just as they had seen it done in the movie. They paid particular attention to the two key ledgers keeping records of cash on hand, not only the current figures, but those from throughout the year. Carefully, they ripped out the pages of these ledgers and tore them to shreds. The insurance investigators later, as well as the police, Hopkins reasoned, would put all this down to simple vandalism. They continued this until the bank was a shambles. Fortunately, knowing every inch of the bank, they needed little light other than that provided by a small pencil flashlight Hopkins carried.

After that, the three got busy on the cash drawers in each teller's cage. They unlocked them first, then broke the locks to make it appear they were jimmied open, then piled what cash was there into the bags. They did not waste much time with this.

It was the vault in which they were interested.

Keep unlocked the iron-grilled entry gate, which ran from floor to ceiling. Then, once inside, he hacked away at the lock, again trying to make it look as professional as he could. Henry Hopkins immediately went to the vault and began to turn the dials. He knew the combination, of course. But he was nervous, and his fingers shook, and he missed the combination three times before he was finally able to open the vault door.

Meanwhile, outside the bank, Hannah Winthrop went through a nerve-shattering ordeal.

A big Stutz open touring car had come screeching around the corner. It was jammed with young carousers, the men in raccoon coats, the girls in furs. They were all laughing wildly and were clearly very drunk. The car skidded in front of Hannah's horrified eyes, the driver slammed on the brakes, and the car rammed into an electric-light pole, only a hundred feet away. There was a loud crash as it came to an abrupt stop, tumbling its occupants around on the seats.

The driver got out of the car and walked drunkenly to the front of the vehicle. The hood and two fenders of the Stutz had been bent in. His friends seemed to think all this was very funny. They laughed in glee and waved around flasks and bottles.

Hannah sat at the wheel, petrified. Her hand hovered just above the horn of the Pierce Arrow. The sound of the crash might attract someone, even another policeman. Or if the driver could not get the car started, he would have to get help somewhere. And that most certainly would complicate matters.

She watched, paralyzed with fear, as the driver got behind the wheel and tried to start the car. The first two times he tried, the car would not start. The third time, however, it did. The driver backed the car off the pole, and then Hannah watched it as it weaved from side to side, then turned a corner at Harrison Avenue.

She leaned back in relief, her heart still pounding. She still had gooseflesh; she was wet with perspiration under her heavy clothes. She wished the others inside the bank would hurry and get it over with.

Inside, the three had already entered the vault, and they

quickly unlocked and opened the big steel compartments in which the cash was kept.

The compartments, now supplemented by the new shipment from the Atlantic Bank of Boston, were filled with cash, now approximately $350,000.

By the light of Hopkins' tiny flashlight, the three began to stuff the canvas money bags they had carried in. Suddenly, they realized they had made a horrible mistake. They quickly discovered that the drawstring bags were far too small to hold all the money. The bags had been made to hold the initial cash, more or less, that the bank had held before the new shipment arrived. This had been in fairly large denominations. But the new shipment was in small bills—five- and one-dollar bills—heavy in weight and huge in bulk. Even if they stuffed some of the cash in their shirts, they would still be unable to get all of it out. And professional bank robbers certainly would not leave a single dollar in the bank—not unless they were insane. They would take it all.

"Dammit, Jonathan," snarled Henry, "why didn't you figure we needed larger bags after this last shipment?"

"Why didn't *you?*" said Keep. "You're running this whole thing. You planned it."

"Look," said Freddie, "we can't just take some of the money. Somebody would smell a rat. How are we going to carry it all out of here?"

Henry Hopkins thought for a moment. Then:

"How many wastebaskets do we have here in the bank?"

"I don't know," said Freddie. "Maybe ten, fifteen."

"Well, empty them and bring them back here. We can carry some of the money in them."

"But we'll never be able to carry everything out at once. I mean the bags, and the wastebaskets . . ."

"Then we'll just have to make two trips," snapped Henry. "Now get going."

Both Freddie and Keep began the task of moving around the bank, emptying wastebaskets and bringing them back to the vault, as Henry filled the money bags and then started to fill the wastebaskets.

Meanwhile, outside the bank, Hannah Winthrop was standing watch in the Pierce Arrow when she noted some movement in the big Peerless parked up the street. It started to move slowly toward the curb in front of the entrance to the bank. Straining her eyes, she could now observe that it was filled with men. To her horror, she saw the men wore masks. And she thought she saw one of them holding a gun.

Her hand flew to the horn button and pressed it twice. No sound came from it. Desperately, she pressed again and again. But still the horn did not sound.

Henry Hopkins had neglected to tell Hannah that on this particular model, the horn would not sound unless the ignition was turned on and the motor was running.

In her hysteria, Hannah Winthrop had only one thought —to warn the others. She opened the car and ran across the street and into the bank. Startled, the men in the vault turned to see her come running toward them, hair flying, her eyes wild. They knew immediately that something was wrong.

"What is it, Miss Winthrop?" said Hopkins. "What's happened?"

"Robbers," she blurted out. "Robbers . . ."

"Robbers?" They stared at her, uncomprehending. And Henry said: "Miss Winthrop, what the hell are you talking about? You know *we're* the robbers . . ."

At this moment, a powerful flashlight beam went on, blinding them. Behind the beam, they saw the shadowy figures of three men and one girl. All of them wore masks, and all of them had guns pointed at the group.

"All right, gentlemen," the leader said. "You just rest easy. We'll take over from here."

He signaled the girl and the other two men to start work. They began dumping the money into huge canvas bags. The syndicate stood motionless, in shock at this turn of events. Finally Henry blurted out:

"What is this?"

"What does it look like?"

"I don't understand . . . "

"We want to thank you, Buddy, for saving us the trouble of getting in here. This is what you could call a friendly little hijack. We've had our eye on this bank for some time. But you just beat us to it." Then he stopped abruptly. His mouth dropped open, and through the eyeslits in his half-mask, he stared at Henry, and then at the other members of the syndicate.

"Well, I'll be damned," he said. "I'll be a brass monkey." He motioned to the girl. "Come on over here, baby. Do you see what *I* see?"

"Jesus," she said softly. "It's the president of the bank."

"Right,"

"Well, what do you know." she said. "What do you know."

"And you recognize these other jokers?"

"I ought to. We've seen them often enough."

The bank robbers, of course, had "cased" the Puritan Bank and Trust, both inside and outside, very carefully. Naturally, in this process, they had been inside the bank several times and had come to know its personnel. The fact that their recognition was delayed for a moment or two was perfectly natural, simply because of the sheer incredibility of the situation. It took their minds a little longer to register what their eyes actually saw.

"Henry Hopkins," said Clive. "That's the name. Right?"

"Yes."

"Well, Henry, you have to understand, I find this pretty

hard to believe. Why the hell would you and your people be robbing your *own* bank?"

"Well," said Henry. "Frankly, we were in a little trouble. Financial trouble, that is. It's a long story, and there isn't time to explain now. I just want to say we're glad you showed up."

"Glad?" said Clive. *"Glad?"*

"More than that," said Henry, "We're delighted."

It was now clear to Hopkins, and to both Keep and Freddie, that the Lord had blessed them, touched them all on the shoulder. The appearance of the Bunny and Clive gang certainly seemed like a miracle sent straight from heaven. Now the bank was being robbed by *professionals.* That let the syndicate entirely off the hook. All they had to do was stand there, let Bunny and Clive take the money, and then go home. In the morning, they could then "discover" the robbery and report it to the police.

"Now I begin to get it," said Clive. "Now I get the drift. You rob your own bank, and then blame it on *us.* "

"That's what we plan to do. Yes."

"You know, Henry," said Clive, "that isn't very nice. I mean, you'll have to admit it. Blaming innocent people. That's a pretty crummy thing to do."

"Yes, sir, I suppose it is. But you see we have no choice."

"Christ," said Clive. "I ought to bash your head in with this gun for pulling something so low-down and dirty. But I won't. You made it easy for us to get in, and you opened the vault for us. So I guess I owe you a little something." He stared at Henry, his eyes reflecting something close to awe. "You know something, Dad. I've got to hand it to you. I take off my hat to you. You're a goddam genius for thinking up a caper like this. In fact, you're in the wrong business."

The girl called Bunny had returned to help the others load the money. She came back for a moment, to talk to Clive.

"Honey," she said, her voice shaking. "This is the biggest heist we ever did see. There's thousands in there. Hundreds of thousands."

"And that isn't all," said Henry. "You'll find a lot more in the wastebaskets. We just didn't have room for it all."

"Why, thank you, Henry," said Clive. "Much obliged for letting us know. That's real nice of you."

"Not at all," said Hopkins.

Clive waved the gun at them. "Now all you have to do, you and your friends, is just stand there, keep your hands up, and nobody will get hurt."

But he reckoned without Hannah Winthrop.

Suddenly, Hannah started to scream and run for the door.

"Stop her," yelled Clive.

One of the men ran after Hannah and caught her by the arm. He swung her toward him. At that moment, she fell into the burglar's arms in a dead faint. The man dropped her to the floor, on Clive's instruction, and went back into the vault to help load the cash.

At this, Freddie Mayhew started for Hannah. His only thought was to see if he could help her in any way. But Clive, who did not understand Freddie's motivation, had different ideas. He clipped Freddie on the side of his head with his gun. And Freddie fell to the floor.

"I *told* all of you not to move!" snapped Clive. He apparently thought he had knocked Freddie unconscious and paid no further attention to him. But as it happened, the blow was a glancing one, and Freddie Mayhew was just barely conscious. In his daze, he saw figures moving about, wearing masks. He saw that they were piling cash in their bags. And in his daze, he lost all memory or sense of reality. He understood, dimly, that there were robbers in the bank, *his* bank, the Puritan Bank and Trust, and they were taking cash from the vaults.

He began to crawl on his stomach around the corner to the

nearest teller's cage. Clive was too interested in the money and his other captives and did not see Freddie. Again, he must have thought Freddie was out for the night and needed no more attention.

Painfully, his head aching and bleeding, Freddie reached the cage. With a great effort, he got to his knees and pressed a button under the teller's shelf. This was a silent alarm and was connected directly with police headquarters, located in the Municipal Building on Court Square, not very far away from the bank itself. Each teller's cage had one of these silent alarm buttons, and there was one located in the executive area at the front of the bank as well. The syndicate had discussed this system and decided there was no point in tampering with it. Naturally, all any burglar would be interested in would be the entry and exit alarms at the doors and windows.

It took the burglars only a minute or two to finish the work of stuffing the cash into the big bags they carried. They were exultant. They had been casing the bank for several days and had, of course, noted the delivery made by the armored car from Boston. But they had not anticipated a haul as big as this.

Bunny and Clive and the two other burglars finally left, staggering under the weight of the loot they carried. They knew, of course, that Hopkins and Keep were themselves bank robbers and obviously would not call the police. By their own calculation, they too, were home free. They would be a long way from Riverside before the burglary was discovered.

The moment they were gone, Keep and Hopkins attended to both Hannah and Freddie. Hannah came out of her faint, but continued to lie on the bank floor. Freddie had lapsed back into unconsciousness. Hopkins and Keep realized that their departure from the bank was urgent. They exhorted Hannah to try to get up. They discussed the possibility of dragging Freddie out of the bank and lifting him into the car.

Outside the bank, the robbers threw their loot into the Peerless. One of Clive's men took the wheel. He started the car, and it began to move up the street. Suddenly they heard the wail of a siren and saw a police car with flashing beacon bearing down on them. They turned right, closely pursued by the police car. The chase was on, and gunfire was exchanged.

Meanwhile, the syndicate was still inside the bank. They were unable to flee at this moment. Hopkins and Keep stood paralyzed, holding up the unconscious Freddie, supporting him under both arms. Hannah rose to her feet dizzily.

When a police sergeant and two patrolmen entered the bank, guns drawn, they were astonished to find Henry Hopkins and the others there.

The sergeant stared at Henry, mouth agape.

"Mr. Hopkins! What are you doing here?"

Again, and almost without hesitation, Henry Hopkins came up with an answer.

"Simply working late, Sergeant," said Henry coolly. "I called a meeting of my staff tonight at nine o'clock. We had an emergency problem to iron out—some discrepancy in the books. It took us almost three hours to straighten the matter out. We were just coming out of the Board Room, ready to go home, when this gang broke in, held us up, forced us to open the vault, and robbed the bank."

"Well, Mr. Hopkins," said the sergeant. "I really *will* be damned."

"Five minutes later and we would have been gone, of course. In that case, nobody would have discovered the robbery till morning." Then he pointed to Freddie: "If you're looking for a hero, there's your man. It's my son-in-law, Freddie Mayhew, here. One of the robbers struck him down with his gun, but Freddie managed to get to the alarm and call you."

"Jesus," said the sergeant. He noted blood oozing from Freddie's head. "He's been hurt." He looked at Hannah, still prostrate on the floor. Then he turned to one of the patrolmen.

"Joe," he said. "Better call for an ambulance." Then, to Henry: "No telling what these crooks could have done to you, Mr. Hopkins. Glad to find you all alive."

"Thank you," said Henry. "Thank you very much."

27

WHAT HENRY HOPKINS and the others needed now was a timely assist from Lady Luck.

And they got it.

The members of the syndicate, unable to draw a deep breath, sat up all night listening to the late radio news reports. They realized that if the gang was caught, the situation could become very sticky. Bunny and Clive, in their anger that the police had somehow been alerted, would not hesitate to describe what the syndicate was really doing at the bank. This, clearly, could be embarrassing. The syndicate would deny it, of course. But there certainly would be some kind of investigation and interrogation.

Fortunately—for the syndicate—a radio newscast early that morning announced that the gang had managed to make a clean getaway after a furious chase. The police, because of the darkness and the speed of the getaway car, had not even been able to identify its make. And Hannah Winthrop, who had actually seen the car, had no idea what make it was and could only describe it as being big and black.

*

The story, of course, made big headlines in the Riverside papers. And it was picked up, not only by all the other New England newspapers, but also by the national wire services.

Later that morning, a series of other events took place. Three other state bank examiners were rushed into Riverside to assist Examiner Alfred Benziger, already on the spot. Working behind locked doors, they meticulously gathered up all the torn ledgers, ripped papers and documents, every scrap of paper they could find, and sealed them in bags and impounded them.

Meanwhile, depositors of the Puritan Bank and Trust, knowing the bank now had no cash, and fearful they would lose their money, pounded at the locked doors of the Puritan, demanding to be let in. They were reassured by newspaper ads, radio announcements, and public statements that they had nothing to fear. In a press conference, Henry Hopkins told them all to be calm, and a little patient. All was well, he pointed out. The Atlantic Bank in Boston was rushing a fresh shipment of cash to the Puritan. The insurance company was making up the deficit. The bank would be closed only until the examiners and auditors were through. Then it would open for business again.

He reminded them once again that the Puritan Bank and Trust had never betrayed a depositor yet. And never would. Moreover, it was, after all, the bank in which Calvin Coolidge himself had an account. Confidence, he said, was the watchword.

Three days later, the Puritan Bank and Trust opened for business.

Both Henry Hopkins and Jonathan Keep were back at their desks. And Freddie Mayhew was still doing business in his regular cage. Only one of the regular staff was gone.

The missing person was Hannah Winthrop.

This absence was due to a meeting between Henry Hopkins and Jonathan Keep the day before the bank had reopened.

"Henry," said Keep. "I'm worried."

"About what?"

"About Hannah. She's as nervous as a cat in heat. Jumpy. I never saw anyone so jumpy. Scares me. She could blab out the truth one of these days, without thinking . . ."

"I know." Henry frowned. "The point is—what can we do about it?"

"Why not give her a vacation? You know, a good long time. A month. Until she calms down."

Hopkins thought about this for a moment. Then he clapped Keep on the back and said:

"Good thinking, Jonathan. Good thinking. I'll take care of it right away."

And so it happened that Hannah Hopkins was given a month's leave of absence. It was explained that she had been close to a nervous breakdown, due to the events of that terrible night. And that she needed a rest to recuperate. The newspapers announced that the Puritan was generously giving her a month's vacation, with full pay, so that she could stay with her sister in Boston and recover from the terrible ordeal.

*

At Riverside Police Headquarters, Chief of Detectives Otis A. Carlton had decided to personally handle the investigation. He had interviewed the members of the syndicate and could find nothing wrong in their testimony. They had all told the same eyewitness story.

He had no reason to doubt any of them. Especially Henry Hopkins, a man of great influence and status in Riverside, scion of an old family, a family noted for its character and integrity, a man who was president of Riverside's most important bank.

Yet, a tiny nerve quivered somewhere deeply within him.

He turned to his aide and sergeant, an officer named Joseph Rafferty, and asked:

"Joe, why do you think the Puritan was trashed before it was robbed? I mean, all those torn ledgers and records . . ."

Rafferty shrugged. "I don't know, Chief. Maybe it was just plain vandalism." He looked at Carlton. "Why? Why do you ask?"

"Well, it's funny," said Carlton. "But Bunny and Clive, in all the previous jobs they pulled, never busted up a bank. They just went right for the money—the cash drawers and the vault." He paused. "Now what do you make of that?"

Rafferty shrugged again. "I don't know, Chief. It could have been they were in a lousy mood. You know how burglars sometimes will rip up a whole room, all the furniture, just for the hell of it, while they're looking for something. Anyway, sometimes banks do get ripped up, you know, by crooks looking for money. I saw it happen once."

"You did? Where?"

"In a movie. Played at the Bijou a few weeks ago. I think it was called *The Great Bank Robbery*. Anyway, they tore up that bank pretty good. The robbers, I mean. Threw stuff all over the place, ripped up everything. At the end, it said the picture was very authentic. In fact, they had a real bank robber as a consultant. Some punk, still doing time at Sing Sing."

"That so?" said Otis Carlton. "Very interesting."

He turned back to his newspaper and felt a little upset at himself. Hell, he thought, I'm getting old. Tired. Too close to retirement. I've been at this so long, I'd suspect myself, let alone my own grandmother.

*

At approximately three o'clock on the afternoon of November 28th, 1929, a big Peerless sedan drove up to a gas pump located in front of a general store in the small town of Wells River, in northern Vermont.

The driver, a woman, was alone in the car. She was a very attractive redhead, richly dressed. She wore a brown cloche hat and brown coat with a fur-lined collar. A clerk in the store, Elmer K. Overton by name, came out to help her. She asked him to fill the tank.

In the course of some small talk, she mentioned that she was just passing through and was bound for Montreal, and she asked him how far it was. She paid him with a five-dollar bill and then drove off.

Elmer K. Overton was a pimply-faced young man who had one great, overweening ambition. That was to become a detective some day. He was taking a correspondence course in this profession from a mail-order school in Scranton, Pennsylvania, and had already earned a bronze badge for his excellence in solving the problems presented in the first ten lessons. After that, if he continued to apply himself, he would receive a silver badge. And finally, when the course was completed, a gold badge, plus a certificate stating that he was now fully qualified in his chosen field.

One of the first lessons Overton had learned was to observe detail. That is, to transfer to memory everything he saw in a single brief impression of a picture or scene. Now, he remembered seeing, as he had cranked the handle of the gas pump, two small round holes in the tonneau of the otherwise perfectly kept and highly polished Peerless. This struck him as being somewhat incongruous.

When the car drove away, it occurred to him that these might be bullet holes.

In addition to this, the face of the girl driving the Peerless began to haunt him. She had told him she was a stranger, just passing through to Canada. Yet, he was sure he had seen her once before. Very recently, and somewhere in the area. He tossed and turned in bed half that night before he finally remembered.

He had seen this same girl come out of the Highway Grocery store, a big establishment for its kind, located in Bradford, a few miles south of Wells River. A clerk was helping her bring out several heavy bags of groceries, far more than would be needed by one single individual.

He had also read in both the Rutland and St. Johnsbury newspapers that the getaway car used by the Bunny and Clive gang was a big, black sedan, although the make was unknown. Now, putting these facts or impressions together in logical sequence, as he had learned to do during his correspondence course, he contacted Wells River's one-man police force, Officer Edmund Creel. He voiced his suspicions, and Creel agreed that the matter was worth looking into.

Overton took time off from his job at the general store and, together with Creel, they began to scour the countryside, looking for the big, black car. For two days, their search was fruitless. On the third day, a local hunter, Jesse R. Wyndham, casually mentioned that he had seen a big, black car parked at the old Gorham place, which was an abandoned farmhouse deep into the woods, in an area named East Ryegate, just a few miles from Wells River itself.

There was an old lumber road leading to the Gorham place, but it had long been considered impassible. Both Overton and Creel examined the road and noted that the brush and rocks had been cleared away. And although the road was full of ruts and potholes, it could now be considered passable for a car equipped with enough gear power.

They then circled around through the woods and, lying on their bellies some distance from the farmhouse, observed it carefully through field glasses. They saw not only the big Peerless, but noted that smoke was rising from the chimney. It was a cold day, and clearly someone was using the fireplace.

They also noted that the house seemed to be occupied by several people. Occasionally, two men came out to get more wood for the fire, and once they saw the girl come out and empty a pail of slops in the field nearby.

After that, Creel called the state police.

The Vermont State Police, aided by the St. Johnsbury police, circled the farmhouse, and Captain George Truscott, through a bullhorn, ordered the occupants to come out with their hands up.

The request was met by a fusillade of fire from the house.

In the ensuing shootout, the three men in the cabin, including Clive, were killed. Clive's real name, it was discovered, was Roland G. Meehan. The girl known as Bunny, who was born Abigail McGreevy, was the only one to survive.

Highly despondent because of the loss of her lover, Meehan, and promised a certain leniency, Abigail McGreevy dictated a formal confession. This included the fact that the gang had actually found Henry Hopkins and the others robbing the bank, when they had arrived. She also led the police to a rocky cave nearby where the stolen money was cached. And she swore that, as yet, they had not touched a cent of it.

The allegation against Henry Hopkins and the others created a sensation in Riverside, and in all the newspapers.

It was, of course, stoutly denied by Hopkins and the others. Hopkins regarded it as some kind of huge joke. He called it totally absurd, malicious, impossible, ridiculous, and laughable. In a statement to the press, he said he could not understand Abigail's motive, unless it was sheer malice against all bank officials in general. He repeated that he and his employees were simply having a late meeting at the Puritan, when the robbers broke in. He put the question to the press:

"Whom do you believe, gentlemen? A female bank robber and thief, a demented and distraught woman who has lost her criminal lover? Or do you believe me, and the honest and loyal people associated with me? Why in God's name would we want to rob our own bank, or any bank, for that matter? To what purpose?" Then he chuckled. "After all, even if we had entered this unusual profession, we wouldn't know the first thing about how to go about doing it." Then he laughed. "As a bank robber, gentlemen, what you see before you is the sheerest of amateurs."

Naturally, there was no question. To the community of Riverside, the accusation was so warped, so monstrous, as to be totally unbelievable. It was put down to dementia, hysteria, and fantasy on the part of the unfortunate girl.

Yet, somewhere deep in the body or psyche of Chief Detective Otis Carlton, the tiny nerve began to quiver again.

He quietly contacted the bank examiners. They had begun to assemble the ripped pages torn from the ledgers into some sort of coherent pattern. The money, still untouched by the robbers, had been returned to the vaults. As a matter of routine, sooner or later, they would match the cash-on-hand ledgers with the amount in the vaults.

On the twentieth of December, the examiners informed the chief of detectives that they had found a considerable shortage in the money returned to the vaults, running into many thousands of dollars.

They did not know, as yet, the exact amount of the short-age, but were working on it.

*

The evening after Hannah Winthrop returned from her vacation, there was a knock on her door.

The visitor proved to be Chief of Detectives Otis Carlton. He had reasoned that she was the most likely prospect to visit first. Hannah Winthrop asked him to come in and sit down. She offered to brew him some tea, which he declined. He told her that this visit was official, not social. And that he would like to ask her a few more questions.

At that, Hannah Winthrop said to him, quietly:

"Captain Carlton, I am glad you have come. If you had not, I might have one day come to you. I can no longer bear the burden of my guilt. It is simply too much for me to carry any longer." She paused for a moment, and then calmly: "Do you wish to just listen? Or do you want to write it all down?"

28

HANNAH WINTHROP'S CONFESSION sent tremendous shock waves, not only through Riverside, but through all of New England. Because of the bizarre nature of the case, it was again picked up by wire services throughout the country, and columnists like Walter Lippmann and H. L. Mencken wrote essays on the syndicate, treating it rather sympathetically. Both made the point that its members had had too much faith in an American system that had proved faulty, and that what they did was inexcusable, but certainly understandable.

The prosecutor, before the grand jury, emphasized that though there was some public sympathy for the accused, "Embezzlement is still embezzlement, gentlemen, a crime is a crime, and the law is the law. Look at it any way you like, the facts are still clear. These trusted employees betrayed their trust. They stole money from the bank—in effect, depositors' money, money really belonging to fellow members of the community—and tried to use it to further their own selfish ends. Knowing all of this, and having obvious and clear-cut proof, I ask for an indictment."

The indictment was granted. The charge was embezzlement and conspiracy to commit grand theft.

The syndicate, having been caught red-handed, and because of Hannah Winthrop's confession, pleaded guilty. The probation officer, after listening to both the prosecutor and the lawyers for the accused, finally submitted his report to Judge Cyrus L. Martin of the criminal court. It was now up to Judge Martin to pronounce sentence.

He deliberated for two days before he made his decision, and on March 8th, 1930, the accused were brought into court and stood before him.

*

Judges, although supposed to be totally objective and impartial, are still human and often unconsciously affected by the milieu in which they live.

The country was now in a depressed and ugly mood, and Riverside was typical of the general malaise. Hundreds of men were thrown out of work in the local factories. Men began to sell apples on street corners. People lost their homes, as banks were forced to foreclose. Some banks—although not in Riverside itself—had already failed and more were going under, depriving people of their life savings. And the banks, at least during this time, became a focal point of people's wrath, a hated symbol of the Establishment which had brought the nation to such a terrible state. There were tales of big New York banks which had turned out to be rascals, joining the speculators and fleecing their small but trusting investors.

The courtroom was filled to capacity as Judge Martin finally pronounced sentence:

"The four who stand before me are guilty, as charged.

"Yet, there are extenuating circumstances. Up to this point, they have all been law-abiding and respected citizens of the city of Riverside. None has any criminal record; this is their first offense. True, it can be said they were motivated by greed. Yet, in another sense, they had a certain faith in America and in American business. They invested in the market, as did many of us. And like many of us, were themselves betrayed. They say that they intended to return every cent to the bank, plus interest, when they reached a certain point, and I believe them. The testimony of many witnesses as to their good character will bear me out on this. Like so many of us, they were hurt by circumstances beyond their control.

"Meanwhile, whatever the intention of these four may have been, they did not actually and physically steal from the bank. I repeat. They had intent, but did not actually commit the deed. The bank was actually burgled, and the money taken, by the so-called Bunny and Clive gang. This very large sum of money was recovered and returned to the bank, and this notorious gang captured, through the courage of one of those accused here, who must have realized that by doing so she would expose herself and her companions. As a result, the Puritan Bank and Trust was able to stay open and preserve its depositors' money.

"These four, then, are not professional thieves. But technically they are guilty, nevertheless. Still, on the basis of the many mitigating circumstances I have described, this case is most unusual. I have pondered long and hard before coming to a decision.

"I sentence all of the accused to five years in jail." Judge Martin paused for just a moment. Then: "Sentences suspended."

It is interesting to note that the entire courtroom, to a man and a woman, rose to its feet and cheered.

The nation was soon notified of the verdict by the wire services, as well as by the radio. The general consensus was highly favorable, and the verdict of most people was that "justice had been done."

Again, it is interesting to note—although it was not generally known—that Judge Cyrus L. Martin himself had lost almost all of his life savings in the market, particularly in Gardner Motor and American Water Works. And that a substantial part of his portfolio had included Sunrise Investment Trust, as well.

It is also of interest that Judge Martin intended to run for political office in the next election, as a member of the United States Congress, and, of course, like any other politician, would need all the votes he could get.

But Judge Cyrus L. Martin was widely known as a judge of the highest integrity, and it would be unfair to assume that this in any way might have affected his decision.

EPILOGUE

As TO WHAT BECAME of the principals in this famous and bizarre case, little really is known.

The Bankers' Association of Massachusetts, after some internal soul-searching, decided to give the $10,000 reward for the capture of the Bunny and Clive gang to Elmer Overton. Subsequently, he became a member of the St. Johnsbury, Vermont, Police Department and served in that capacity for many years.

Of all the conspirators, Hannah Winthrop was the only one who remained in Riverside. Her plight had excited considerable sympathy in the community, and it was thought that she had been led on, a naive victim of the others. Dr. James Ricardi, the famous plastic surgeon in Boston, aware of the publicity value to his own practice, gave Hannah Winthrop not only a new mouth but a complete face-lift, free of charge.

Eventually she married a local man in the hardware business, Edgar Morton by name, and bore him two children.

Henry Hopkins was divorced by his wife, Helen, and moved to Coral Gables, Florida, a suburb of Miami. It was rumored that he was selling real estate in that community.

The whereabouts of Jonathan Keep is not known. He disappeared from Riverside as though the earth had swallowed him. It was rumored that he had bought a small chicken farm somewhere in Wisconsin or Michigan.

Freddie Mayhew and his wife, Ellie, now the parents of a baby boy, moved to Philadelphia. There, because of the publicity value of his name, he was hired by a small radio station as an announcer.